# ANICES BARGAIN

MADELINE MARTIN

*All rights reserved.*

No part of this publication may be sold, copied, distributed, reproduced or transmitted in any form or by any means, mechanical or digital, including photocopying and recording or by any information storage and retrieval system without the prior written permission of both the publisher, Oliver Heber Books and the author, Madeline Martin, except in the case of brief quotations embodied in critical articles and reviews.

PUBLISHER'S NOTE: This is a work of fiction. Names, characters, places, and incidents either are the product of the author's imagination or are used fictitiously. Any resemblance to actual persons, living or dead, business establishments, events, or locales is entirely coincidental.

Copyright Madeline Martin

Published by Oliver-Heber Books

0 9 8 7 6 5 4 3 2 1

# CHAPTER 1
MARCH 1336, BRAMPTON, ENGLAND

It was not their first siege, but it was certainly their longest. The Grahams were determined.

Lady Anice Barrington, second daughter to the third Earl of Werrick, regarded the dismal larder with her father at her side. Their gazes were mutually fixed on the lone sack of grain.

"The last," he muttered. His brow furrowed into a complex map of creases, carved by a life of sorrow and hardship.

"Is there nothing else?" Anice asked. The large red brown dog sitting near her feet shifted and gave a low whimper as though he could understand their dismal discussion. Piquette was not allowed to receive his own ration of food and so Anice split her meager portion with her beloved pet. It was hardly enough to fill either of them. They were left persistently desperate with hunger, though neither offered up complaint.

Nan, the cook of Werrick Castle, crossed her arms over her chest in a show of authoritative knowledge. "Nothing left save any vegetables we manage to grow in the garden, my lady. But they get eaten as soon as they're plucked from the earth."

"We'll need to reduce food distribution." The earl nodded absently to himself, content with his decision.

Nan cast Anice an anxious glance, the steel in her back melting. "We've already done that several times. The people are starving." The cook had once been round and plump, the way one in her position ought to be—or so Nan had said. The lean months, however, had left her sharp chin jutting from sagging skin and her kirtle swinging around her once generous frame. They were all too thin, too hungry.

Anice stood mutely, unable to come up with a solution. They would be out of food within days. Reducing their rations further would do nothing but anger the people of Werrick and prolong the inevitable by a day or two at best. But what would happen when it was all gone?

Anice shivered at the possibilities, all of them awful.

Lord Werrick dragged a hand down his tired face. "I wish Marin were here," he said quietly. "She would know what to do."

Anice bit the inside of her cheek and focused on the sharp pain rather than the cut of her father's words. He had not meant them, after all. Or at least, he had not meant for them to hurt. Anice's eldest sister, Marin, had been gone from Werrick for almost three years, living in their mother's favorite castle in England. Hunger made Anice's head swim. It was all too easy to remember the peaceful life there with lovely rose gardens and sunlit gardens. And food. So much food.

Sweet, fresh apples with juice that ran down one's chin when she bit into the crisp flesh. Crusty bread that broke under her fingers and revealed the soft, steaming doughy center. Slathered with butter. Greasy, salty—

*Stop.*

"Perhaps we can speak to the Grahams," Anice suggested abruptly. Anything to take her mind off food. "I've heard reivers will sometimes bargain."

Her father shook his head, his stare going distant. It tugged at Anice's heart when he did that, lost to the horrors she wished she could blot from his memory.

"I cannot lose another messenger." He looked down at her with his large, solemn eyes—eyes that had shone with joy when Anice had been a girl. How she missed those long-ago days, back before her mother died.

In a brave attempt to bring a message to the king requesting his help, their messenger had rushed past the Grahams, gotten caught, and paid with his life. He'd lived only twenty summers, the same age as Anice, and had volunteered hoping to save the lot of them. Anice's father had reluctantly agreed. The young man's body had been left in front of the gates the following morning with the missive torn, the dozens of pieces fluttering in the grass about him like macabre, blood-spattered moths.

Several more men had followed that messenger, either to escape the stomach-gnawing hunger within Werrick's walls, or in an attempt to help. And while Anice did not know if any of them made it through, they remained without aid.

"We haven't tried discussing it with the Grahams ourselves," Anice protested.

"And who would go?" he asked.

Anice straightened. "Me." She ran her fingers over her dog's soft fur. "Me and Piquette."

At the mention of his name, Piquette stiffened to attention, always loyal, always brave.

He blinked and his face reddened. "Absolutely not."

"Mayhap they wouldn't kill a woman."

"Nay, you know what they would do to a woman." His jaw flexed beneath his gaunt face. Anice opened her mouth to protest, but he swept a hand in front of her. "I'll not discuss the idea of sending one of my daughters to be left at the mercy of those barbarians. "He turned on his heel and strode from the kitchen. His footsteps rang out on the flagstones until the door closed behind him, muffling his derisive departure.

A little black cat wound its warm body around Anice's feet and cast Piquette a wary glance. Poor Bixby hadn't been the same since Marin left. Though in truth, it was most likely her husband, Bran, who the cat missed the most. Bixby flopped in front of her and she gently nuzzled his chest with the toe of her shoe, much to Piquette's grumbling agitation. Anice bent and rubbed her fingers at the little white star on Bixby's chest, while scratching behind Piquette's ear. It was easier to offer affection to the animals than to regard Nan and the pity dulling the older woman's eyes.

Anice wasn't Marin. That much was obvious with each passing day. She didn't help their steward, William, with the books the same way Marin had; she didn't have the soothing patience; she wasn't as organized and couldn't keep the castle together as Marin had. As with much else in Anice's life, she was failing as others succeeded, no matter her immense effort and good intentions.

Nan's warm brown eyes fixed on Anice. "I'm inclined to agree with your da. There now, you needn't be upset." Nan settled a hand over Anice's cheek. Though there was little food to be had, the comforting scent of baking bread still clung to Nan's sleeve.

Since Marin had left, Nan had taken on more of a maternal role with the remaining four sisters—yet another area Anice had been found wanting.

Bixby rolled abruptly. His ears flicked and he darted into a shadow. At least one of them would eat well today. He always knew where to find the rats.

Piquette watched him with a furrowed brow, too big and clumsy for an attempt of his own.

"If I went down there, mayhap I could make them listen." Anice kept her back held straight as she spoke. She was a woman of twenty, running the Werrick Castle as lady of the keep. Had Timothy not been slain in combat she would also be a wife.

If only he hadn't been pulled to the battle of Berwick with her father. If only he'd returned home, they could have resumed their plans to wed. Memories of her time with Timothy twisted at something inside of her, the same as it always did when thoughts of him surfaced. Not with the regret of a lover, but rather, with a pang of guilt.

"How about a smile on your lovely face instead?" Nan smoothed Anice's hair from her brow. "Your beauty is enough to cheer up the whole of Werrick."

Anice swallowed the rising ire within her and complied. Not for herself, but for Nan.

She kept the smile pitched to the corners of her mouth until she was out of the kitchen and she let it fall without ceremony. Piquette nuzzled her palm with his big wet nose.

No doubt her father would have trusted Marin to go speak to the Graham reivers. He might go so far as to allow Ella, whose intelligence could unravel any stitch of trouble. Or Catriona, whose immaculate aim with an arrow could knock a feather from a bird mid-flight a hundred yards in the air. Or Leila, with her ability to foresee what was to come.

But Anice had none of those qualities. She was simply beautiful. A dull, shallow label she loathed. Regardless of how much she despised it, she clung to the praise. While paltry, the notoriety was better than being nothing.

Despite her father's refusal and Nan's warnings, Anice knew best how to aid her family. And it had everything to do with her beauty.

She waited until the castle went still that night, then crept down to the kitchen. In more ordinary times, servants would have been awake still with dishes to scour and foods to prepare for the following day. In their new life, everyone went to sleep early, even the servants, conserving their little strength remaining.

She slipped into the pathetically empty larder, where wine barrels were piled against one another. Beneath the collection lay a secret door, leading outside the castle walls. Piquette padded silently behind her.

Though she'd tried to get him to stay in her room without her, he'd refused. Forcing him would have resulted in a fuss she could ill afford, so she had finally conceded to allow him to join.

He sat and watched her with his head tilted, as she shifted about the casks, long since empty of their contents. The barrels were easily moved, the passage opened and within seconds, they were navigating the earthen tunnels beneath the castle. Anice cupped her hand over the candle flame to prevent it from snuffing out in the dank, cool air. Outside of the flickering light, darkness pressed in on them, threatening to swallow them whole.

In truth, she was grateful for Piquette's presence, for the warm comfort of his massive body hugged up against her leg. He brought what she needed most—strength.

At last, they made their way to the gate of the narrow exit. She pulled the key from her pocket, clicked the lock open and eased out into the night through the tangle of concealing vines. Above, the stars winked down at her with such brightness, they appeared to be slivers of forgotten sunlight caught in a blackened sky.

Once the gate was locked and the vines rearranged to conceal the spot Piquette had barreled through, Anice hid the key beneath a large boulder. In the full face of a brilliant moon, they made their way through the dewy summer grass to the scattering of firelight below.

She had spent hours preparing for this moment, ensuring

she'd chosen the right gown, that her hair gleamed like spun gold; her scent was feminine, but not overpowering. Mayhap everyone was correct. Mayhap there was nothing more to her than being attractive. After all, what she was about to do lacked skill and thought. If she stopped and truly thought of her actions, she would no doubt run back into the safety of Werrick's walls.

She spun the small ruby ring on her right hand, the one her mother had given to her before their world had abruptly changed. Anice did not intend to quit this mission. Not until she was at the Graham encampment and had the opportunity to speak to whoever was in charge of the marauding band of murderers.

They had to listen. And if her beauty was the only way to make that happen, so be it.

James Graham regretted having come to Werrick Castle. He'd been fool enough to think he might be able to sway his father from the war-torn path he had blazed for years over the border between England and Scotland.

"We're wearing them down, lad." The elder Graham grinned in the light of the campfire. Shadows danced over his aged face and gave him a ghoulish appearance. His hair, once a deep brown like James's, fell in wisps of white around his skeletal cheeks. He bobbed his head in slow consideration. "I can feel their surrender coming, deep in my bones."

Such words used to bring pride to James. Back when he had believed their way of life was the only way to live, prior to his acknowledgment of the damage left behind their success. Back when he looked up to this father and contemplated his words wise.

No doubt the laird of the Grahams was correct now, but it did not mean James took joy in such truths. They'd been camped at the base of the massive castle for nearly five months now. In the last month, their fires roasting freshly caught game had lured soldiers to the parapets. No doubt the scent of cooking meat made them wild with hunger.

The people of Werrick Castle would be on the barest bit of grain, if they had any left. The village nearby had not suffered at the hands of the Grahams, not when they were too important for their purpose in supplying the camping force with food, ale and women.

James hoped the sparing of the village also had to do with the lessening of his father's blood lust, mayhap even a modicum of guilt. The acts of their prior years had been more than James could bear. He suppressed a shudder.

"Just think, Son. When they surrender, ye can have the land ye've been wanting." Laird Graham bumped his elbow against James's arm.

He cast a dark look at his father. "I dinna want the land like this."

"Ach, aye." Laird Graham nodded to himself. "Someone is just going to give it to ye then, provide ye with heaps of coin to start anew and we'll all sprout rainbows from our arses." He gave a wheezing laugh that bled into a wracking cough.

James looked away to afford his father privacy, while the old man gathered his breath once more. He was dying. They both knew it, but neither bothered to say it aloud.

"We have enough coin," James ground out.

"For caring for the land." His father cleared his throat in a great, rattling hum. "We dinna have enough for land *and* living. These people dinna need a farming tenant. Especially no' when its frozen or been buried under rains like in the past. Nay, lad—

our people need a laird. They are used to battle, to being led into war and winning, no' tilling soil."

"Better to till soil than to murder." James met his father's gaze. "To live a life they dinna have to regret."

Laird Graham stared at James, his eyes glittering like flecks of onyx. "I liked ye better before that witless English bastard got to ye."

This argument again. The one about the man who had saved James first from death, then from a life of lies and theft. He'd showed James there were other ways to live, ways Laird Graham might never agree with.

Somewhere in the distance came the shouts of several men, followed by the clatter of weapons striking. Another fight. Sieges led to bored men and bored men seldom possessed good intentions. They wanted a fight, something solid and ripe for their blades to split. They wanted war, a break from the tedium of endless waiting.

"Ye should settle into the life ye used to have." His father's tone was impatient. "Find yerself a wife, have a few bairns."

It was a tender spot and James's father knew it. There'd been no other woman since Morna. James scowled.

Laird Graham gave another winded laugh, this one shallow in his obvious attempt to prevent another coughing fit.

"Ye're always on about having me change my ways." The elder Graham smirked at his son. "Mayhap I'll consider altering my set ways when ye decide to wed."

It was no secret Laird Graham hoped to see grandsons prior to his death, to pass on his marauding influence, more likely. For James's part, he wanted his father's remaining time to be spent in peace, in a world built on hard work and honesty rather than theft and greed. As it was, the old man's dark heart would send him straight to the flames of hell. Before that, as death was stretching a hand toward him, there would be the reminder of all the hurt he had caused.

James knew all too well how horrific those final moments truly could be. "Dinna ye see I'm doing this for yer own good, old man?"

Laird Graham scoffed. "As do I, lad. As do I."

James pushed up from the roughhewn bench and stepped away, desperate to let the cool night air smooth the ragged edges of his irritation. His father's wheezing laugh followed him, until it became distant enough to fade into the backdrop of the camp. James drew a deep breath to calm his racing pulse and appreciated his ability to do so without the lancing pain in his chest he'd experienced so many months ago.

The scar stung at times in a sharp, internal way; nothing he could soothe, but for the most part, he had recovered from the thrust of a sword into his chest. He'd used the idle time at camp to strengthen his body once more and was grateful to have recovered so fully.

He knelt at the edge of the small creek, cupped water into his palms and splashed it over his face. It was cold against his hot skin. Refreshing. He sighed and leaned his head back. It was then he realized he was not alone.

He put his hand to the hilt of his dirk, his muscles tensed to spring from his crouched position as he slowly glanced to his left. He went still.

It was no warrior standing several paces away, but a woman. Nay—a goddess of the old ways—for truly no mortal woman could possess such an ethereal presence. Moonlight glowed off her in a radiant sheen, from the purity of her white gown, to the perfection of her fair skin and the brilliance of her golden hair. She was a moniker of peace, a symbol for everything pleasing and right in a world that had gone so damn wrong.

A massive dog, the size of a small pony, came from behind her and stood in front of her like a sentry.

The woman beheld James with long-lashed pale eyes, her gaze beseeching. When she finally spoke, her voice was soft, gentle, far too appealing. And completely English. "I need your help."

## CHAPTER 2

Anice's pounding heart had been unexpected, as had the rush of memories of her mother. The days after their mother's attack by a Graham, the despondency of the child she'd been left with, and their own dear Leila whose birth had been so violent, it had taken their mother's life.

All because of the Grahams.

At once, rage, horror and disgust flooded Anice. Her stomach roiled with nausea and her muscles went tight.

Piquette bristled at her side, protective, as though sensing his mistress's discomfort.

"Are ye injured?" The man rose.

Anice followed his ascent, watching the tallest, largest man she'd ever seen rise to standing. Her skin prickled, acknowledging her fear. These men had attacked Werrick Castle fourteen years prior. They had killed Anice's people, plundered fine goods and raped her mother. Her idea to come was truly foolish.

"Are ye well, lass?" He stepped toward her.

She flinched and then berated herself for having done so. These men were beasts. Showing them weakness would be like giving a hound the scent of a fox during a hunt. She notched her chin upward in what she hoped would appear as a show of strength. "I have come to speak to the man in charge of the Graham reivers."

"Who are ye?" he asked.

"Lady Werrick, Countess of Werrick," she lied. She had put much thought into this answer prior to leaving the safety of her home. Name and position held great weight. As simply the daughter of an earl, she was an easy target, one whose innocence was as tempting as the opportunity to besmirch the Barrington name. But a countess carried clout, far more than a mere daughter.

Though her mother had been dead for well over a decade, it was entirely plausible that Anice's father would remarry. In fact, it would be expected, especially with five daughters and no sons.

Anice hoped this warrior would assume her to be a new wife rather than a daughter. She needed every advantage she could get. The man stood with his back to the bright moon, his face cast in shadows. He observed her for a moment, then walked away. His large hand beckoned, and she followed with Piquette at her side.

Her heart danced in her stomach, her body alight with trepidation and wariness. Ahead of them was a sea of tents, the little triangular tops of white welling in the night like capping waves.

Several men stopped, gaping as she strode proudly by. She did not look at them, but she could feel their stares on her like something greasy and slick, as if they groped her with their eyes. In that instant, she regretted the kirtle with its low-cut bodice and its fitted waist, and the belt that hung tightly around her hips. Piquette issued a low, menacing growl.

"Have ye no' ever seen a lass?" The reiver leading her spun around to glare at the eyes feasting on her.

As suddenly as the men had surrounded her path, they now disappeared. This time when the man faced her, the full glow of the moon shone on him, revealing a straight mouth beneath a cropped brown beard and pale eyes. Not a handsome man, but nor was he ugly. Not like she'd expected of the Grahams. She'd remembered them with pockmarked faces and gaps of missing teeth, a child's memory of terror.

The man folded his arms over his chest. "Go on." He nodded her forward, and Anice had the sudden suspicion she might be more prisoner than guest.

Of course, she had anticipated such a possibility when she decided to go through with her scheme. It was a risk she was willing to take to aid her family.

There were a lot of things she'd considered. They might try to kill her, or threaten her at the gates of Werrick as Marin's husband had done with their younger sister, Catriona, years ago. For those reasons and countless others, Anice had taken care to strap a dagger to her thigh and cut the bottom from her dress pocket, ensuring she could reach the blade at a moment's notice. Whether to defend herself and Piquette or, if she were to be used as bait to lure the castle gates open, to end her own life.

The deeper they wound into the camp, the more pungent was the scent of roasting meat. It had been so long since she'd had more than simple grain or a bit of vegetables from the garden. Meat. Poultry. Fish. Venison. Beef.

Her heart drummed faster and spots of white blossomed in her vision. Fat hissed on flames, skins charring with tender meat roasting within. She desperately longed for the tear of it against her teeth and her mouth filled repeatedly with saliva.

She kept her head held high, but she could not stop her lingering gaze at a bit of beef slung over the fire. Piquette's head bobbed upward with each inhale, his stare fixed on the meat they passed. Still, as hungry as she knew he was, he stayed with her.

She strode toward the large tent standing out among the

myriad smaller ones and conceded once more that perhaps this decision would cost her life.

The large man pushed at the tent flap, lifting it from her path in an unexpected show of chivalry. Anice gathered closer her courage, nodded her thanks and passed through it. The air inside was thick with the heavy, smoky odor of tallow dips on several tables around the large tent. Oily black smoke curled up from the bit of cloth set in the saucers of pooled fat.

The man inside, Laird Graham presumably, rose from a chair as she entered. While larger than her, he did not stand nearly as tall as the man who guided her into the tent.

Thin strands of white hair hovered like fine threads of cotton over his otherwise glossy pate. There was a gauntness to his sharp featured face, lending him a skeletal appearance. He narrowed his glittering eyes at her and then turned to the tall man.

"Who the hell is this?" He demanded.

Piquette sat forcefully in front of Anice as though he meant to shield her from this man. "I am Lady Werrick, Countess of Werrick," she replied for herself. "I intend to treat you with civility and would expect likewise from you."

"Why would ye do that?" His lip lifted in a partial snarl.

"Because I feel as though everyone deserves the opportunity to disprove rumors spread about them."

He barked out a harsh laugh and his dark eyes bore down on her like a beast about to devour its prey. "And what have ye heard?"

A shiver slithered down her spine. She was grateful for Piquette and his strength. She gently ran her fingers over the thick reddish-brown fur of Piquette's neck for comfort. The dog did not move, but kept his stare fixed with lethal intensity on the laird of the Grahams.

Her gaze slid unintentionally to the man who brought her to

the tent, the one who had acted with chivalry. His glare was fixed on the laird she spoke with, his body tensed as though he intended a fight, as though he was not her jailor, but her protector.

JAMES COULD KILL HIS FATHER. The old man leered at the young countess, letting his gaze slide over her breasts and the sensual flare of her hips beneath the fitted dress. James's stomach roiled in disgust. How had he gone so many years without ever questioning his father's judgments, his tactics?

Lady Werrick regarded his father with scrutiny. "I've heard more of you than you've heard of me, I assure you," she replied levelly. "The Grahams have quite the reputation."

"What part of that reputation is it ye're here for?" The laird stepped closer and stared pointedly at the swell of her bosom rising above the fine silk gown. The massive brown dog in front of her issued a low, rumbling growl from deep within its chest and readjusted its stance.

James's own body tensed at his father's obvious attempts at intimidation. True, he had never seen his father strike a woman, or take one by force, but with the countess's slender arms and the narrowness of her waist, it was obvious she was a slight woman, as delicate as she was beautiful. And she *was* beautiful.

The room swam with her delicate jasmine scent, and the glow from the various tallow dips played over her curls. While she seemed fragile, her strength lay in her appearance. And a woman like her knew how best to wield her only weapon. In fact, she most likely had spent considerable time preparing herself for this meeting with his father in the hopes to disarm him with her loveliness.

The thought allowed him to pull his gaze from where she

stared up at his father with wide blue eyes, her full mouth carefully parted in a way meant to be becoming.

"I want to plan a meeting, a negotiation." She licked her lips. "For peace."

Aye, she played her game well.

"What do ye have that I want?" Implication was ripe in Laird Graham's tone and gleamed in his eyes.

James stepped forward and glowered at his father. The old man was going too far.

The countess narrowed her eyes. "I think you'd be surprised what can be offered."

"Oh, I doubt that." Laird Graham smirked. "And why is it yer husband sent his wife to do his speaking for him?"

"Will you meet with us or not?" Her fast reply gave way to what James was beginning to suspect. She had come alone, and without her husband's blessing.

"And how do we know ye willna kill us if we agree?" the laird demanded.

"You would have to trust me."

"What do ye think, lad?" James's father cast a pointed look in his direction.

"The Earl of Werrick has great wealth," James replied slowly. What was the old man playing at? He knew James's position. "It would be worth the attempt."

"I dinna trust well, especially regarding the English." The laird nodded to the massive brown beast. "Leave yer dog with us."

The countess put a hand to the dog's shoulders. "Nay."

James's father shrugged. "Then we willna meet with ye."

She glanced back at James, as though she expected he might intervene on her behalf. For the first time, the defiant strength in her eyes dimmed. Indecision warred on her face. Surely, they were nearly out of food in the castle at this point. Her people would be starving. Most likely that had forced the countess beyond the protective curtain wall of Werrick Castle.

For his part, James could not help the rise of pity in his chest for the woman. Mayhap it was that concern for her that made him step forward. "If ye leave the dog here, I'll mind him myself."

She knelt and curled her arm around the dog's chest, hugging him closer. A ruby ring glinted on her right hand.

"I'll guard him with my life." James held out his hand to the dog. When it did not growl at him, he moved his hand closer and gently scratched the underside of the brown chin. While it did not crane into his hand with affection, nor did it bite him. Instead, the dog fixed large amber eyes on him, as though conveying its lack of trust.

"I'd rather you keep me instead," the countess said with finality.

"Aye, but yer beast canna relay the message to yer husband." James's father said. "The dog stays, and we will meet ye tomorrow when the sun goes down."

She was silent so long, James thought she might refuse. Her head bowed toward the great beast and the soft breathy notes of indiscernible whispers rose from her whispered words to her dog. When she lifted her head, her eyes held a glossy sheen. She drew in a deep breath and rose. "Not when the sun goes down. You will meet us at noon."

James almost laughed at her brazen demand.

"If we can come to agreeable terms," she continued, "then your men can begin leaving the castle grounds. And my dog will be returned to me." She lifted her chin with the authority of her esteemed position.

"Noon," the laird declared. "And the beast stays, or ye'll all die in those walls."

The countess' eyes met James's. "If you harm him, I will kill you." For all her prettiness, there was an edge to her tone that told him she would make good on her threat or die trying.

The laird scoffed and nodded to the tent flap. "Take this wench back to her husband."

"Piquette walks with us," she said.

James's father waved his hand dismissively, decidedly done with the whole mess.

The countess regarded James with her long-lashed blue eyes before turning on her heel toward the tent flap. There had been something in the way she'd looked at him—a fearlessness, almost a challenge. This was no woman to easily tamp down. Piquette trotted after his mistress, the beast's shoulders jutting up like bony sticks from his haunches.

James followed after her and put himself at her unoccupied side. "Yer dog could use a good meal."

When she did not answer, he glanced down at her. The moonlight hit her just so and shadowed the hollows in her collarbones and cheeks. She was nearly starving herself. No doubt she tried to feed Piquette as well as was possible, given their limited means.

Disgust coiled low in James's belly. He hated being part of this life, scraping people's misery for their own gain.

"I'll see he is fed well," James offered.

The countess stopped and she regarded him with a large-eyed hope that bore into his soul. It gave him a glimpse of the hurt she'd suffered during this siege, of the desperation leading her to make this great sacrifice of leaving behind a beloved pet. She looked away abruptly and strode onward, severing the connection.

"That would be good of you." She spoke softly, the charged defiance in her tone softened by evident gratitude.

The shift in her demeanor was that of a woman made hard only through circumstance, a woman who might be entirely different under another situation. And though he had thoroughly learned his lesson when it came to alluring women, he could not help the stir of sympathy.

He leaned slightly closer to speak, to ensure they could not be heard by the tents falling away behind them. "I could get food for ye as well if ye like."

Her breath caught. But she swallowed and shook her head. "Nay but thank you. I ask only that you care for Piquette. He is dear to me."

James put up a hand to still their forward progress. Several arrows jutted from the ground a few feet in front of them, marking where the range of arrows could not strike them. He waved his hands and shouted out to the English soldiers along the castle wall to get their attention. "Yer countess wishes to return to the castle," he called. "Dinna shoot."

Atop the battlements of Werrick, the archers lowered their bows. The countess knelt beside her dog and wrapped her arms around the great beast. Piquette's high-pitched whines rose to James, as though he understood the transaction.

"I promise ye I'll give him the greatest care." James spoke as the countess rose, before she could issue any more of her ready threats.

Except there were no threats on her tongue. But there were tears in her eyes, gleaming and unabashed in her regret at leaving her beloved beast.

"I anticipate his safe return." She turned away with great hesitation and made her way to the castle. While she strode forward, she glanced over her shoulders several times like an anxious mother leaving a child.

Piquette whimpered again and shifted his position, restless with unease. On several occasions, he tried to follow, but each time Anice put up a hand to still him and he settled beside James once more.

"Dinna worry." James reached out to the dog and rubbed his hand over the large brown head.

The dog eyed him with a wariness a few strips of venison would doubtless ease. Ahead, the countess waited at the great gates as they opened to her.

For her sake, and for that of her people, he hoped an agreement could be reached between the Earl of Werrick and Laird Graham.

Especially as James's father's negotiations did not come cheap.

## CHAPTER 3

The following day, a few minutes prior to noon, Anice trailed after her father as he swept from the solar. Her clipped pace matched his, as did her determination.

"I told you not to come," he muttered. His mood had been sour since her return from the Graham camp the prior evening, going first from shock to outrage. Initially he'd declined any meeting with the Grahams, until Anice pleaded for Piquette's safe return.

The Earl of Werrick was a formidable man whose primary weakness was his love for his five daughters. Anice might not be the most intelligent or talented of them, but she had always had a knack for coercing her father to her will.

"You have told me not to attend." Anice did not slow her pace. "But I refuse to be left behind."

"Anice," her father bellowed in a tone he had not used with her since she was a child. "I do not wish to have you there."

She went hot with humiliation. "Because I am not Marin?" she demanded. "Do you think me so incompetent that you doubt my ability to manage at your side throughout the negotiations?"

His face softened. "I was thinking more of what happened to your mother." He averted his gaze and the muscle along his bony jaw went tight.

He had been like this for some time now: nostalgic, melancholy. Anice's heart flinched. He missed their mother, though it had been many years since her death. But Marin's leaving had caused his sorrow to dip deeper. No matter how hard Anice tried to take her elder sister's place, the feat was impossible.

"I coordinated this meeting; I intend to see to the discussion as well." Anice tried to keep her voice steady. After all, she knew well how to fake confidence.

Her father sighed and appeared every bit of his two and fifty years with the exhaustion and weariness emphasizing the loose skin under his eyes. "Very well, but I expect you to leave the speaking to the men." He motioned for her to walk in front of him on their short journey down to the great hall. Not that there was much great about it anymore, save its massive size.

The trestles lay in neat lines, empty and nearly useless with so little food to be had; the once-lively chatter now rendered quiet with a general darkness of foreboding; the bustle of servants gone still with the grinding pain of hunger in their bellies. Rats didn't dare enter the castle anymore for fear of encountering a desperate inhabitant of Werrick.

Even the rushes underfoot had long since gone bad and been swept away with nothing to use in replacement, leaving their steps echoing off the walls with a despondency that resonated in Anice's heart. William, their steward, stood beside the dais at the ready, as well as Drake, their new Captain of the Guard after their former one, Sir Richard, had sought a quieter life in the country in his older age.

The heavy thud of shoes on stone sounded outside the hall as Anice and her father took their seats upon the raised dais at the rear of the great hall. Her father curled his hands around the carved arms of his chair, his knuckles white.

Mayhap the meeting had not been a good idea. But their alternative was what— to starve slowly?

The doors opened and the laird entered along with the man who had promised to care for Piquette. However, her dog was nowhere to be seen. Her heart lurched.

"Where is Piquette?" she demanded when they entered.

Her father shot her a look of stern warning to be silent. Marin would never have warranted such a reprimand.

The large man inclined his head in apology. "Forgive me, Lady Werrick. To ensure our safety, I was forced to leave him behind. Know that he is quite well and in eager spirits to see ye."

Quite well, indeed. Anice shifted in her seat, unable to still the restlessness burgeoning inside her at this unwelcome news. As it was, she had not been able to sleep, not with images of Piquette being beaten or threatened, or worse—killed. Her heart flinched at such terrible musings.

"Piquette is with a man I'd trust with my life," the man continued. "Yer dog is in fine care and has eaten his weight in venison after ye left."

"Lady Werrick?" her father said with obvious irritation. "Lady Werrick died nigh on fourteen summers ago, and we've got you to blame for taking her light from our lives."

Laird Graham scowled. "We're here to come to an accord, are we no', Lord Werrick?"

Anice's heart was pounding with rage at the injustice her mother had suffered at the hands of the Grahams. But anger would not aid her in a time of negotiation.

Her father narrowed his eyes with obvious suspicion. "Aye."

"Ye want us to leave yer lands." Laird Graham let his glittering gaze shift around the barren room before coming to rest on Anice's father. "What are ye willing to give us to make it happen?"

The Earl of Werrick did not answer. Anice turned to her father and found him clenching his jaw with stubborn determination. "Papa," she urged quietly.

Her father pulled in a long inhale. "I imagine one such as yourself would arrive with a price in mind."

"Ye're a perceptive man, my lord." Laird Graham grinned. His gaze slid over to Anice and lingered with clear consideration. "Yer daughter is unwed, aye?"

Anice stiffened. Surely the old man did not mean to ask for her hand. Time had shriveled him into a husk. His shoulders curled downward, shrinking what might have otherwise been an impressive height like the younger man with him. Laird Graham stood hunched, his stomach protruding like a woman swollen with child. His face was puckered like an apple left too long in the sun and his eyes glittered with gleeful malice.

"Aye, Anice is unwed." Her father's words were heavy with trepidation.

"Yer eldest?" Laird Graham surmised.

"Second eldest. My eldest was wed several years ago." Was there a note of sadness to her father's tone, or had Anice imagined it?

"Pity." Laird Graham's mouth puckered and he sucked at his teeth. "This chit still comes with a dowry, aye? Coin and land?"

Irritation rankled through Anice at the man discussing her as though she were a transaction to be handled. As though she was not within earshot of both men.

Beside her, the Earl of Werrick cast a deep sigh. "She does come with a dowry of coin and land."

"Verra well. I have agreement then." The aged laird nodded. "My men will leave so long as the lass will agree to marriage."

Though she'd been somewhat expecting such words, shock

still rocked through Anice. Shock and disgust. To imagine kissing this man, letting his fetid breath near her mouth and his spotted, age-pruned hands on her body. She suppressed a shudder. There was no other choice, though. Her people would starve if she refused, and her sweet Piquette would no doubt be murdered. Her life with this man was a small sacrifice for all that would be gained.

A lump settled in her throat at the dismal options she faced. She would not allow Piquette to come to harm for her decisions.

Her father shot to his feet. "Absolutely not. I will not sell off my daughter like a piece of horse flesh. Certainly not to the likes of you."

She stared up at him in gratitude for his consideration, to not so easily cast her away for his own well-being. There were few fathers who so loved their daughters as he did. It was for that reason she spoke up, as well as for the love she held in her heart for all the people within Werrick, and for her dear Piquette who was both loyal and brave.

Anice got to her feet beside Lord Werrick. All eyes shifted to her. Her blood raced uncontrollably through her veins, powered by the raw energy of the decision she had made. A decision she had to swiftly speak lest she lose the nerve.

"All is well, Father." She regarded Laird Graham, the crumpling figure of a man who would surely kill all her girlhood dreams of love and passion and replace them with the reality of survival and necessity. To think, all those wasted hours trying to get poor Thomas to kiss her, all the nights she'd lain awake imagining what it would be like to be well-loved by a brawny man. All those blossoming girlhood fantasies withered away under her decision.

She inclined her head to her soon-to-be husband. "I will agree to marry you."

Disgust curdled in James's stomach at the woman's agreement to wed Laird Graham. Anice, her father had called her. An earl's daughter, one of youth and incredible beauty. James's father aimed high, even for a laird.

She kept her gaze fixed on Laird Graham, her face an emotionless mask. Surely, she could not be pleased with her decision, and yet he knew she did this to save her people. The lass was brave.

Exceptionally so. A woman willing to sacrifice anything to save those she loves.

Laird Graham threw his head back suddenly and laughed. The barking depth of it echoed off the stone walls surrounding them. James regarded his father with confusion. Had the old man's mind deteriorated along with his body?

"Ach, I'm flattered, lass. Truly." James's father wheezed out another laugh and panted for breath before speaking again. "I dinna want a wife. I've had enough nagging and harassment in my years." He slid a sly glance toward James. "Ye're for my only son."

James stilled. Surely his da jested. "I dinna want—"

"Marry the lass," Laird Graham said. "Or ye condemn these people to die in this castle."

Anice's stare settled on James, her face unchanged, her expression still shielded. He wished he could see into her mind at that moment, to read her thoughts. James was not the withered man his father was, but nor was he handsome. Experience had taught him all too well how beauty craved beauty.

Bitterness frosted over his heart at the memory he never fully pushed away. Anice would be trouble.

"Dinna ye want to marry the lass?" James's father slapped

him on the back, urging him forward, but James held his ground. "Dinna ye think she's bonny?"

Contrary to her impassive expression, Anice's cheeks blushed and her back went stiff. This was not going well.

"I dinna want to marry," James replied as delicately as he could.

"Why no', lad?" Laird Graham gestured to the woman and lowered his voice. "She gets ye everything ye want. If ye decline, these people will die." He shrugged with clear disinterest either way. "Do ye agree to wed her or no'?"

James glared at his father, hating the decision forced on him. He'd never wanted a wife. Not with the life he currently led, not with the fear of letting himself be so vulnerable again. But he could no sooner allow more innocent lives to be lost. Damn his father and the impossible decision he lay at James's feet.

James regarded Anice and nodded. "Aye. I'll marry her."

Her eyes burned into his, but he still could not read her expression.

"I have one other demand." Laird Graham drew their attention with his declaration. "I request that my son and I remain at Werrick as guests until the wedding. To ensure ye canna back out of the arrangement once ye have yer stores replenished, aye? And I want the wedding to be proper, with the banns read. I dinna want ye sneaky bastards to find some way to have it annulled."

The Earl of Werrick sat mute, his face slack with stunned shock at what had transpired. In truth, James felt much the way the man looked.

"Very well," Anice replied. "So long as your men are gone today by the time the sun sets."

"Consider it done. We'll remove our men from yer lands and return to be shown to our chambers." Laird Graham clapped his hands with the finality of a job done and departed.

James stared at the woman he would soon wed. Her fair brow furrowed in a pained expression. While he was a better choice than his father, James doubted this was a marriage she wanted.

She lifted her head and stepped off the dais toward him. "I have not been afforded the opportunity to make my own demands."

A smile quirked on James's lips. The lass had spirit, and he liked it.

"Ye are no' in a position to ask for anything," Laird Graham said from the doorway.

James put a hand up to stop his father. "Have a care how ye speak to my wife, da." He threw a warning look over his shoulder prior to returning his attention to Anice and nodded. "Go on."

She flicked her tongue over her lips, the only sign of nervousness she had exhibited thus far. "I want my dog back. And I'd like to know your name, please."

"Nay," the Earl of Werrick said suddenly, as though the grip of his shock had finally loosened. "You need not do this, Anice."

*Anice.* It was such a lovely name, sweet and delicate, like the woman.

"It is my decision to make, Papa." Anice lifted her arched brows at James in silent reminder that she still waited on his reply.

"I'll have them fetch Piquette posthaste. And I am called James Graham." He inclined his head. "Well met, Lady Anice."

"Well met," she murmured and offered a short curtsey.

The air between them congealed into something thick and uncomfortable.

"Damn it, Anice," the earl hissed. "Do not do this."

"It is done." Anice's tone and manner were strong with confidence. "My dog," she said to James, giving him leave to sever the awkwardness burgeoning between them.

James was all too eager to accept her offer, ready to remove himself from the aged, shocked earl's presence and that of the woman he was to wed.

Once outside, his chest swelled with an inhale of fresh, clean air to sweep away the stink of the castle's desperation. It clung to him like a second skin and made his body itch with the need to bathe. The people had watched him intently, large eyed and hollow cheeked, hungry for food and safety and peace. His clan had done this to them, turned them into such miserable creatures they didn't bother to shield their stares or shy from his path. They craved life as they were shadowed by death.

His father waited for him just beyond the castle gates, which had been thrown open in a show of peace. The old man leaned over with exhaustion from the show of force he'd exhibited in the bowels of Werrick Castle. James suppressed a shudder. He did not ever want to go back into that castle again, especially not in compliance with his father's demands—that they remain until the wedding.

Laird Graham's spine jutted from the thin fabric of his leine and he reached out blindly when James's shadow fell over him. James caught his father's withered hand in his and held fast. "No' much farther now, da."

"Ye've no' thanked me yet." His father's body weight bore shakily against James through the heel of his palm. After a moment, the old man straightened upright with a wink. "I dinna ever have so fine a wife."

James grunted.

His mother had been one of the laird's wives, a woman known for her ability to heal. Regardless of all her skill and knowledge, she had not been able to save herself when the baby she carried had died in her womb.

James remembered her in bits of broken memories, blurred from the time passed since his boyhood when she'd died. The delicate notes of lavender that perfumed her embraces, the warm gentleness of her hands when she tended his many scraped knees and cuts, the way her silky brown hair tickled his cheeks when she bent over him to kiss his forehead. Her kind, green eyes had sparkled every time she looked upon him.

To James, she had been beautiful. Perfect. Too good for his father.

Laird Graham had remarried immediately after her death, never loving any of his wives.

They neared camp and Piquette barreled toward them at full tilt, not stopping until his body slammed into James's thighs. The dog stared up with his sad brown eyes, as though imploring to be taken to his mistress.

James grimaced, knowing he had to return the dog to Lady Anice, that he had to face that castle, those people, and her again. His future wife, a woman too fine-looking for her own damn good. And certainly, for his own.

## CHAPTER 4

Anice's father was vexed.

He paced up and down the lushly appointed solar, his face furrowed into a map of hard lines. "There has to be another way."

Anice had looped through the circular conversation again and again with him. She swallowed down her sigh. Marin, after all, would have been patient in such a situation.

"You know there is no other way," Anice said levelly.

"First your mother and now you." The earl scrubbed a hand at the back of his head where a lifelong cowlick had begun to reveal a patch of flesh beneath his thick gray hair. He stared at her, his eyes large and haunted. "You're too beautiful, my sweet Anice. They'll destroy you, crush that loveliness and leave you wilted."

"I'm no flower, Papa." Anice said it as gently as she could, but it was hard to keep from giving way to her frustration. She was his beautiful daughter, the one whose merit of note was relegated to her appearance. How she longed to be more, to have a talent or a skill worth noting.

"Do you want to do this?" he queried.

She hesitated. It was the first time he asked what she truly wanted.

She met his gaze, sure of her answer as it rose from her heart. "I want to see our people fed and healthy. I want to ensure the family I love remains safe and comfortable. I want this for all of you."

Her father's gaze searched the floor. "Marin would have known what to do."

His words ground at Anice's nerves like salt. "Marin is not here." Her heartbeat pounded at her temples and the air was growing thick. She couldn't stay in this room any longer, going over the same conversation, bearing the reminder that she was the lesser daughter.

"*I'm* here," she said. "And I did find a solution." Nothing more could be said to that. Anice strode toward the closed door, desperate to be free of this bothersome discussion with no logical end.

"What of Timothy?" her father demanded of her back. "This is not like what you shared with him. This is no love match."

Her cheeks went hot with rage or guilt or shame, or possibly a combination of all three. "Timothy is dead."

With that, she pushed through the door and strode with clipped steps to the quiet privacy of her own room. Or rather, Marin's former room—the one that had once belonged to their mother. Regardless of its ownership, it would be silent within.

Anice didn't want to think of Timothy even as his image edged into her mind. The thick golden waves of his shoulder length hair, his clear blue eyes. He had smiled solely for her, always thinking to send her trinkets and flowers and poetry.

Anice's heart flinched.

He had loved her.

His life had been lost as it had been lived, in the service of chivalry and employment to his noble birth. While Anice's father had survived the battle at Berwick, Timothy had fallen in battle.

Her guilt had been great when he'd been alive, heavy with the knowledge she had agreed to marry him based on his being a wealthy earl's son, one of the king's favorites. With no other viable talents to her person, she'd tried to benefit her family with her one attribute. Surely, marriage was the only thing a woman of considerable attractiveness was good for.

But no matter how handsome Timothy was—and he was certainly handsome—nor how chivalrous or kind or smitten, Anice could not bring herself to love him.

Her stomach twisted at the internal admission, the same as it always did. While marriages were often made without love, her inability to return his affection weighed on her. A burden that had become heavier to bear after his death.

A sharp bark from outside broke through her unwanted reverie and her heart leapt to attention.

*Piquette!*

She broke into a run, not caring what she looked like as she sprinted to her returning dog. James Graham met her in the large entryway of the castle with Piquette, who appeared healthy and happy as he trotted affectionately at the Graham's side. Anice skidded to a stop. Piquette cast a hesitant glance up at the reiver, no doubt won over by the food he'd been given.

"Piquette," Anice called. It was all her dog needed and he promptly bounded over to her, nearly knocking her to the ground when she knelt to welcome him. His dark brown eyes were bright in a way they hadn't been in months and his whip of a tail would not stop wagging.

The Graham approached her slowly, as though he feared frightening her. "He was well cared for."

She could see the truth in what he'd said for herself and hated the stab of jealousy at his ability to give Piquette what he had needed to be healthy. Or rather, she hated her own inability to provide for her dog. Doubtless Piquette had been given fresh meat while she had only been able to offer grain and bits of gritty bread.

She rose, but kept her hand settled atop Piquette's soft head. "Thank you."

She studied him for a moment then, this man who had cared so well for her dog, who had kept his promise, who had agreed to marry her when clearly, he did not wish to. Her cheeks heated at the amount of convincing Laird Graham had needed to get an agreeable reply from his son.

*James Graham.*

He was not unattractive, and he had treated her kindly thus far in their limited interactions. A beard bristled over his large jaw and she could not help but wonder how it might compare from the smooth caress of Timothy's freshly shaven face. Not that Timothy had truly kissed her the way she'd seen other men kiss women. He'd been too aware of her femininity, too protective of her virtue.

But what would it be like to kiss this man? To be kissed *by* him? His arms were large, thick with bulky muscle. Surely a simple embrace would swallow her against him. And what must his beard feel like? Scratchy prickles? Or was it soft? His lips showed beneath the thick strands of hair, pink and full. What might he taste like?

The brine of salted meat? The earthy musk of home-brewed ale? Her head spun. Dear God, she was so ravenously hungry. Even her fantasies were laced with tasting food on men's lips.

He shifted his weight from one foot to the other. The slight movement broke the spell of her curiosity and she jerked her gaze away. She'd been staring.

How embarrassing.

"Ye dinna have to do this." He spoke low, his voice barely above a whisper.

Anice tilted her face up to him. "Your father's grand speech would indicate otherwise."

"Ye dinna want to marry me," he said smoothly.

"Is that an opportunity for escape? Or a warning?"

Not that his answer would alter hers. She would marry him. No matter how large or intimidating he was. For he was truly large.

And intimidating.

But Anice was never one to fall quiet under intimidation.

"You don't want to marry me," she stated bravely. "Is that what this is about?"

His gaze narrowed and didn't once trail down the length of her body. He was perhaps one of the only men in Scotland and England to not pay her beauty any mind. All men, including those who claimed to be chivalrous, had slid appreciative stares her way when they thought she would not notice.

Not this man. His eyes did not move past her face, as though he were assessing her worth as a person rather than her beauty as a wife. As though he could see into her soul.

Why could he not be like other men and take in her appearance, rather than leave her nearly squirming like a worm baited on a hook?

"Do you not find me attractive?" She'd intended her question to pull his eyes from her face to her body, something she was used to. Something she could bear. Only the words came out sounding arrogant and ugly.

She licked her lips, giving in to the nervousness twitching through her. "Isn't that what all men want? A woman with a title who is appealing and comes with a hefty dowry?"

"There are more important things in life," he answered with a slow, steady patience.

Another unexpected response. The man was insufferable. "There are few men who would agree with you," she countered.

"There are many men who are fools." The clatter of footsteps echoed around them. He slid a glance to the open hall at their left and stepped closer. His presence was too great, it seemed to suck the air from the massive room and left her heart pounding.

"There is more to the world than titles and coin." His gaze did slide down her now, but not with appreciation. "And beauty."

Her cheeks warmed. "Such fascinating words when spoken from the mouth of a Graham." She could not keep the harshness of her hatred from her words.

"Ye'll be a Graham soon, too."

She drew in a harsh breath at the revelation. Her thoughts swam in a dizzying mix of uncertain emotions made thick with hunger. She could not do this. Not until she'd had something to eat, until she could properly think. She turned to go.

"Anice," he said her Christian name in a low voice. There was something soft to it, sensual, beckoning, and despite her irritation, it made a warmth stir deep in her belly.

She faced him once more.

"I will only wed ye if ye come willingly," he said. "I'll no' force ye."

She understood then of what he spoke. The heat of her cheeks stoked to blazing.

He took her hand in his massive one and ran a thumb over her palm. Sunlight streamed in through the open shutters and shone on eyes that were more green than blue. He searched her gaze with those exquisite eyes, and she no longer felt as though she needed to squirm beneath his observation.

"What say ye, Anice?" he asked softly. "Will ye come to me willingly?"

JAMES'S REQUEST hung in the air, poised between them with a discomfiting tension. Anice gazed boldly at him.

"I will comply as is my duty." Her tone was neutral and cool, thoughtless to what those words implied. She drew in a breath as one does when they intend to say more, but then did not speak further.

"I will be a good husband to ye." His voice filled the silence but did nothing to make it less uncomfortable.

"I must take my leave." She began to turn away.

"A moment."

She hesitated and fixed her gaze on him once more. Her long-lashed eyes were pale blue and rimmed in a darker shade. Beautiful. Wary. The skin tightened around her eyes.

"I know we are being pushed into this." James drew the parchment-wrapped parcel from the satchel he carried. "We both have our roles to play. Mayhap we can be allies."

"Allies?"

He handed her his gift, which she took cautiously. The parchment puckered against her grip and the briny scent of salted venison blossomed into the air. Her nostrils gently flared.

"What is this?" Her voice was soft with breathy hope.

"Consider it a betrothal gift." Seeing the hunger widen her eyes made James wish he'd pinched more meat from the cook's tent. "I've also sent several men to notify the village of the castle's need for supplies."

She clutched the gift to her chest. The slender bones of her hand stood out against her pallid skin. "I haven't anything for you."

"Ye needn't give me anything."

Her nostrils flared again, no doubt taking in deep breaths of the savory dried meat she clung to. "It doesn't seem right to not have anything to give in return." She swallowed and extended the parcel to him.

Footsteps echoed off the stone walls, indicating their time alone was drawing to a close. He shook his head as she tried to return his present. "Give me a secret, then," he said. "Something ye've no' ever told anyone else."

She furrowed her brow at his request but drew the meat tight to her thin chest once more.

"No one has ever truly known me." Her words were rushed, as if she wanted to purge the secret from her lips. The parcel wrinkled in her grip. "I must—I must go."

The footsteps were closer now. He didn't stop her this time, but instead watched her thin frame dash down the hall with Piquette following at her side.

Two young women entered the great hall then, hand in hand. They were younger than Anice and shared her golden hair and large blue eyes. Fine dresses of costly fabric hung from their painfully skinny bodies. The women slowed and gazed up at him, the taller one appearing thoughtful in her assessment, while the younger one beamed broadly at him.

"You are James Graham?" the younger asked.

He nodded. "Aye, I am. Are ye Lady Anice's sisters?"

"We are. This is Ella and I'm Cat. Well, Catriona, really. I would say you could call me Cat, but I suppose Lady Catriona is more proper. Though I would not mind if you called me Cat." She smiled. "I hear you are to stay with us."

Her friendliness was unnerving. His clan had been trying to starve the inhabitants of Werrick Castle, but she seemed pleased to be in his presence.

The concerned glance by the older sister, the one Lady Catriona referred to as Lady Ella, was more what James had expected. Wariness. Skepticism. A hint of fear and contempt.

Still, James inclined his head graciously to the sisters. "Well met."

"My sister trusts too readily." Ella stepped in front of the other girl. "I, however, have questions regarding your motivation. Why was it you laid so long a siege upon us? Was this what you wanted? A marriage to a daughter of the Earl of Werrick, Warden of the English West March?"

James frowned. "I have never been in favor of this siege."

"You were there regardless though." She gave an inquisitive tilt of her head. "Why?"

In that moment, he might have mentioned his attempt to save a lad in one of their raids and how it had changed his life, or his many conversations to sway his father to a life of good, or his own aspirations to see his people living a life of honesty. However, the young woman did not seem one to indulge another's contrition.

Her lip lifted with censure, an indication he had paused for too long. "Your silence is reply enough." She gazed up at him once more, unabashed in her study of him, then caught her sister by the shoulders and swept them both from the room.

Dear God, this was going to be an interminable stretch of time. Perhaps even greater than when he'd thought he would die in that raid. Then again, at least death would have ended his suffering. As it was now, there was no hope for reprieve.

His grating exhale echoed off the stone walls and empty floors. His father had backed him into a corner, forcing him with a woman who did not appear to want to marry him, sisters who resented his presence here, and an earl who no doubt would gladly kill James rather than see him marry Anice.

And worst of all, James did not fault them, for he knew his own sins, and they were truly great.

## CHAPTER 5

Anice swallowed, but saliva continued to pool in her mouth. The frantic walk to her room left her inundated by the salty perfume of dried meat. It emanated from the wrapping she clutched and released little bursts of scent with every step. It rose around her like a miasma, fogging her brain and leaving her nearly mad with hunger.

She practically ran into her chambers and slammed shut the door behind her. Without bothering to go to her dressing table, she unwrapped the worn parchment to reveal a fist-sized hunk of dried venison. Her hands shook with such desperation she nearly dropped it to Piquette who waited with an eager gleam in his eyes.

"Oh pish," she chided. "You've had several meals while you were cared for. This is one meal I cannot share with you." Yet, as she spoke, she drew off a single sliver and tossed it to her beloved pet.

Piquette snatched it from the air and swallowed it without bothering to chew.

Anice peeled off another sliver of dried meat and lifted it to her lips. The saltiness of it hit her tongue, flavor exploding in her mouth. Herbs, salt, smoke from the curing flames. Pleasure radiated through her body. She leaned her head back against the smooth wood of her door and chewed and chewed and chewed the small bit of meat, savoring it as much as reigning in her control.

It would be too easy to blindly devour the meat in great, savage bites and gnaws. But such a delicacy should be shared with her sisters. She tore off another strip and ate that one with less decorum, giving in to her desperate hunger.

Only two months prior, meat was eaten daily, something sure and commonplace. Yet it had now become so rare and cherished.

Piquette flicked a glance up at her. She tossed a curl of venison to the floor. "No more. I believe you've had more than your share when you were with James."

*James.*

She slipped another piece of dried meat into her mouth, and slowly ate, knowing she ought to stop soon lest there was no more to share. His gesture to bring her food had been kind. Yet he had appeared no more eager for the union than she. Was there another he loved? What was his opinion on her being English?

Her thoughts stirred to life in her mind, the starving stagnation of her ability to concentrate finally returning due to the bit of food. She ripped off another small chunk, her final one. It would be enough to provide the energy she needed for her body as much and her mind.

James did not wish to wed her.

And he'd asked for a secret as his betrothal gift. She groaned and bowed her head forward beneath the crush of humiliation from having revealed that secret to James.

It had all happened so fast, been so confusing with her muddled thoughts. The tantalizing scent of the venison had overwhelmed her. It had sent her system into a wild response where her pulse raced as though she were near death and her gums ached for the pressure of solid food while she chewed. She had not been able to think properly with her head spinning thus. Rather than come up with an interesting reply, a safe reply, she had offered the only thing that would rise through the cloudiness of her muddy thoughts—the truth.

In fact, it was far truer a secret than ever she'd confessed.

"Did I truly say that aloud?" The scraps of food in her stomach went sour.

Piquette's large head lifted to regard his mistress, but Anice shook her head at him. "No more. The rest is for the others, at least until supper. Which we shall have tonight." A giddy bubble of excitement tickled in her chest. "We shall have supper every night. Oh, Piquette, we will have food."

The dog gave an eager chuff in celebration with her. The last few weeks had been miserable for everyone.

She wrapped the venison in its simple parchment. Her sisters were as hungry as she and would benefit from some of the meat. She opened her door and quickly located Ella and Catriona in the corridor leading to their shared room.

"We saw your future husband." Catriona clasped her hands to her chest and grinned.

Anice winced. "Dare I ask what you thought of him?" She handed the wrapped bit of meat to Ella.

"He seems a fine man." Cat watched Ella open the parchment "He is quite tall and—" Her eyes went wide. "Is that venison?"

"A betrothal present." Anice put up her arm to keep Piquette from snuffling the precious food with his large, wet nose. "I thought it best to share."

"It was kind of you to do so." Ella stared down at the gift in her hands.

Cat swallowed, as her large stare fixed on the food. "We can't, Anice. He gave it to you."

Anice put her hands to her hips. "Pish." The way she said it, she reminded herself of Marin, who said the phrase in moments such as these. "It is mine to do with as I please and I want to share it with the two of you. Besides, this will prepare our stomachs for food tonight."

The sisters both pulled off small bits and smiled gratefully as they handed it back. Cat devoured hers with a haste even Piquette might envy, but Ella savored hers as Anice had done.

The girls were too thin, their young bodies painfully skinny. The famished gleam in their eye as she passed them a second chunk made her grateful for her decision to share. No matter how bad it might be to marry a Graham, it would be better than watching these sweet girls slowly starve.

"It was kind of James to offer this to you." Cat grinned. "As I was saying, he is very tall and strong. Did you see how large his arms were? Like tree trunks." She spread her fingers in the air to demonstrate their size.

Ella tilted her head in ponderous consideration. "To me, he seemed conflicted."

Anice wrapped the remainder of the meat to share with Leila and Papa. Little more than a knot-sized amount remained. "What do you mean?"

"He stated he didn't approve of the siege." Ella shrugged. "And yet he was still there. Either he was attempting to placate us by wiping himself free of culpability for his association, or he lacks conviction."

Ella's explanation implied Anice's future husband was either a turncoat or a coward. And while that might bother some women, Anice was simply happy to have her family fed.

For now, at least.

Reivers were always ready to be on the move, even when they'd been stationary for months. James's life was a nomadic one, filled with constant movement and no real place to plant roots. If nothing else, he hoped this union would offer his clan a much-needed change.

The reivers had cleared their camped position around Werrick Castle, despite the driving rain, leaving patches of the wet ground scarred by evidence of their occupation. When James entered the castle once more, he found Anice waiting for him with Piquette and the earl by her side. Another man stood with them, with reddish-brown hair and a face with creases at the corners of his eyes as though he smiled often.

Piquette's tail wagged with such excited ferocity, it rocked the dog's massive body back and forth. He appeared the only one eager to see James and his father.

The earl regarded them with his lips tucked downward in a sour expression. "Per the agreement, we bid you welcome to Werrick Castle." Lines of tension wrinkled his forehead contrary to his civil tone. "I assumed you would prefer to look over your newfound wealth upon arrival. This is my steward, William."

His final words were hard with bitterness, not that James could blame the man. In one day, he'd lost a daughter and a portion of his fortune to his most hated enemy.

The man with reddish-brown hair offered a slight smile at the introduction and nodded his head.

"I dinna care to see." James shifted the weight of his pack onto his shoulders. "But I'd like to be shown to my room."

"Ye may no' wish to see," Laird Graham said. "But I do."

The older man's claim did not surprise James. Nor did the earl or his steward appear surprised.

The earl inclined his head toward James. "I will call a servant."

"That isn't necessary." Anice waved James toward her. "I will show him to the guest chamber."

The earl frowned. "I do not think that would be appropriate."

"Forgive me, Papa, but I do not see any of this as being appropriate." She lifted her brows. "Besides, Piquette will accompany us." She stroked the dog's large square head. With the ease of one who always got what they wanted, she turned to James. "Follow me."

The earl settled a hard stare on James in silent warning and motioned for Laird Graham and the steward to join him.

James lifted his bag and made his way beside Anice. He wanted this time with her. Alone again. Where mayhap she might elaborate more on what she'd said earlier.

"You do not wish to see your fortune?" Anice slid him a long stare as if she expected him to react. "Interesting."

"It was my da who wanted it, no' me."

"What did you want?"

"To stop the siege." He adjusted the weight of his heavy pack from digging into his right shoulder. "How did ye acquire Piquette? He doesna seem like the typical lady's dog."

"We are not in a typical location." Anice's hand reached out and stroked Piquette's large head. The beast immediately gazed up with adoration, his jowls swinging with each step. "As you know the border can be a dangerous place. Our castle was breached once, and the destruction was...harrowing." She paused, her gaze lost somewhere else. Her jaw clenched tight as she continued on.

James tightened his grip on his bag. He knew well what she spoke of, but from a victor's perspective. The raid had been traumatic for the people of Werrick Castle. He thanked God he had not been old enough at the time to join his clan in the attack.

"Papa immediately set to building the castle wall to ensure our safety," she continued. "To keep out those who would attack women and children."

Implication laced her statement like poison. She was obviously referring to reivers, and more specifically the Grahams.

The reivers still told tales of their great spoils of war from that night, prior to being run off by the remaining soldiers. Ever since, his clan had been clamoring to get back in while the earl did everything in his power to keep them out.

"My father wanted to ensure we would always be protected, especially after..." She looked away. "Especially after what happened to my mother."

James's stomach clenched. Apparently Lady Werrick had been attacked, or killed. Or worse. He wanted to ask, but a cowardly part of him wished to remain ignorant to the extreme of their suffering.

"My father had us—" she pressed her lips together. "He wanted to ensure we had protection at all times. Not that Piquette was much of a deterrent when we received him." There was a curl to her mouth which pressed James to ask her to go on.

"He was a squirmy warm thing." Anice smiled at the memory. "Small, if you'd believe it. With a ready tongue for bestowing kisses upon us all and a brow that furrowed as though he were contemplating the world with an old man's careful assessment." At this, Anice puckered her brow, dramatically intimating the appearance of an old man. "And now..."

She bent at the waist and took Piquette's massive head in the cradle of her palms. Piquette's tail whipped back and forth as he gazed affectionately at his mistress.

"Now that he's fully grown, all that thinking has made him serious and loyal and wonderful." She gently ruffled her fingers through the dog's fur, much to Piquette's obvious enjoyment. He lapped eagerly at the air between them. Anice laughed, a sweet, clear note, and ducked her head to avoid the onslaught of canine affection.

James couldn't stop his own grin. This was a side of Anice he hadn't expected, one of playfulness. In a moment such as this, her heart seemed open and kind.

"Enough, my Piquette." Though she spoke in a delicately chiding tone, the dog immediately stopped and sat. Anice bestowed a kiss to the top of the beast's head and then straightened. "He has always been such a good and loyal companion."

Her joy reached her eyes in such a lovely way, James found himself mildly jealous of the large dog. Together, the three of them continued walking.

"Ye said he was for the lot of ye," James said. "But ye're the one he follows about. How did ye come to win over his affection?"

She laughed again. "Oh, I didn't intend to. In truth, he seemed too serious a pet for me. But every time we would all sit beside the fire, he would wander his way over to me in that dreamy, sleepy way puppies do." She danced her hands through the air like a wobbly puppy. "And he'd fall into my lap and sleep. He was so precious, I hadn't the heart to wake him, and so I'd remain motionless until he woke and bounded off once more."

"It appears he's no' left ye since." James wanted to keep her talking, to observe the happy expression glow over her fine features, and the graceful movements of her hands as she illustrated her story.

"He hasn't." She leaned a bit closer and whispered, "And I'm glad for it."

They'd stopped walking as they came to a door. "This is where you will be staying until…" A flush crept up Anice's neck. "This is your chamber."

He regarded the blank door. He'd been so captivated by her story of Piquette, he hadn't paid any notice to the path they'd walked to get there. Mayhap she would be kind enough to guide him there again later if he could not find it again.

He nodded his thanks to her, but she did not leave, and he was glad for it.

"I wanted to thank you," she said slowly.

He lifted his brows.

"For the betrothal present of dried meat." She twisted a small ruby ring on her hand. "It was much needed by me and my family."

James frowned. It hadn't been meant for her to share. If she shared it with all of her sisters and her father, there wouldn't have been much left for her. "Ye're to be my wife, Lady Anice. I will always care for ye."

She stared up at him and silence stretched between them. However, where it had been long and uncomfortable previously, it was now pleasant, more intimate. Her expression was soft with consideration and for the briefest of moments, her gaze dipped to his mouth. The way a lass looked at a man she wanted a kiss from.

## CHAPTER 6

James let his gaze linger on Anice's lovely face, getting to truly study her for the first time. Her features were without flaw; so exquisite, she made Morna appear plain by comparison. A feat James would have thought impossible.

The idea did not sit comfortably in his stomach. Nor did the thought of kissing Anice. Not now, at least. He knew well the reputation of the Grahams, and of what some of the crueler men in their ranks were capable of doing. He'd been disgusted by such things, but his father never sought to punish the offenders. Yet another change he would implement when he was laird.

But he would not now kiss Anice for fear of making her assume he was like them. "I should go inside." He indicated the door.

"Aye." Anice set one graceful hand to the latch and opened the door for him.

To his surprise, she entered first, leading him into his chamber. The furnishings inside were fine, the kind his father and the older men of the clan discussed often when detailing their raid nearly fifteen summers prior.

The great four-poster bed had green velvet trappings on

either side so one might close themselves within at night, and a large trunk at its foot. A far Ïcry from his bedroll in the pele tower. Tapestries hung from the wall, the colorful thread glinting with silk and gilt. If all the rooms were as well appointed as his, and all the daughters dressed as finely as Anice, it was no wonder his father had circled back to Werrick to test its impenetrable walls.

James put his bag on the floor beside the bed, unwilling to set the dirt-crusted leather upon the neatly made bed. "This is verra fine." He glanced at Anice where she stood just inside the threshold of the room.

Piquette strolled past her and settled onto the floor by the unlit hearth with a great whump. Anice considered the dog first, then turned her attention to James. "Why did you not go with your father?"

Her question had been asked casually enough, but the intensity of her expression indicated his answer was of great import. He decided to go with what he knew best—the truth.

"I dinna want ye to think I was marrying ye for yer fortune."

"Ah, yes. The man who does not want power or influence or wealth." She recited the words coyly. "Or beauty." She smirked and held up her hand with her fingers splayed. "However, you are a laird's son." She folded down her pointer finger. "You will marry into a good amount of land in one of England's prime locations along its border." She folded down her middle finger. "Those lands will yield a considerable amount of coin." She folded down her ring finger.

"And then there's ye." He gently folded down her small pinky. He'd spoken without considering his words and immediately regretted them. Flattery to beauty was as dangerous as oil to an open flame.

She lifted a brow. "It would appear you have everything

anyone else would want without wanting any of it. Tell me, why did you agree to marry me?"

"Ye're clever." He stepped closer to her and Piquette did not so much as stir, apparently comfortable with him after their time together at camp outside the castle walls. "Ye dinna take things at their immediate worth, do ye?"

She said nothing, but nor did she move back as he stepped closer still, so that they were nearly touching. Her floral scent teased at him, light and sweet and delightful. Like her.

"I dinna want this siege." He smoothed a hand down his beard.

Her gaze remained locked on his, a challenge, or perhaps an invitation. "Why didn't you leave?"

"I thought I might do some good in staying." He could practically sense the warmth of her body radiating through his clothing. He should move back, put space between them.

Her lips quirked. "It would appear you did."

"Aye."

Her mouth was perfectly shaped, plush and entirely too kissable. Had she been kissed by another? Would he be her first?

Her breath drew in softly and her body swayed slightly closer, as if she were being drawn toward him. He tentatively put his hand to her cheek and her lashes swept down. Her cheek was warm, her skin soft. So, so soft. He swept the pad of his thumb over her high cheekbone and she opened her eyes to gaze up at him.

Desire burned her gaze, bright with curiosity and unmistakable. Another woman had looked at him once with the same smoldering innocence, and he'd sacrificed too damn much for her.

He wished Anice was not so appealing, or that he was handsome, the kind of man worthy of such loveliness. And he wished like hell he didn't want to kiss her.

Like a moth drawn to a fatal flame, he lowered his face to hers. He had meant the kiss to be gentle, a delicate brushing of their lips, a taste of that full mouth. It had started off as such. At first. The initial connection had been almost imperceptible. Not enough.

He nudged the underside of her chin with his fingertips and she lifted her face toward his. Her lips were petal soft, warm and wonderful and sent a delightful sizzle of desire through his veins. Still, he'd carefully held back, until her mouth moved against his own, bold and inviting.

He caressed her bottom lip with the tip of his tongue and she gave an eager gasp. His hands cupped her face, cradling her as he swept his tongue into her mouth. She tasted fresh, like water, clean and pure. It made him hungry for more, for her.

She gave a soft moan and the length of her body pressed against him.

A powerful knock sounded, and they leapt apart like guilty children. Anice gave a shy laugh and tucked a lock of stray hair behind her ear. James smiled in spite of himself and went to the door, which had thankfully been closed. Piquette continued to sleep soundly at the cold hearth.

A Werrick soldier entered, his handsome face stern. He looked first to Anice and then to James and his jaw went tight. It was only a simple reaction, but it was enough.

The soldier was clearly protective, displeased to find James and Anice together alone. This man might very well be in love with her, as was the way with men when it came to bonny women.

"Drake." Anice stepped forward and touched the man's sleeve. It was an innocent touch, but it sank into James's chest in a shard of bitter jealousy.

He was doing it again. Irritation at his own weakness lit like fire in his veins. He was letting himself warm toward a bonny woman. Surely, he'd learned his lesson the first time.

The ruby ring winked on Anice's right hand. Her kiss had been too eager. Had she had a lover previously? Mayhap the ring had been a gift from one.

He forced his thoughts from the idea. He may have to marry Anice, and he would share her bed, but he would keep his heart well-guarded. The pain and humiliation of his last betrayal had ached more than his near-fatal battle wound.

The soldier, Drake, turned his intense black gaze on James. "I was told to summon ye. Laird Graham is gravely ill and has been taken to his chamber."

James went still with the news. His da had been ill, and certainly weak, aye, but James hadn't expected his death so soon. Not yet. "Has a priest been summoned?" he asked.

"Our healer is exceptional," Anice said to James before giving her attention back to the handsome man. "Has Isla been sent to him yet?"

"I tried, my lady." Drake offered. "She refuses to come. She's in the kitchen with Nan—"

"Take James to his father's rooms. I will see to Isla." Anice stepped through the open doorway and called over her shoulder for Piquette. The dog blinked open tired eyes and hefted himself to his feet to trudge after her. Anice quickly departed the room without ever having glanced in James's direction, no doubt regretful at their shared kiss.

Drake did not speak as he led the way to Laird Graham's room. It was for the best. James had nothing to say to the handsome young man.

Inside, the chamber was thick with heat from the newly started fire, the windows shuttered against the outside air. The curtains to the massive bed were parted to reveal a slender frame lying prone.

James rushed to his father's side, surprised how frail the great Laird Graham appeared. His da's skin had faded to a gray pallor and his narrow chest rattled with each wheezing breath.

Never had James seen his father in such poor condition. So withered and shrunken in on himself, it was as though the old man was already dead, as though James had already lost him.

∽

THE RICH SCENT of cooking stew drew Anice toward the kitchen as surely as did her purpose. Her mouth watered and her stomach clenched with the want of nourishment. For food and the pleasure of taste, of chewing.

Hunger buzzed through her and Piquette panted at her side with intermittent whines.

"I know." She smoothed a hand over the top of his head. "We must get Isla though, for the sake of Laird Graham, and for the sake of all of us as well." Speaking aloud was more for her resolve than it was for Piquette's benefit.

It would be all too easy to sit down with a large bowl of stew, the gravy thick and rich, the meat tender and savory. She could practically feel the greasy thickness of it against her lips and gave a whimper of her own.

Such thoughts were impractical and detracting. *Isla.* She needed Isla.

She found the aged healer locked in deep discussion with the cook.

Isla peered around Nan toward a large pot sizzling over the fire. "Dinna use so much goose fat."

"I don't instruct you on the art of healing." Nan swelled out her bosom. "Don't you dare instruct me on the cooking of my food. This is my kitchen and I'll have you gone."

Various food stuffs were piled in neat stacks, more food than any of them had seen in months. However, it was not nearly as much as they had received in prior deliveries. No doubt the Graham forces had depleted the village of their usual stores.

"Isla, you're needed," Anice said.

The arguing stopped abruptly and both women turned to stare at her.

Isla narrowed her tawny eyes, which made them nearly disappear beneath the etched wrinkles on her aged face. "If this is about Laird Graham, I dinna care to aid the whoreson."

Nan pushed in front of Isla. "She won't leave me be." The cook set her hands stubbornly on her hips, her apron streaked with fresh flour. "She insists I'll make everyone ill with my cooking."

Isla rolled her eyes and dramatically pushed in front of Nan's obtrusive frame. "The people havena had a sufficient meal in nearly two months. Ye canna give them strong food or their stomachs will rebel." Isla stared pointedly at Nan. "I've told her as much, but she doesna listen and has given every person who has wandered down here a whole loaf of bread, a bit of cheese and ale. 'Tis far too much."

Anice put up her hand to still their remonstrations. "Nan, your cooking is always delicious and will not require much seasoning or fat. The supplies do not appear to be as plentiful as they'd once been. Mayhap it might be prudent to utilize restraint. For now. I am certain your meat pies will be as delicious as ever, regardless."

Nan flushed with pride, her face creased and kindly once more. She handed Anice a roll, still warm from the ovens, hot where it rested against her palm.

Isla slid a look of smug censure in the direction of the cook. The old healer pulled the roll from Anice's grasp, tore it in half and gave a satisfied nod.

Anice stared at her halved roll. She wanted to shove the

mass of it in her mouth. Instead, she swallowed down her desire and addressed the healer. "Isla, if Laird Graham dies, his clan will assume it was done with purpose. Every soul in this castle is once more at risk if he dies. If anyone can save that old goat, it's you."

Isla grinned, flashing the brilliance of teeth so straight and white, it was rumored she took them from the mouths of corpses. Anice, however, refused to believe such gossip. Just as surely as she'd cast aside the gossip that the woman was over three hundred years old.

"Aye, I can do it." Isla lifted her large basket of assorted items for common ailments. Isla's gaze fixed on a servant clutching a bowl of flour. "Bring up a pot of boiling water and some fresh linens to Laird Graham's chambers, aye?"

The young woman nodded and Anice waved for the healer to follow her to the stately room, one both worthy of welcoming guests and keeping them easily guarded. No sooner had Anice turned away than she bit into the bread. It was soft under her teeth, and still hot enough to burn her tongue. She did not mind and devoured the entire bit of it, sharing a pinch with Piquette. Though it had been a meager amount, her stomach felt stretched to its limit with the meal and she realized her gratitude to Isla for the restraint.

She brushed her hand over her mouth to ensure no flour remained on her lips. James's kiss popped into mind as surely as it had the entire walk to the kitchen from his chamber. Timothy had always been tepid in his affection, offering delicate pecking kisses, delivered more often to her hands than her lips.

Guilt singed her cheeks. Timothy was dead. It would not do well to think ill of him, especially when he had truly loved her so much. James though—that kiss.

Her breath caught to think of it. His large hand had been so impossibly gentle when he'd nudged her chin upward. The way his tongue had swept against her own, the way it captured her world in the grip of blazing lust. She wanted to clutch him to her, to kiss him more, let him lick her mouth, her neck, her breasts, every part she'd ever heard others discuss and had never experienced herself. A pulse of desire settled deep between her legs and made her long to rub her thighs against one another to experience the delightful ripples of pleasure.

In truth, it was what she had wanted of Timothy. She had agreed to his marriage proposal for the benefit of her family. She did not fully relish the idea of the children, not yet at least. But passion…oh, how she longed for passion.

And she had a sense James might be able to provide such lustful endeavors.

Midway to Laird Graham's room, they came upon a man bent over the sturdy wall, his hands braced over his head while he retched. Chunks of bread and cheese sat in the clear liquid on the floor.

Isla tsked. "I told her no' to give ye so much." She lifted one side of her basket and rummaged about until she pulled loose a small satchel. "Put this in a bit of boiled water to steep and drink it all. It'll cure yer pain."

The man reached up without lifting his head and accepted the pouch of herbs with muttered thanks. Isla pointed a bony finger at him. "And dinna eat too fast next time, or this will happen again, aye?"

The man retched once more, and Isla waved him away as though he were a lost cause. They continued on their way, pausing thrice more for other inhabitants of Werrick suffering from the same affliction.

Anice had a new-found appreciation for Isla's warnings and was glad to have followed her advice. "What is in the teas you are distributing?"

"Common remedies for disorders of the stomach." She

shrugged. "Chamomile flowers, root of ginger, a bit of linden. All soaked in heifer piss and left to dry in the sun for a sennight."

Anice suppressed her grimace, suddenly gladder still for having heeded Isla's warnings so as not to require the cure.

The healer pushed through the door to Laird Graham's chamber. Anice could make out James's large form in the dark as he knelt at his father's bedside. He leapt to his feet at their arrival, his face anxious. In spite of his father's malicious demeanor and their obvious disagreements, it was clear James held an affinity for the old man.

It was tempting to admire the sweetness in James. And yet, she did not know him. Not only did she not know him, he was a Graham, a member of the marauding reivers who once destroyed her home and ultimately killed her mother. She would do well to keep such thoughts forefront in her mind.

Isla strode to the bed and pressed her ear to Laird Graham's narrow chest. Not that it seemed necessary when his wheezing breath whistled through the room. The laird truly was unwell.

Isla set her basket of herbs on the table and began to rifle through its contents, pulling out several herbs. She bound them together in a thick stalk, secured it with a bit of catgut, and lit it with a flint. Smoke rose from the bundle and filled the room with the musty scent of sage and several other herbs Anice could not name.

Isla bent over Laird Graham's unmoving body and gently blew the smoke toward his face. He gave a chuffing cough and tried to turn his face away.

"Dinna fash yerself," Isla chided. "This will help ye." She waved a hand at James's towering frame looming over her. "Yer son floating about my shoulders, however, willna offer any good."

James didn't move. "Will we need the priest?"

A slow smile blossomed over the healer's thin lips, tinged

with malice. Of course, the healer wanted Bernard called. Not for last rites, but because the twitchy priest's fear of Isla brought her great amusement.

"Isla, nay." Anice put her hand to her hips. The last thing she needed was Isla and Bernard sniping at one another over the dying laird.

Though in truth, it might benefit them all if Anice did go to the chapel within the castle to pray. If Laird Graham died in their care, it would not bode well for the inhabitants of Werrick Castle. There could be a war, another siege. One they might not escape from.

Anice shuddered to think how much worse it truly could have been. It was too easy to see how they might starve to death if they'd been forced to go on another two or three weeks.

Instead, she put her attention to James. "You needn't worry. I do not think your father needs a priest. Isla is the best healer in all of England and Scotland."

"Aye, 'tis true." Isla cackled to herself and blew huffs of smoke toward the laird once more.

A knock rattled the door. Anice ran to answer it so Isla would not be disturbed from her work.

A man stood on the other side, his face pale, one arm clutched over his stomach. "Isla needs to come to the great hall. We're in dire need of the healer."

## CHAPTER 7

James cast a nervous glance at his da's deathly pallor. If the healer was needed by the people of Werrick, then surely, she wouldn't stay to attend to a man who'd been set on killing them all.

For certes, choosing them over his father would be far too easy. But the withered old woman did not depart from Laird Graham's side.

She waved James toward her. "Blow this in yer da's face for a bit, aye?"

James gently exhaled and a wash of gray white smoke swirled over his father's face then dissipated into the air.

"Ye take these packets," Isla said to Anice. "And tell them to steep it. I knew many would try to eat too quickly. I prepared these a while back in the event we were saved." She winked at her own foresight.

A knock sounded at the door again. James blew on the steady stream of smoke curling up from the bundle of dried herbs and glanced over his shoulder as a petite redhead walked into the room with a steaming pot held with a cloth.

The healer's withered face crinkled more with her eyes narrowed. "Ye two can go now. I have the help I need."

James hesitated, his hand still clutching the cluster of smoking dried herbs.

Isla hefted the steaming pot from the young woman's arms without the benefit of the cloth, her fortitude and grit far more than James would have credited for the spindly woman. She was so wretchedly thin, she looked as though she might break.

She motioned to the young maid. "Get the herbs from him and wave them about the old goat's face."

"I'd like to stay." James tightened his grip on the herbs and pulled them back, away from the young woman's reach. The servant cast an uncertain glance toward Isla.

Isla set the pot by the hearth with a puff of irritation, strode over to him and plucked the herbs from his hands with wiry strength. "Ye'll do me no good hoverin' about. Off with ye."

James opened his mouth to protest when his father gave a rattling cough. He immediately kneeled at his da's side.

Behind him, Isla gave a long-suffering sigh. "Do ye see what I mean? How am I to get to him with ye in my way?"

A hand rested gently on James's shoulder. He turned abruptly, expecting to see the sour, wrinkled visage of the old healer and instead saw Anice's comely face, her brows pinched with sympathy.

"Mayhap you could join me in distributing the herbs?" She held up the basket she held in her other hand and offered a kindly smile. "It would give you a chance to know the people of Werrick Castle. And the distraction might be welcome."

James cast one more glance at his da's pallid face.

"Dinna worry, lad, he'll no' die." Isla edged around James and glared down at the Graham laird. "He's too stubborn to go, I'll give ye that. And he's too bloody important to us. Off with ye now."

Reluctantly James got to his feet, cast one final, regretful stare at his father. He lifted the basket from Anice's arm and allowed her to lead them from the room.

As they walked, his mind churned with turbulent thoughts. What if Laird Graham died, and he wasn't there to say goodbye? What would happen if his father was no longer in charge of the Grahams?

Certainly, he wouldn't have to marry Anice. He would have full reign of the clan to do with as he pleased without his father's interference.

He would have everything he'd been wanting. But he could not bring himself to wish for his father's death. Laird Graham might be mean spirited and blinded by avarice more times than not. But for all his gruffness, the old man loved James and showed his oldest son affection in his own peculiar manner.

After all, Laird Graham had sacrificed his desire for Werrick Castle to offer James the opportunity to fulfill his wish for a life without marauding. James knew how long his father had wished to take Werrick Castle again. And he'd given it all up for James.

"It is difficult to see someone you care for suffer." Anice's soft voice drew him out of his ruminating.

He made a low hum of consideration and shifted the basket more comfortably against the crook of his elbow. Its weight made him grateful for having insisted on taking it from her.

She twisted the small ruby ring. "My mother died during childbirth. I was by her side when she finally succumbed."

There was a quiet pain in Anice's voice James could not ignore. It was one with which he was familiar regarding his own mother. "I imagine that was difficult to have been there for," he said. His own mother had died in childbirth as well, to a sister who also had perished, but he hadn't been allowed to be present. Not that it had kept him from hearing her screams.

Anice drew in a heavy breath. "She was beyond comprehension at that point. Carrying the babe had been difficult as she was so filled with despondency after—"

The baritone of male voices came from the open doorway to the great hall. James stopped and caught Anice's free hand. "After what?"

"After the attack on our castle." Anice slid her gaze from his. "After what happened to her. She walked about the castle empty-eyed, as though already dead. In truth, we feared for her child as much as we feared for her."

"Did it live?"

Anice smiled to herself. "Aye, by a miracle. Another magnificent sister we named Leila." She peered into the great hall and nodded in the direction of a girl wearing fine blue silk dress and a somber expression. "There she is now."

Unlike the other daughters of Werrick, this one had dark hair and appeared to be…

His heart squeezed. Little Leila appeared to be approximately thirteen years old, the same age she might be if…

"Yer mother." James spoke slowly, dreading the answer as much as he hated voicing the question he suddenly needed to ask. "What happened to her before her death?"

Anice drew a slow, steadying breath and refused to meet his gaze. "She was attacked when your clan took Werrick Castle. She tried to keep us safe after Papa had been struck down. A man took her." She curled her hand into a fist at her side. "He dragged her away where he beat her, raped her and left her for dead."

∽

ANICE THOUGHT UNVEILING the truth behind her mother's death to James would allay the burning anger inside her chest, but it did nothing to dampen the flames. For his part, he remained silent.

A glance at his face showed a furrow of pain on his brow. Guilt cut into her for goading him with the story. Guilt!

It was foolish, of course, but she could not still the twist of discomfort.

Leila made her way toward them, oblivious of their prior conversation, and slipped her hand into Anice's while staring up at James. "You are James Graham, correct? The one who will marry Anice."

Of all the inhabitants at Werrick Castle, Leila was the most well fed with the sisters all saving a bit of their rationed food for her to eat. Regardless, the youngest was little more than skeletal arms and gaunt cheeks. Evidence of her pathetic appearance was obvious in James's sorrowful expression.

He set the basket to the floor and knelt in front of Leila, so his eyes were level with hers. Piquette licked at the air beside James's face, but he backed farther out of reach with a light chuckle. "Aye, that is right. And are ye the wee Lady Leila?"

She nodded.

"Well met, my lady." He lifted her free hand and brought it gently to his lips. as though she were a great lady at court and he a cultured courtier.

To Anice's surprise, Leila beamed at James. "Indeed."

It was a rare thing to see so wide a smile from the youngest Barrington sister. Leila pulled her other hand from Anice's and put it to James's bearded cheek. "You didn't want this siege." She lowered her head in reverence. "Thank you for helping to bring it to an end."

If the smile had surprised Anice, her sister's words left her speechless. Leila had not offered any foretelling or emotional insight to people in over three years. Not since she had missed Marin's attack and fell victim to her own self-doubt.

James blinked. "Thank ye for understanding."

Leila lowered her hand from his cheek. Piquette lapped his tongue near James's face once more, but he eased back with a carefree grin and rubbed the dog's giant head.

"Will you take him out for a bit, Lamb?" Anice asked. "We've got several people to attend to." She nodded to Isla's basket on the floor at James's feet.

Leila nodded enthusiastically. "Come, Piquette. We can finally go outside." Her lips pursed with an unladylike whistle and she patted her thigh.

Piquette gave an excited hop with his massive front paws, then stopped and hung his head in Anice's direction, as if seeking permission. She laughed. "Go on with you both. But mind you bring a soldier."

"Of course," Leila tossed over her shoulder as she ran from the room with Piquette galloping at her heels.

"That is Isla's, is it not?" A man pointed to the basket at James's feet. "We were told she was coming to the great hall with teas. Is she following you?" the man craned his neck to peer at the empty doorway.

"Nay, she is detained," Anice replied. "We have been sent with items in her place. Do you suffer from stomach pains?"

The man slid a wary gaze in her direction, evidently uncomfortable answering her. His hands slid around his belly, which gave a rumbling gurgle. Sweat shone on his pale brow.

Anice bent to retrieve a packet of herbs from the basket and tucked it into his hand. "Steep this. It will aid your digestion."

The man muttered his thanks and ran off with an awkward, clenched gait.

"Mayhap I speak with the men and ye see to the lasses." James nodded toward a woman approaching them.

Anice slipped several bags of the tea from the basket and made her way to the woman as two more men entered. James's attempts to offer the packs of herbs went without receipt; the men opted for the embarrassment of their irritated stomachs with Anice over acceptance from the enemy. It did not escape her notice that James even attempted to sit at a table, minimizing his intimidating height. Still no one approached.

Anice's vassals did not appear to be as accepting of the large reiver as were Piquette and Leila.

"James can assist you, if need be." Anice smiled pleasantly at several people waiting for their turn to get their tea from her. The people remained in place.

Not that she could blame them for their suspicions. She harbored them herself. James had been kind, and Leila seemed to trust him, but he was still a Graham.

Regardless, only good would come of him getting to know her people better.

She made her way to James's side and set her hand to his massive shoulder in a public show of solidarity. The people were forced to approach them both. Except instead of handing the packet to the sufferers directly, she delivered the instructions and allowed James to pass out the herbs.

Werrick's young priest, Bernard, stepped forward when it was his turn, and cast a helpless gaze at Anice, with more nervousness than the twitchy man usually exhibited. Sweat shone on his bald head and beaded on his upper lip. He licked his lips and stayed back a step more than anyone else. But then, it was no secret the man was deathly afraid of reivers.

An unholy rumbling sounded from his bowels. He clenched his teeth and clapped a hand over his stomach. "My stomach."

Isla ambled into the room. Her stare settled on Bernard and a smile stretched over her face. "Ate too much, did ye, Priest?"

His eyes bulged. With a trembling hand, he made the sign of the cross and muttered a prayer to himself, the bag of herbs held stiffly between his fingers. "This came from the witch?" He nodded toward Isla.

She folded her arms over her chest, an unctuous gleam in her eyes. "Aye, of course. Where else would it have come from?"

He pushed his hand to Anice's and unfurled his sweaty fist, so the damp bag fell into her palm.

"I shall be fine on my own." He swallowed thickly and staggered from the room.

Isla cackled, bending her bony body in half with the force of her mirth. "Do ye see where his stubbornness will get him?" She tsked gently, a smile still in place. "Too bloody high and mighty for his own good."

"My da?" James asked.

Isla took the basket from Anice and waved her hand dismissively. "Ach, the man is fine. Just having a bout of weak chest. He's as beastly as I imagine he always has been and is waiting to see ye."

Anice breathed a discreet sigh of relief. The old laird would live. She realized that meant her fate would remain strapped to James, but it also meant her people would remain safe from an attack. At least for now.

∽

HANDING out the herbs had been a difficult feat. At least to James. Beneath their tunics and kirtles, many of the people were skeletal. Not only men and women, but children too, their eyes overlarge in their skinny faces. They'd been so starved that the bit of food had left them ill.

James had been hungry in his life. Who hadn't? But never to that level of depravation.

His heart clenched. As much as he did not want this wedding, as much as he had his reservations of marrying a woman of Anice's beauty, he was glad for the decision. If marrying would save these people, he would gladly fulfill his side of the agreement.

He opened the door to his father's room, expecting to see the old man withering in his bed. Instead his father was sitting upright and drinking tea, his gaze bright and alert.

"Dinna get yer hopes up, lad." He winked at James. "The devil isna done with me yet." He drained his cup and held it out for James to collect. "Where have ye been? Off wi' that bonny lass of yers? Or discovering the new fortune I got ye?"

"I've been handing out herbs." James ignored his father's action. "The ones whose stomachs were so weak, they canna take the simple bit of bread, meat and cheese they're receiving."

Laird Graham waved the cup in the air in silent demand for James to take it. "Ach, they'll be fine. Nay doubt finer than if ye'd said 'nay' to wed the lass." He laughed at his own macabre joke and broke off in a feeble wheeze.

"These are people's lives, Da. Lives ye almost took without care." James still ignored the damned cup.

Laird Graham shrugged. "I dinna know these people. I know we've been starving for years and they've no' ever come to our aid. I know they have enough coin to afford fine clothes and costly horses, while we dinna even have a home to call our own. They've had everything, and for the first time in their lives, they've had to struggle. I canna feel bad for their loss." He tossed the mug and sent it flipping toward the floor.

James lunged forward and caught it with his fingertips, a mere second before it could smash on the fine wooden floor. His ire flared up. "Ye talk about a life of struggle, and I'm offering ye an alternative, one where we dinna have to steal and hurt others, and ye dinna seem to care."

"I'm too old to care," the old laird said in a petulant tone. "But ye've got yer opportunity to change the lot of the Grahams.

Thanks to me." Laird Graham grinned. "Off wi' ye now. Go look at the advantage I'm giving ye, one I dinna ever have. And while ye're about, see if ye can find that healer again."

James frowned at his aging father. Aye, he was sitting up in bed, but his skin was still an unhealthy pallor, the lines around his mouth etched more deeply.

They had once been nearly inseparable, Laird Graham and his only son. And through it all, at least until James's recovery, they'd fought like fishwives. If only his father could see the world as Lord Bastionbury had presented it; mayhap then his father could make amends prior to his death.

"Are ye feeling unwell still, Da?" James asked, unable to keep the concern from his voice.

Laird Graham waved a hand dismissively. "Nay, lad. I'm fine. But that woman has a bawdy sense of humor that gets a man's mind going." He grinned. "I've a mind to see what she's all about."

James stared at his father. "Isla?"

"The one with the fine white teeth?" Laird Graham nodded emphatically. "Ach, aye. Send her up." He rubbed his palms like a greedy child.

James gaped at his father, unsure of what to say, but without any intention to summon the aged healer. The idea of them... James grimaced.

"Rest well, Da." He nodded to his father and quit the room, disgusted not only by his father's request for Isla, but also by his lack of remorse for the hardships he'd exacted on Werrick Castle.

A cloud of anger hovered over James as guilt nudged into his mind. He wished he had the Earl of Bastionbury's patience. Were it not for the kindness and exceeding patience of the elderly Englishman, James might never have acknowledged and accepted the idea of a peaceful life.

James, however, lacked such diligence and composure.

Two people rounded the corner, nearly running into James. Anice. And Drake.

The latter churned at James's ire all the more. The man was too bloody good-looking and might have been mistaken for a lass, were it not for the undeniable bulk of his strength.

"I was coming to inform you supper will be served soon," Anice said, oblivious of his assessment of the other man. "Thank you for walking me, Drake."

"Of course, my lady." The man bowed slightly but lifted his brows at her as he rose. "Think on what I've said, aye?"

Anice's smile did not waver. "Aye, I will. Thank you."

There was something unspoken between them, and James did not care for it. He'd once been made foolish over an attractive woman. He would not be again.

"I dinna want supper, thank ye." James shifted directions to go to his room.

"How is your father?" she asked.

He stopped. Piquette ambled toward him and nudged his palm with a cold, wet nose. "He claims the devil isna done with him yet."

Anice offered a tight smile. Only then did James realize how unwelcome such words might be, when his father was the very devil who had mere hours ago threatened the castle with death.

"I'm no' like him." He didn't know why he said it, why he wanted this woman to like him. But he could not stop staring at her, desperate in his hope for her approval, while he scratched at Piquette's large head.

"I do not believe you are like him." She lifted her chin as she said it. Mayhap in an attempt to convince herself. "I bid you a good night and will see you tomorrow for mass."

"Aye."

She turned and strode away, her face stony. Piquette flicked a lick at James's hand and then trotted off after her.

*Mass.* The announcement of their betrothal would be called there. James found his way to his room without issue, thankfully. But the clench at his gut did not abate. Not when the banns would be read the following day. And while he told himself it would not be as bad as he feared, he knew deep down, it would probably be worse.

## CHAPTER 8

James was often aware of the attention he drew when he entered a room. His size alone was enough for most to turn their eyes on him. Entering the surprisingly large chapel within Werrick Castle was no different.

The low murmur of conversation eased upon his entry, and a sea of faces turned toward him with quiet curiosity. Those stares followed him to the end of a pew four rows back.

The woman he stood beside gazed up at him. "Where'd you come from?"

She clutched the hand of a small child, as did several other women around her, all of whom gaped at him. He could not fault them for their curiosity.

They were emaciated, their arms and legs stick-thin and practically lost in their oversized garments. James was thick with healthy muscle, his skin glowing with youth and vigor. In a room of skeletal frames, he stood out more so than usual.

"Ye'll find out soon enough," he muttered.

A glance about the room confirmed James's father was not in attendance. While Laird Graham was not a religious man, James had assumed he would at least suffer through a mass in order to witness his scheme coming to fruition.

It appeared, however, that Laird Graham had decided to refrain from his victorious moment. For that, James was grateful.

"Excuse me." A breathless voice panted at James's right.

He turned to find the priest at his side, the man's hands tightly clasped together. Bernard, if James remembered correctly.

Sweat dotted the top of the priest's bald head. "You may sit with the family." He unfolded his hands and indicated the balcony with a trembling finger.

James followed the direction and discovered Anice sitting in a gilded seat beside her sisters and her father. It did not escape his notice how Drake stood behind them all, ever the protector.

James hadn't thought to look for the Werrick ladies when he first entered the chapel, but then he'd just wanted it all said and done so he could move on with his day. Whatever that might entail in his new location and role.

"I'll be fine here," he muttered.

Bernard's eyebrows inched higher on his broad forehead. "I beg your pardon?"

"I'm fine here." James folded himself into the hard-backed wooden pew. Better to sit among the masses than over their heads in a clear indication of superiority.

The priest darted a nervous glance at the balcony and once more clasped his hands. "Can I not change your mind?"

James settled back, grinding the wood against his spine, as if he were perfectly comfortable. "Nay."

Bernard cleared his throat and gave a tight-lipped smile. "Very well." With that, he darted to the front of the chapel. All at once the lazy hum of conversation among the parishioners cut off into silence, followed by a collective rustling as the congregation sat.

The priest opened his hands in benediction. "Let us pray." He bowed his head forward. The multi-hued light from the stained glass caught in myriad colors the shiny smoothness of his freshly shaved pate.

The inhabitants of Werrick Castle lowered their heads obediently. Bernard's prayer thanked God for granting them peace in a time of war, and food in a time of famine. Simple notes of gratitude that were folded into several ornate speeches of a very, very long prayer.

"Prior to my sermon," Bernard said at last. "I have a unique announcement to make." He folded his hands over themselves in front of his waist and cast a coy expression. "Our own lovely Lady Anice is to wed."

He paused and a collective gasp sucked through the congregation.

"God save Lord Clarion." A woman in the pew in front of him made the sign of the cross.

James frowned. He'd never heard of Lord Clarion. Whoever the man was, he evidently had been tied to Anice in some way, and it seemed her Lord Clarion was dead. Mayhap she had loved him. And now James was to marry her.

At the pulpit Bernard cleared his throat and his cheeks flushed. The announcement had evidently not taken the path he'd intended. "Her newly betrothed is among you today. Three weeks hence after the final reading of the banns have been called, Lady Anice will wed James Graham." He indicated James with a great flourish.

Silence ensued, followed by turning heads and horrified gazes. Their eyes burned with accusation; their mouths twisted with censure.

And James could not blame them for their hatred.

Bernard, oblivious to their malice, continued in his smooth, level tone. "Let it be known, I publish banns of marriage between James Graham and Lady Anice of this Parish. Once graced by the will of God and consummated, their union will seal a pact with the Grahams to enact a treaty between our people and provide peace."

James had to resist the urge to glance behind him to the woman he would soon wed, to witness her reaction.

Bernard let the silence drag out while his words settled over the congregation. "If any of you know cause of just impediment as to why these persons should not be joined together in Holy Matrimony, you are to declare it here and now."

James did not have only one objection—he had several. But he remained seated in the hard-backed pew, resigned to the deafening quiet of the church, and his own inevitable misery.

∽

ANICE SQUEEZED her clasped hands in her lap in an effort to remain silent. She didn't want this marriage any more than the man she would have to marry. Aside from the woman who had remarked on her former betrothed, no one spoke a word.

*Timothy.* Anice hated the twist of her stomach at the mere thought of him. When their banns were read aloud almost five years prior, he'd sat beside her as a guest of the castle, contented with the announcement, as though suddenly the world was right.

James had declined joining her, from what she'd gathered from his exchange with Bernard, and now he did not so much as glance up at the balcony.

Bernard's pause dragged on for some time, as though encouraging the congregation to protest. His pale eyes swept over the balcony and lingered on her, as if to say, "Now is your chance, my lady."

But it was not her true chance. Bernard was deathly afraid of marauders, even more so than he was of Isla; however, he must realize that Anice's sacrifice was integral for their survival.

When the silence had stretched too far, Bernard slapped his hands together. "Then there it is, the first of the banns." He nodded and proceeded with his sermon.

Anice ought to have listened to his preaching, however, her gaze continued to settled on the head of wavy brown hair sitting higher than all others around him. *James.*

An uncomfortable hollowness echoed within her heart. She wished the woman had not mentioned Timothy. Wasn't it bad enough that Anice was being forced to marry her greatest enemy? Did she now have to be reminded of her former betrothed?

The air held a clamminess that stuck in her throat and left her with a sense of suffocation. Bernard's monotone voice droned on and on and on. She was glad she sat, for surely her legs would have given way if she'd been standing.

Anice remained in her seat after the sermon drew to an eventual close and waited for the room to clear so that she might light a candle for her mother. The same as she did most days after mass. She glanced down as James lifted his gaze to the balcony when rising from the pew. His stare hovered on her for a moment, long enough for her heart to suspend mid-beat, and then he was gone.

She made her way down the narrow stairway and to the front of the chapel. Her footsteps rang off the stone walls in the large, empty room, reminding her she was gloriously alone.

Except she wasn't alone. Another figure bowed over the flickering flame of a candle. Her father.

He lifted his head at her approach. "Anice."

"I came to light a candle."

Her father eased himself up from his knees. "I wanted to speak with you."

"Here?" Surely, the solar was a better place for a discussion.

He gave a good-natured smile. "Do not put on pious airs with a man who knows you better."

Anice said nothing, as they both knew he was right.

"The banns appeared to go well," he offered.

She did not want to think of the banns, or of how James had not bothered turning to look at her. "There were no protests."

Her father nodded slowly, obviously mulling over an idea. "While he's here, I want you to keep a watchful eye on your betrothed."

"You want me to spy on him."

The earl tilted his head in quiet confirmation. "We'd be fools to trust any of them, and you keep that forefront in your mind. See where he goes, who he talks to. Be with him at all times."

"I'm to be his guard?" Anice asked with incredulity.

He gazed down at the flame and his jaw tightened. "Aye."

She folded her arms over her chest, but it did not calm her heart's rapid beat. "This is my punishment, I presume? For allowing him to remain here."

"Daughter, your marriage will be punishment enough, though you've done nothing wrong. In fact, you've done a very brave thing, and you did it for our vassals and those you love. Your decision is commendable."

"And now I am to guard him?" She hoped she was able to keep the petulant frustration out of her tone.

He put his hand to her cheek, the way he had done when she was a small girl. But now the warm power of his palm had gone cool and dry. "My sweet, lovely Anice, I want him to have time to get to know you. For surely once he does, he will fall in love with you and will have no choice but to treat you well."

Anice lifted her brows. "I do not think the Grahams capable of such a thing as love."

"Everyone is. Including the Grahams." He released his hold

on her. "And if ever there was one to lighten a dark heart, it is you, my beautiful daughter."

Anice pressed her lips together to still her argument. Her father did not understand James and his inability to be swayed by a woman's comeliness. Now she would be spending the final few weeks of her independence leashed to James's side. Her eyes stung with tears of indignation.

"Go on, then, Daughter, light your candle for your mother." Her father stroked a hand over Anice's hair. "And then find your betrothed."

She studied her feet. A small stain showed on the toe of her right slipper, a splotch of black on the otherwise smooth leather. "How did you know the candle was for Mother?"

Her father lifted Anice's hand and gently touched the small ruby ring she wore, a gift from her mother. Before the Grahams had attacked and their world had fallen into chaos.

"I assumed as much." There was a sad wistfulness to her father's tone. "For my candle is always for her as well."

He pressed a kiss to her forehead, released her hand and was gone. Anice stared down at the candle her father had lit and fought back tears. How she wished her mother was alive to offer guidance, or at least that Marin might be here with her sage advice.

As it was, Anice had nothing but this foolish plan of her father's and a significant amount of dread.

## CHAPTER 9

In the following week, Anice came up with reasons to remain near James's side. If he was suspicious, he did not indicate as much. Their interactions remained cordial; their conversations often centered on Laird Graham's improving health, the weather, or the reserve of food being restored at Werrick. At no point did either one of them bring up their impending marriage.

Though Anice suspected it was not any further from his thoughts than it was from hers.

The upcoming wedding was the very reason she had not donned the white and gold gown for the feast that eve. The celebration had been anticipated by all ever since the portcullis of Werrick could once more be opened safely.

Isla, however, had maintained tight control on the mass quantities of food filling the larder. While unpopular, her orders were obeyed. Especially after an older man, who had been giving half his meager rations to his grandson, had died following his first hearty meal.

Over the days following the Graham's departure, various foods had slowly been added to their diets until Isla deemed it safe for them to consume as they like, which had then resulted in Anice's father declaring a feast.

She smoothed a hand down the green gown, skimming over the beads she'd sewn carefully onto the costly silk. The beads caught the light and twinkled with each movement. The perfect distraction for how the bones of her hips from the months of rationed food showed against the fabric.

Her hair was left unbound and in soft curls, her cheeks and lips gently rouged to compensate for the naturally rosy glow lost during the siege. The darkened surface of the polished copper mirror reflected a woman still fine-looking even after hardship and starvation.

She touched jasmine water to her neck and wrists and smoothed a bit over Piquette's head as she bestowed a kiss onto his soft, russet-colored fur. For his part, Piquette looked quite handsome with a smart collar of dark blue silk studded with gemstones. Perhaps a trifle delicate for the dog whose breed had been trained to fell bears, but Piquette appeared to be rather proud of his distinguished appearance.

She opened the door to make her way down to the great hall to discover James waiting in the empty hallway. He stood with his feet spread and his hands clasped in front of an elegant doublet, evidently borrowed, given how his thick wrists jutted out from the sleeves. His shoulder-length brown hair had been bound back from his face with a thong, revealing the definition of his strong jaw beneath a carefully trimmed beard. He smiled sheepishly at her, an endearing expression on such a large and intimidating man.

He gave an apologetic shrug. "Ella insisted I wear this for the feast."

"You look very fine." Anice replied. And truly, he did.

James's eyes ran over her and his brow furrowed. The bolster of confidence she'd gotten from the sparkling gown immediately fled, replaced by uncertainty.

Did he not care for the dress? Or possibly the way she'd styled her hair? She patted at her tresses to smooth away any strands that might have strayed out of place.

He smiled and it set her at ease. Until he spoke. "I see ye've put Piquette in a bonny collar."

Piquette's ears perked up at his name and the crinkles on his forehead deepened. Anice rubbed a hand over Piquette's head, careful to not muss his brushed hair, and was rewarded with a stare of adoration. "I thought he ought to dress for the occasion." She paused and added with some significance. "It seemed only fair since we all have taken such pains to prepare."

James held his arm out to her as a courtier might do, entirely oblivious to her implication. She had spent the most considerable time of them all to ready, and he had not said a single word about how she looked.

Anice suppressed a sigh, slid her hand into the crook of his warm arm and allowed him to lead her to the great hall. The lilt of music in the distance grew louder as they approached, along with the most heavenly aroma of all the foods they hadn't eaten in months: roasted vegetables and gravy-laden meats and buttery rolls. A true feast.

Anice's mouth watered with the memory of such tastes. Every step led her closer, and her heart pounded so loudly with anticipation she could scarcely hear anything else. Her sisters already sat upon the dais with their father, and beside him was Laird Graham, engaged in lively conversation with Isla, his face glowing with good health.

James led her to the table, and both took their seats to discover a goblet of fine wine waiting for them and a massive trencher of food. The earl gave a speech, short and nearly unheard by the salivating masses who merely waited for the opportunity to indulge.

And once they were eating, the only sound to be heard was that of the musicians. Though Anice was no longer starving, her hands still shook as she brought the flavorful food to her lips. She drank deep from her wine and asked for another helping from the servant with the flagon, and then another still. All too soon, she discovered herself full and her spirits uplifted with the cheerful music. Most important of all though was the company of her family nearby, happy and safe.

"Are ye still hungry?" James indicated her empty plate.

Anice hesitated to answer. While her tongue craved the taste of more, she was far too full. James lifted the silver tongs left behind by the servant and raised his brows in silent question. As though he meant to serve her.

She put her hand to her stomach and shook her head. "I fear I've already eaten too much."

"So then I should wait to ask ye to dance with me?" He grinned. "Or should I simply walk over to the musicians and wait for ye to follow me?"

She stilled at his words and immediately drank a sip of wine to cover the reaction. Had his question been intentionally specific?

"Ye have been following me, haven't ye?" he asked, this time undeniably blunt.

Mayhap she ought to be indignant, but he'd said it with such a pleasant tone, and the wine had left her relaxed and joyful. "Whatever do you mean?" She widened her eyes in feigned ignorance.

He laughed and lifted his empty goblet for the servant to fill from the flagon. It would appear she was not the only one who had over-imbibed. "Ye dinna have to lie about it, Anice." He winked at her, as if they shared a secret. "I know."

"What is it you think you know?" She sipped her own wine and let the rich liquid sit on her tongue before swallowing.

He leaned close to her, the cedar scent of him spicy and delicious. He whispered in her ear, his voice so deep and sensual, it elicited delightful chills dancing over her skin.

"I know ye're spying on me."

~

JAMES SETTLED back in his seat, expecting Anice to protest about his accusation. At the very least, to continue to feign innocence. He had not, however, anticipated the carefree laugh.

Her eyes sparkled and her cheeks were flushed with drink. "Is it so very obvious I've been following you?"

James considered the way she shadowed his every move, appearing at the exact location he happened to visit. He chuckled at her lack of discretion and nodded. "Aye, verra obvious." He leaned in close once more, enjoying the tease of her delicate jasmine perfume, and lowered his voice. "Are ye spying on me?"

She laughed again and traced the rim of her goblet with one long, graceful finger. "My father told me to. He said if I did, you'd be sure to—" She tucked her lips together, as if physically stopping herself from saying more.

"I'd be sure to what?" James lifted his cup to his lips and drank with enjoyment of the finest wine he'd ever consumed in his life. His blood hummed with inhibition, and he was completely at ease, happy to be in the company of this incredibly beautiful woman.

She matched his posture and leaned closer; her blue eyes slanted with a coyness that made his groin tighten. "Do you not like me going everywhere you do?" she whispered in a breathy voice.

How she lured him, beckoned him with the sly glance, and the slow arcing of her finger over her goblet's rim. He wanted that finger to trace as delicately down the length of his body, teasing him into arousal, their bodies naked, their hearts racing. He swallowed, unable to reply.

Her gaze shifted away, to her sisters who danced together near the musicians, leaping and clapping in their revelry. A wistful smile touched her lips.

"What if I told ye I do like it?" He was flirting, and he didn't give a bloody damn. Wine and lust ran hot in his veins and left him bold.

"Do ye want to dance?" he asked. In truth, he hadn't danced much in his life, but it looked to be easy enough.

"Aye, I do." Anice pursed her lips. "But you are forewarned that I do not dance as well as Ella."

He looked toward the cleared space where her sisters danced. Discerning which sister was Ella was impossible from his vantage point. Leila's dark head made her easy to identify, but the other two young women wore their blonde hair in braids twisted around their heads, and white gowns. He certainly couldn't identify one dancing better than the other.

"I dinna dance as well as her either," he offered.

Anice grinned up at him. "I promise not to be disappointed."

Together, they rose. Piquette remained under the table, happily gnawing on a large bone. Much as James liked the large dog, he certainly didn't need him underfoot while dancing. It would be hard enough as it was with his limited skill.

In fact, it was impossible. He didn't know any of the proper movements and continued to trip over himself for the better part of the first song. At least until Anice took his large, clumsy hand in her small one and carefully guided him through the steps. Her dress glittered like the night sky as they moved, and several times she put his hands to her narrow waist.

Whatever part of the dance that bit was, he liked it best. He wanted to remain thus, with his palms secure against the silky fabric, sensing the heat of her body.

But she pulled his touch away with a smile and spun around. "Do you see?" she asked with flushed joy. "It's just like fighting. You learn the motions and you repeat them."

Aye. Like fighting. That he knew. And then it all suddenly made sense. Instead of a parry, it was a leap. Instead of a jab, it was a step.

By the fifth song, he was dancing, truly dancing, like a bloody courtier. And he was having a jolly time of it. The night passed quickly with laughter and more wine until the music ceased.

"I believe the feast is over." He spun Anice one final time. The hour could not be as late as it was, not when he still had so much unspent energy.

"It would certainly appear as much." She came to a stop and gazed up at him. Her face glowed with happiness and her eyes were locked on his.

God, how he wanted this woman. To draw her against him, to let his hands skim over that lovely gown and taste those lips smiling so radiantly.

"Will you walk me to my room?" Anice asked. "Piquette seems to have abandoned me."

Indeed, the large dog was no longer under the table with his large bone.

"As ye've been deprived of yer escort, I think I ought to ensure ye are seen safely to yer room." He offered his arm to her.

"How chivalrous." She slid her hand into the crook of his arm. "After all there could be marauders or reivers."

He led her from the room as sleepy servants cleared away the final cups remaining on the trestles. "Aye, they are the worst sort of people. Without exception."

Anice shifted closer to him. "I disagree."

"Oh?"

Her delicate fingers stroked over the fabric of his sleeve, a movement both enticing and overtly sexual. "I suspect there might be an exception."

James swallowed. "And who might that be?"

She shrugged with seeming nonchalance. "Someone of your acquaintance."

"My da?"

She gave a soft, purring chuckle and nestled closer to him. "Nay, but did you see how he and Isla danced?"

He couldn't have avoided the pair if he'd wanted to. His da's hands had been quite free as they roamed over the ancient woman during one particular song. They'd broken apart afterwards and blessedly gone their separate ways.

James groaned aloud and Anice giggled at his reaction. He liked this side of her: relaxed and sensual.

All too soon, they reached the door to her room. He stopped and released her arm to offer a bow. "My lady is safely delivered to her chambers."

She turned to face him, her eyes bright with blatant flirtation. God's teeth, but she was an alluring woman. Even if she knew it, he couldn't deny how very attracted he was to her. Her bonny face with long-lashed blue eyes and full lips; her body with firm breasts, slender frame, and her long, graceful limbs.

"How could I possibly thank you for such bravery?" She tilted her face up toward him.

Unbidden, his hand moved to caress her cheek. His fingertips met impossibly soft skin, smoother and more luxurious than he'd imagined. She drew in a breath and closed her eyes, leaning into his touch.

He tilted her chin with the pad of his pinky and lowered his mouth to hers, claiming the woman who would be his wife with a searing kiss.

# CHAPTER 10

James couldn't still the roaring in his veins as his mouth nudged Anice's, especially not when she gave a little whimper of desire. She swayed closer, the embodiment of temptation.

And God help him, he could not resist.

She rested her palms against his chest and rose on her toes to deepen their kiss, as eager as he. He swept his tongue against the silky warmth of hers and was rewarded with a gasp.

He shifted his hand to cradle the back of her head and slanted his mouth over hers. Her hot tongue stroked at his, clumsy with an innocence that surprised and delighted him. The headiness from drink mingled with the fire racing in his body and left him overwhelmed by lust.

His free hand glided down her side, over the swell of her breast. She gave a breathy moan and pushed into his hand. Encouraged by the sound, he let his fingers sweep over the hard bud of her nipple.

Her head fell back slightly, breaking away for only a moment before she slid her hands up to the back of his neck and resumed the kiss hungrily. She leaned closer to him, so their bodies were flush, and the hardness of his cock strained against her stomach.

She arched like a cat into his touch, pushing into him as though she wanted more. Without thinking, he cupped her bottom in his hands and pushed his pelvis to hers with his erection pressed between them.

He ought to stop. For her innocence, for his own foolish heart, for the lesson he'd learned previously about an attractive woman who reveled in lust.

Try though he might, the fullness of her mouth on his, and her firm rump in his hands, chased away all argument.

He drew up one side of her skirt and ran his hands over the smooth skin of her outer thigh. Her breath caught and her naked leg curled around him. His hand cupped the top of her leg, holding her in place, while his fingers carefully teased toward her center. His fingertips brushed over the sweet place between her legs. She gasped and her standing leg nearly gave way. He carefully eased her backward so the wall behind her supported her, as well as his body pressing her against it.

He slid his hand over her arse and this time traced her slit with his finger. Her head dropped to his chest and she gave a breathy sigh. James clenched his teeth and tried to ignore the growing tightness of his bollocks. Only a few kisses and Anice was slick with ready wetness.

She arched her hips to grind herself more firmly against his hand. He wanted to find the nub of her pleasure and roll it gently with his thumb; he wanted to slide a finger into her sheath, one at first and then two, stretching her for him. His cock ached with all he wanted to do.

What he might do if he let himself be too overwhelmed by his own lust.

A warning blared in his mind, a reminder anyone might see

them where they were, a reminder of her innocence. "We shouldna do this out here," James said between kisses.

Anice gave a hum of acknowledgement but did not still her kisses. Her hand at the back of his neck trailed away for her own brazen exploration. His chest, down lower to his stomach, down — God's teeth. Her hand grazed over the tip of his swollen prick.

With a growl, he shoved open her door, pulled her through while she remained attached to him, closed it and pushed her against it. Desire pounded through his body and his kisses came with abandon as his hand found the heat of her mound beneath her skirts.

Her fingers curled around the hard outline of his erection and his breath hissed between his teeth. His bollocks clenched. Her touch moved over him, up and down, creating the most delicious friction between his trews and her delicate palm.

His fingertip discovered her bud and circled it until she cried out once more. She ground herself into the heel of his palm, riding his hand the way he wanted her to ride him. He captured her mouth and drank in the sounds of her passion.

The musk of sex hung in the air and made him nearly mad with wanting. A tug came from the lacings of his trews. She pulled at the soft leather thong with shaking hands.

"Nay." With an impossible willpower James did not know he possessed, he put his fingers over hers to allay her intent. Once his cock was free, there would be no putting it back, not until he'd had this woman he'd vowed not to want.

"We are to be wed." She gazed imploringly up at him.

He drew back and let her dress fall over her naked, shapely legs. "We are no' wed yet."

Her teeth sank into her lower lip and made him want to kiss her again. Again and again and again, until he lost himself enough to comply with her desires.

She leaned her head back on the door and closed her eyes,

slowly and with obvious pleasure. "How can you kiss me like that, touch me like that, and then stop?" Her eyes opened and she met his gaze with a searing challenge. "Does it not make your body burn as it does mine?"

He swallowed and found his throat strangely dry. "Aye."

"But you will not touch me again."

He nodded in confirmation. "Ye're to be my wife and deserve my respect."

She gave him that coy look once more. "Just one more kiss?"

Against his better judgment, James touched her face and lowered his mouth to hers, this time delivering a chaste kiss, a simple brush of his lips over hers. The scent of her sex on his fingers tangled with her jasmine perfume and left his mind whirling.

"Good night, James." There was a throatiness to Anice's voice that sent chills of delight racing over his skin.

He stroked her cheek and drew his finger over her plump bottom lip. "Good night, Anice." His hand fell away. "Will ye be following me on the morrow?"

A grin pulled at her lovely lips. "If it's expected, I'd hate to disappoint."

"Ach, aye, I have many expectations." He hadn't meant his statement to be quite so sensual.

"As do I." The gleam in her eye told him she definitely had meant it that way.

She rose on her toes once more and pressed a kiss to his lips. Her tongue dipped in and swept over his. "Good night." She drew away from him and pulled open the door, dismissive.

The long, empty hallway held no appeal, especially not when compared with the alternative. Already the pleasant flush of heat to his cheeks and body were beginning to cool. Though he told himself not to, he was already anticipating the following day when he would see her again.

Aye, he would need to mind himself with Anice, to ensure he guarded his heart, so he would not once more be love's fool.

～

ANICE CLOSED the door behind James and gave a little twirl of elation. Her body was hot with thundering lust, her mind alight with a virgin's imagination. She flung herself on the bed and closed her eyes to plunge into the decadence of her own desire.

She might have shied from his mouth, if she were meek. But she was not meek; she was curious, hungry, eager. For too long, she'd wondered at the intimacy between a man and woman.

Now blind fantasy was becoming tangible reality.

The wine still humming in her veins pushed aside her inhibitions and allowed her to think of Timothy. Her attempts to kiss him had been disastrous, the awkward moments smoothed away by his protests of decorum and maidenly expectation. As though maidens were immune to passion.

While many women would have swooned over a betrothed as chivalrous as Timothy, Anice had been disappointed. She hadn't wanted the marriage. She could admit that to herself openly now, with her state of intoxication emboldening her thoughts. Chivalry hadn't been what she wanted. She desired strength, confidence, and assuredness.

She wanted a man who would cradle her face in his large hands and kiss her until she melted. She wanted those powerful hands on her body, igniting every part of her so brightly that the rest of the world dulled. Exactly the way James had done.

Aye, if maidens were immune to passion, she was the exception. She rubbed her thighs together, a slight movement to increase the delicious pulse between her legs. Thoughts of Timothy were shoved aside. She didn't want to brood over him and fall prey to the stark chill of guilt. Nay, she wanted to relive

James's kiss, his touch, the way he'd grazed her center with confident skill.

She let her fingertips skim over her breasts as his had done. Her nipples tightened beneath the silk of her kirtle. Tingles spread from the pebbled tips through her breasts and down to the place between her legs that he'd touched with such intimacy.

Rubbing her legs together was not enough. She needed more. Like what James had given her. Slowly, she drew the fabric of her skirt upward. Cool air graced her fevered skin.

In her mind, James slipped his hand between her legs. She gently touched her fingertips to her sex and gave a startled gasp of pleasure. Her intimate place was slick with desire.

What she did was sinful. She knew this and was equally aware she ought to stop. Her middle finger grazed the swollen nub of flesh and a bolt of euphoria drew her back to repeat the motion. Her breath caught. She settled her touch over the spot. Rubbing it sent thrilling ripples of delight across her body and left her panting.

She did not want to stop any more than she had wanted James to. Would he have continued to stroke her if he'd been there? Would he do it on their wedding night?

She rubbed harder and her enjoyment intensified. Her nipples prickled with something she didn't understand. She imagined James's large fingers moving carefully over her, bringing such wicked delight. The heat of it burned impossibly hot and something inside her exploded. She locked her legs around her hand and let overwhelming pleasure wash over her until she was happily drowning in it.

When finally the euphoria eased its grip on her, a sense of peace washed over her that left all of her feeling buoyant. A languid smile spread over her lips. If such bliss was to be had in one's marital bed, mayhap being wedded might not be terrible.

The thought stayed with her through a night of passion-fevered dreams of James and into the next morning when the second calling of the banns would be read. James did not sit with her again, but she discovered she was less repulsed at the announcement.

In fact, she thought of him so much through the service, she'd been compelled to say as much in confession with Bernard later. Not only for the distraction through his sermon, but also for the sinful touching of herself the previous night. The priest had suggested prayer for forgiveness and refraining from repeating such behavior. His recommendation had come out in a stammered speech accompanying a face so flushed, it was almost purple.

Even as she vowed to refrain from her intimacies with James, she knew it to be a lie.

She couldn't wait to be alone with James again.

As fortune would have it, she did not have long to wait. Following supper that eve, James made his way to the castle gardens. She, of course, had no choice but to follow.

She settled on a stone bench at his side beneath a rowan tree. They stared off in the distance where the sun set in an array of gold and pink amid patches of fluffy clouds cast in gilded light. The air was crisp and tinged with his wonderfully masculine scent. Though subtle, it was enough of a reminder of their intimate closeness the prior night that her nerves tingled with lust.

James shifted his attention from the sunset to her. "Forgive me for last night."

"Don't," she whispered.

His brow furrowed. "Ye're to be my wife. Ye deserve my respect, especially with ye being of such fine birth. I shouldna have kissed ye." He winced. "Nor should I have touched ye as I did, especially no' out in the open."

"You caused no offense." She put her hand on his and the heat of his naked skin burned against her palm. "You are to be my husband. The banns have already been called twice."

His gaze sifted over her in a slow, careful way, as though he were taking all of her in. She was grateful to have worn the dark blue kirtle, the one which dipped lower on her chest, revealing her smooth collarbones and the swell of the tops of her breasts. He licked his lips and she leaned toward him, anticipating a kiss.

It did not come, though he continued to stare down at her.

"I enjoyed your kisses," Anice confessed. "And your touches. I could not get them from of my mind, not at all last night, nor even still today."

A muscle worked in his jaw. "Who was the Lord Clarion?"

Anice flinched away. *Timothy*. She didn't want to talk about him. Not when she'd longed for another taste of desire, a tease of pleasure.

She pulled her hand away and settled back in her seat where she'd started, before she'd thought James might kiss her. Such a ridiculous notion now when it had been so plausible an expectation a moment ago. "He was my betrothed."

James's eyes tightened thoughtfully. "A man worthy of marrying the daughter of an earl, no doubt."

"His father was an earl, and he would become one as well," Anice answered.

"I take it he was chivalrous, aye?"

*To a fault.* Anice nodded in silence rather than voice the thought.

"Did ye love him?" he asked, his expression unreadable.

Despite it being such a simply stated question, it widened the chasm of hurt in her chest. He might as well have asked her for details on the night her mother had died in childbirth after nine months of emotional torment.

Even now, after years had passed, Anice could still not speak the truth. As though doing so might do some great disservice to the memory of Timothy, who had died so bravely in battle. A man not deserving of the cards life had dealt him: unrequited love and an early grave.

Instead she leaned in close to James once more and gazed up at him in the way she knew men found becoming. "I told you a secret the day we became betrothed, but you have not told me one. I'd like you to do so now."

He smirked. "I dinna have secrets."

"I find myself unconvinced." She leaned closer, further still. "Tell me what you want more than anything in this world."

At first, she did not think he would answer, but then he drew in a slow breath and regarded her earnestly. "I must confess, I lied to ye."

## CHAPTER 11

James did have secrets. Ones he'd declared only to his da, who had promptly disagreed and then ensnared James in this present mess.

Moreover, he knew her question for exactly what it was: a diversion. She had not yet answered him as to whether or not she had loved her former betrothed, which was in itself surely answer enough.

A dull pang echoed in his chest.

"I lied to ye," he repeated.

The playful look on her face earlier had furrowed into an expression of confusion. "What did you lie about?"

"I do want land."

She gave a soft smile of bittersweet victory, for he'd proven her correct. "So, you are not immune to the spoils of war after all, I see."

"Aye, but no' for the reason ye think."

"Not to claim vast amounts of coin to burn through on drink? Or keeping a well-appointed whore waiting nearby to attend your every pleasure?"

Her crass speech momentarily silenced him. This amused her, for she laughed then.

"Do you not think a lady ought to know of such things?" She folded her arms over her chest. "My father has taken us to court several times. Ladies are told to ignore such things, aye, but that does not mean we do not see."

"That is what some men do," he replied hesitantly.

"But you are not most men," she surmised.

Piquette ambled toward them, bumped a clumsy wet nose against both their hands and settled in a snoozing heap at Anice's feet. Her face warmed with affection and her hand reached down to absently stroke his golden red fur.

"Aye, I'm no' most men. I dinna prefer a life of stealing and theft." Though James had lowered his voice, Piquette's ears flinched at the sound.

Anice raised her brows, but her skepticism was not as sour as it had been when they were first betrothed. "What do you want land for then, pray tell?"

"I want it for my people." His pulse ticked up a notch merely saying the words aloud. "A place for them to be safe, to stay out of harm's way. To have the opportunity for a life without theft and lies."

Silence met his confession and the cool air filled with the tinkle of voices and chatter wafting from the castle. James gritted his teeth.

Clearly, she did not agree with his plan, the same as his da. Mayhap it was a foolish hope, and there was no place in his life for a living built on honesty and fairness.

Anice lifted her large blue eyes up to him. The golden light from the setting sun washed over her and turned her loveliness into something ethereal. "Do you know the lands you will acquire from my dowry?"

He shook his head. In truth, he'd felt too guilty to see everything he would get with their marriage, like a thief pawing through his purloined treasures.

"It is a prosperous estate, befitting the daughter of an earl." She lifted her chin up a notch with a note of pride. "The lands are in Carlisle, excellent for farming."

He didn't know England well enough to gauge if the land were good or not, but if the soil were rich, his men could learn to tend it.

"It would appear in your solicitous appeal to your father for our well-being, you have been delivered exactly what it is you were seeking." Her smile held no weight to whatever emotion played behind her eyes. "You are fortunate."

The final rays of the sunset went all at once bright, before being snuffed out as it lowered into the land beyond.

"I hope ye're right." He reached down and rubbed behind Piquette's ear. The dog didn't stir.

"Do your people know how to farm?"

"Some." James got to his feet and held his hand out to Anice. "It grows dark, Lady Anice."

"Call me just Anice when we are alone." She put her small hand in his and rose gracefully to her feet. "Please."

Her pulse tapped quickly against the heel of his palm where their skin connected. "You said some know of farming. What of the others? What of you?"

James guided her to his side and threaded her hand in his arm, for he too could be chivalrous. Mayhap not as much as her former betrothed...

He hated the rise of his jealousy.

"I confess I dinna know much of farming," James replied. "Half my people were once farmers, men so heavily taxed, they took to raiding for survival. They were forced into it."

"My brother-in-law was a reiver." Anice stopped at the stairs leading into the castle. "I'm aware of more than you think. I also know something of farming."

His lip quirked in an unbidden half-smile at this surprising woman, whose milky white hands did not appear to have ever come into contact with any amount of land work.

"Don't act so shocked." She ducked her head in a way suggesting she was pleased by his reaction.

"Ye dinna seem the type of lass to be digging about in the dirt."

She laughed, and the light spilling from the castle played over the delicate lines of her neck as it flexed around the sweet, joyful sound. "I confess I am not the most adept of us all. Leila has always been the one with true skill when it comes to planting and harvesting."

He thought of the small, dark-haired girl with the somber expression and his heart flinched, a reminder of what his clan had done. Did the population of Werrick Castle feel the same way? Was wee Leila a reminder of all that had gone wrong between their people?

Anice turned away from the staircase and pulled him back to the garden with her. "I am not ready to retire as yet."

He let her lead him, content to walk the paths a thousand times over with her at his side. She leaned into him, sharing body heat in a way that was quietly intimate.

He stroked her hand at his elbow. Most likely not the thing a chivalrous earl's son might do, but certainly the thing *he* would do. "I get yer land, and yer knowledge on how to farm it. I have the chance to draw on an opportunity that might never have been extended to me otherwise."

She turned her hand upward and allowed him access to the softness of her palm, while her fingers stroked against his. The trail they followed took them down a darkened path. Heat fired in James's veins. There were many things one might do by cover of night on such a path.

"It seems unfair." His steps slowed to prolong their time in the dark, to continue the silly act of petting one another's hands. It was ridiculous how the graceful sweep of her fingertips over his made his stomach tighten, or how circling his middle finger over her palm drew a similar sexual energy as when he'd circled the bud of her center.

"What seems unfair?" she asked in a breathless voice.

The way she spoke was far too alluring. *She* was far too alluring.

"I gain much from this union." He faced her with their hands still joined. "Yet aside from having saved yer people, ye get nothing."

~

JAMES'S WORDS sank into Anice with the weight of a stone. He was right, of course. He did have the better end of the bargain, but in times of desperation, there was no room for fairness.

Her fingers stilled against his, and the heat of desire cooled. "My people are safe and will remain thus. Our marriage will end the Grahams's persistent threat against Werrick."

"What can I give ye, Anice?"

She couldn't make out his face in the shadows, yet she was all too aware of his nearness. The heat of his body against her kirtle, the strength of his hands over hers, the way his soft burr held a note of tenderness.

A snuffling sound came from the ground and Piquette strode away. Anice turned her attention to the dog in an attempt to gain reprieve from having to answer James's question. Nose to the ground, her beloved pet and protector shuffled off in pursuit of something delectable.

"Do ye want me to truly know ye?" he asked.

Her breath hitched. "What do you mean?"

"The first day when I asked ye for a secret, ye said no one has ever truly known ye." He shifted closer and the pressure of his massive body against the front of her skirt increased. "I think ye want someone to know ye, or ye wouldna have said as much."

"I was beside myself with starvation." She waved her hand and gave a short laugh. "It was merely the ramblings of near-madness you heard."

A pause hung between them. He ran a finger down her palm, slow, and with a deliberate sensuality. A shiver ran down her back and her nipples tingled.

"I dinna think so, Anice." He released one hand from hers and cradled her face.

She exhaled a shaky breath. His touch was rough with calluses, but warm and lightly scented with cedar. He wanted to *know* her, to make her happy.

Why had she uttered that ridiculous secret? Of all the things she might have said, why must it have been that one?

"Tell me, Anice." His caress was soft as a butterfly's wing as it drew over her cheek. "Who are ye? Who is the secret lass ye dinna want others to see?"

Her heartbeat thundered in her ears. This was too much. Too quickly. She had only met him days ago. This man was her *enemy*. The reminder fell flat in her mind, for he did not act like a foe, not when he was so very much like a lover.

Regardless, it would be impossible to tell him the truth, especially when he saw her exactly the same as everyone else: a dowry, an opportunity, a woman of great beauty with no other true value.

However, he had never told her she was beautiful. While many others had composed sonnets and sent gifts to praise her appearance, never once had James so much as said she was lovely.

She opened her eyes and found he stared down at her with quiet, glittering determination. As though he truly did want to understand her.

"Passion," she whispered. "I want passion."

She waited for a heated kiss, for that delicious press of his hardness against her pelvis. But he did not pounce upon her as other men might have. Instead his hand fell away from her face. "Passion? That is truly yer secret?"

His skepticism was obvious in the slow repeat of the word. Her throat went dry. She had to work harder to see him convinced.

After all, it was something she wanted. And it was a far safer confession than the truth, than facing her own inadequacies in life about being nothing more than a beautiful face.

"Aye." Anice swallowed, her throat so dry, it stuck to itself. "I have always been handled delicately, like a flower that might wilt in one's hands. I...I want passion. I want strong hands on my body, searing kisses, a man who can push at the boundaries of my imagination."

He tilted his head. "Push the boundaries of yer imagination?"

Mayhap that had gone a trifle far, but there was no backing out now. "Aye."

"And what are the boundaries of yer imagination?" he asked, after another long pause.

She bit back an irritated sigh. Why couldn't he just launch himself at her as any other lusty courtier might? Why did he have to be so considerate? So thorough?

"I..." She bit her lip. "I liked what we did last eve." Her cheeks scorched with heat. "When you..." Words failed her and required searching. "When you touched me."

He gave a soft chuckle. "Ye're giving me a fair amount to consider, lass."

Anice's tension splintered with a laugh. "I know."

"It's what ye truly want?" he asked.

The playful awkwardness melted into sensuality and drizzled over her like warm honey. "Aye," she said again.

He put an arm around her waist and drew her against the wall-like strength of his large body. "Ye liked it when I kissed ye?" His fingers brushed over her lips so gently she might have thought it was the wind, had she not caught his wonderful scent.

She hummed her approval. Her stomach fluttered with anticipation where this might go. More kisses. More touches. More. More. *More*.

"When I cupped yer breast, did ye like that as well?" The pressure of his hand was unmistakable against the side of her breast.

Her breath caught. "Aye."

"When I teased yer nipple too?" His fingers toyed unabashedly over the hard peak of first one breast, then the other.

Her knees went soft and dropped from underneath her. He tightened his hand around her waist, keeping her fully upright, being her support.

"And when I drew up yer skirt?" His voice was a low growl against her ear.

Prickles of delight raced over her skin. She could not so much as speak over the power of her own longing.

"Lady Anice?" A man's voice sounded from the castle. Drake.

Anice stiffened. It was one thing to whisper of such inappropriate touching among themselves in the dark, and entirely another to be caught. She quickly slipped her hand into the crook of James's arm and urged him forward. "Pretend as though we were merely walking," she hissed.

Which was exactly what he did. He strode as easily from the shadows as though they had been out for an innocent stroll, rather than discussing his illicit deeds from the previous night and setting her body to burning.

"Good evening, Drake." Her greeting was overly cheerful, a fact confirmed by the narrowing of his eyes in obvious suspicion.

He inclined his head respectfully, but not before shooting a dark stare in James's direction. "Lord Werrick grew concerned when ye did not return after the sun went down."

It was too late to be out, she knew. Regardless, she hadn't expected Drake to come after her as though she were a child. Irritation vexed her. She climbed the stairs and called for Piquette, who took several moments to appear, most likely having been chasing squirrels about in the orchard.

Her irritation with Drake dissipated suddenly when he strode past her and discreetly pushed a bit of parchment into her hand.

# CHAPTER 12

The note. James had seen it pass from Drake's damned hands into Anice's and had rescued it from the flames. Ire rose in him like bile.

*The stables tonight.*

Anice hadn't seen him do it. And for all her talk of passion, she was doubtless already well-versed in such matters of intimacy. Innocence at kissing could always be pretended. He'd known her excuse for passion to be a flimsy mask for what she'd meant by her confessed secret, but he hadn't presumed she'd been protecting Drake.

James could scarcely contain the energy pumping hot through his tensed muscles. But what he was about to do required a warrior's stealth. Control. He drew a deep breath to rein in his anger and silently cracked open his door to reveal a guard standing in front of it.

James waited until the man looked down the opposite end of the hallway, then shoved the door open completely. It smacked into the guard, catching him off-balance. Without allowing the man to recover, James jerked his elbow upright and caught his opponent under the chin.

The Werrick soldier dropped to the ground like a heavy sack of grain. He'd rise later, once James was down the hall and on his way to the meeting point to witness the planned tryst.

Undoubtedly, Anice thought she'd been discreet when she read the note and deposited the scrap into the hearth. She hadn't accounted for the bit of parchment to float just outside the reach of the flames as she checked about her.

He'd been a witness, unseen, and had rescued the missive from the fire.

*The stables tonight.*

The three words ground into him like splintered wood. Anice had played him a fool, the same as Morna. Fire burned in James's veins so intensely, he wanted to roar.

The handsome warrior was Anice's lover. James would interrupt them, catch them in the act to have his proof and discover the true secret she'd been so unwilling to bare.

A tight band squeezed at James's chest, brutal and unexpected. He ought to have anticipated such from Anice. After all, she was the most incredible beauty he'd ever laid eyes on, more so than even Morna. Still, he'd thought Anice above that. Their interactions had suggested a woman of better bearing.

But then, she too had lied.

James avoided the soldiers as he navigated the darkened halls of Werrick Castle, until he made his way into the cold night air through one of the side entrances. The guard there had been as easily handled as the one outside his room. Not slain, of course. He'd simply knocked the sense from the soldier.

The moon was bright that evening and shone down upon him with more light than he preferred. He skirted the castle walls, moving soundlessly among the shadows to ensure he was unseen. His heart hammered in his chest like a war drum. He'd initially been so eager to catch Anice in her betrayal, but now he was apprehensive. His stomach roiled with disgust.

He needed to face what she was. He crept into the barn through an open doorway and stopped. A figure stood in the shadows. One he recognized to be Anice.

She squirmed and writhed. *As though in the throes of passion.*

The world shrank around James and suddenly he did not want to be there. He didn't want to witness her deception. The air became too thin to breathe and he was immediately transported to that awful day. When he'd stumbled upon Morna.

These stables at Werrick were empty, so like the ones he'd found Morna in, the motion of her moving. Except Anice did not cry out with pleasure.

She gave a growl as she twisted about. Her arm stretched behind her back. The sound did not seem to be laced with passion.

She uttered a very unladylike curse.

Piquette laid on the floor by the wall, a massive lump in the dark.

The edges of James's panic softened. Anice was alone, or certainly she would have asked for assistance as she was obviously struggling. She wouldn't be alone long, however, or there would be no point to the note.

She might very well be attempting to disrobe, given the awkwardness of her movements.

No sooner had the understanding struck him, the sound of footsteps came from outside the stables. Anice stilled at once and her attention snapped to the front of the stables. She uttered another curse and ducked deeper into the shadows.

As though she were frightened.

Piquette lifted his large head.

James's heartbeat came faster, this time with concern rather than dread. The air crackled with awareness, the way it often did prior to battle. His body tensed and he crouched lower in the darkened stable, prepared to strike.

The footsteps went silent, but James could sense an additional person in the stables with them. It was in the pressure of the air, the tension in his gut. Was it Drake? Someone else?

Why was Piquette not getting to his feet?

The shadow of a man stretched over the front wall, arms drawn back, hefting something upward. A sword? Or a hammer? An axe, mayhap? James did not pause to see. He flew from hiding like a beast and launched himself at Anice's attacker with his full weight.

~

Anice had been expecting an attack. She had not, however, anticipated a giant to spring from the shadows, like a nightmare, to thwart the impending battle.

James sat atop the Master of the Horse's chest with one massive fist raised to bring down upon the man's face. Peter, for his part, was very brave in not cowering from the man who easily outweighed him twofold.

"Stop." Anice grabbed James's large shoulders and hauled him off the Master of the Horse.

"Peter," she gasped. Piquette was at her side now, prancing from paw to paw with his apparent unease.

Peter slowly got to his feet and dusted off bits of hay from his clothes and shaggy dark hair. "No better practice than with an actual Graham, eh?" His full mouth lifted in a half-smile that showed a dimple in his cheek.

They all had met in the stables for years to practice: Anice and her sisters with the Master of the Guard and Peter. After the initial attack by the Grahams, when Peter had been too young to aid anyone, he vowed never to be helpless again. He wanted to be a part of their training so that he could defend not only himself, but others as well.

"Pish." Anice regretted the phrase as soon as she said it. The word made her sound too like Marin, when she so clearly was not. After all, Marin would never have allowed James to escape his room and follow her.

In fact, how *had* James come to escape his guard to follow her?

She had been so careful, only reading Drake's note after depositing James at his chamber, and then burning it. But she'd been so excited that they would finally have a serious practice after so many long months without it, when they had been too weak to expend energy on mock battle.

She spun on James. "How did you get here? *Why* are you here? And what has become of your guard?"

His face remained a mask. "It appears we've both had our trust betrayed tonight." The mask broke, however, when he slid a stabbing glare to Peter. "With yer dallying with the stable lad."

"I would never so disrespect one of Lord Werrick's daughters." Peter's hazel eyes flashed. "And I'm the Master of the Horse."

"James, this isn't as it appears." Anice kicked the padded armor she was trying to put on beneath a bit of hay.

"Ye could have told me ye had a lover." James spat the words out and indicated Peter's sword on the ground. "Though what ye two were about, with him coming at ye with a blade, is beyond me." He cut his glare to her this time. "Mayhap it went beyond the boundaries of my imagination."

Anice's stomach flipped at her own words being flung back at her. He didn't understand. And, of course, she couldn't tell him about their meetings to train for battle. If he were spying like her father suspected, that knowledge could make them lose their advantage. She had to figure out a way to get him from the stable before—

Drake appeared in the doorway then with her sisters at his

heels. Cat popped around behind him and took in the scene with a wide smile "Are we allowed to tell James now?"

"He isn't supposed to know." Ella peered around with obvious curiosity. Her mouth fell open. "Peter, are you injured?" She rushed to him at once and began fussing over him. But then, Ella had always held an affinity for Peter.

"It's fine to tell him," a soft voice said from behind the older siblings. Leila slowly walked around her sisters and made her way to James. She settled a small hand on his arm. "I trust him." Her nose wrinkled. "He is not like his father."

James tilted his head in a nonchalant show of agreement. "The lass is a wise one." While less angry, he did not appear any less confused. "What is all this about?"

Geordie entered the stable with a sword buckled at his hip and glanced around. The young man had been squire to Sir Richard, but now awaited a station with another knight somewhere in England to conclude his training. In the meantime, he could always be found with Cat, same as when they were children. His gaze fixed on her, and an affable grin stretched over his wide mouth in his usual lovestruck manner. Cat, as always, was completely oblivious.

Anice sighed, at the sisters, at James, at the ridiculous situation. Leila said they could trust him, but Anice had her doubts. He was, after all, a Graham.

Leila met Anice's gaze and nodded slowly.

"We intended to train," Anice said slowly. "Though we anticipated doing so without your knowledge."

"Train?" James frowned and looked at Anice and her sisters, as if seeing them for the first time. She could understand how they appeared from his eyes: her with a sword propped behind her, the daggers shoved in Leila's belt, a bow and quiver slung over Cat's back and the battle axe propped at Ella's shoulder. "Ye mean in weaponry?"

"Of course." Cat bounced on her toes. "We haven't been able to do it for half an age because we had to conserve our energy, or so Isla said. Now that we have had enough food again, she's told us we can resume our practice."

James indicated Anice's sword where it was propped against the wall. "I can show ye a bit, if ye like."

"I've already been trained." Anice couldn't help the note of pride in her voice.

James put his hands up in surrender and backed up a step. "I leave ye to yer training then, but I'd like to stay to watch."

"Aye," Leila answered. "Mayhap you can offer advice on how to fight a Graham, should the need arise."

"If any Graham attacks here from this day onward, I'll be fighting at yer side," James said with sincerity.

Anice studied him skeptically. Did he truly mean he would go against his own people?

She put her back to Ella and set the question from her mind. If they were going to train, they ought to start soon, or it would grow too late to continue. "Help me with my armor, if you would please. It's given me a beast of a time." Ella turned from Peter and helped strap the thick padding to Anice's chest, an impossible feat earlier while wearing her kirtle.

While they usually donned breeches and shirts for practice, they'd agreed dresses would be prudent in the event James or Laird Graham saw them coming to or from the stables. While Leila trusted James, Anice did not anticipate she would do so with Laird Graham.

Once her armor was securely in place, Anice swept her sword from the wall and strode past James. All the others followed her, except Ella who glanced toward Peter. "Would you spar with me tonight?"

The handsome Master of the Horse often trained with Ella, which most likely had only increased her affection for him.

Anice didn't have the heart to tell her sister how often Peter slipped away from supper early in the evenings with his arm around one of the various female servants of Werrick Castle.

"Come, Ella." Anice nodded to the cleared space of the bailey behind the stables, an area unable to be seen from the castle. "You're with me."

Ella gave one last, lingering look at Peter as she walked outside.

Anice shot James a glance. "I hope you can keep a secret."

The corner of his lip curled up. "Ye know I can."

Before the implication could stain her cheeks, Anice followed Ella from the stables with Cat bounding after them.

Geordie was at her side in an instant. "Do you want me to set your target?"

"That would be lovely, thank you." Cat beamed a smile that no doubt devastated the boy, and he ran off, casting glances back at her.

Not that Anice had much time to observe such displays of unrequited love. Not when Ella drew back her axe and swung.

Anice ducked low to avoid the blow and bolted upright with a jab of her dulled blade. Of them all, Ella had to utilize the most care during their mock battles. While the edge of her weapon had been dulled to render it safer, the impact could still shatter bone.

Ella leapt back, avoiding being struck by Anice's blade, and the battle began in full.

## CHAPTER 13

James could not take his eyes from the women who parried and feinted with padded armor over their kirtles. These were not mere noblewomen whose talents were related to needlework and running households. Nay, these women were warriors.

All around him, the Earl of Werrick's bonny daughters fought like men, each with their own specialty. Cat landed every arrow she launched into the middle of the target. Even wee Leila wielded her dual daggers with dexterous hands that moved with a nimbleness his eyes could scarce track.

Ella spun around and brought the axe with her, but Anice arced her blade in time to obstruct its path toward her head.

Forgotten where he stood on the outskirts of their melee with Piquette sitting at his side, James observed the woman who would be his wife with a fresh perspective. Battle enhanced the usual grace of her movements, in the same manner as when she danced. Only far more lethally.

Her words came back to him then from when they'd danced, when she'd instructed him the moves were like those in battle. He'd been too heady with drink then to wonder at what she'd meant. He felt almost foolish now for having offered to train her on her sword.

She was no novice to the art of war.

Her well-timed thrusts and blocks were the result of countless hours of concentrated practice. While Anice was bonny in daily life with her careful eye for fine clothing and the lovely sensuality of her face and lush body, she was stunning in battle.

Her eyes glittered with determination, locked on her target with confidence. It was no wonder she did not want a meek man who would treat her like something delicate. She was no fragile woman at all, but a pleasant surprise.

Ella's axe whirled through the air toward Anice's face. Too fast. Too hard. James's heart lurched in his chest, but before he could get to his feet, Anice stopped the weapon with only one inch between her nose and the heavy block of iron.

Without hesitation, Anice circled her wrist and forced the axe to the ground, then lifted her blade to Ella's throat. A cocky half-grin announced Anice's victory.

The battle was done. James approached the ladies and lowered his head respectfully in Anice's direction. "I was wrong about yer level of skill. I've no' ever seen a woman fight like ye. Ye handle a sword better than most men."

Anice beamed at him and ducked her head, as if to hide how much his praise had pleased her. The action was both humble and endearing.

"You should see Marin with a sword." Ella set the heavy head of her axe to the ground. "She moves so fast that you would swear her sword was enchanted."

"It's true," Cat called out from the side of her bow and released another arrow. The lad at her side darted off to reclaim the lot of arrows bristling at the center of the target.

"Aye, it is." Anice lifted her head. Her smile was now absent its proud sheen. "Marin possesses far greater skill than me."

There was a hurt there, tucked in the back of Anice's happy expression, and in this exchange, James realized he was glimpsing that internal pain for the first time. Nay, mayhap there had been other times and he had not recognized it. James folded his arms over his chest to keep from reaching out to her. "I havena seen Marin fight, but I've seen ye and am in awe of yer skill."

"Thank you." Anice lowered her head again and hid her expression from him.

"In fact, I'd like to test yer skill."

That got her attention. She snapped her head up. "You want to fight me?"

He grinned. "Aye."

The moonlight played off her features and highlighted the sharpness of her gaze at the anticipation of such a challenge. "Ella, get the man a practice sword."

"And I can spar with Peter." Ella dropped her axe and ran off to comply with Anice's request.

It was obvious the sister held affection for the handsome Master of the Horse. Better Ella than Anice.

Within moments, Ella was happily sparring with the Master of the Horse, and James had a practice sword in his hands as he stood opposite Anice in the small fighting ring. The weapon was awkward in his hands, short and off-weight, much different from the longer claymore he typically used in battle.

He didn't have a chance to adjust to the foreign heft of the weapon, though. No sooner had he braced himself in front of Anice than she set on him. Her blade swung at him, smooth and swift. He feinted and jabbed his weapon toward her.

A sudden note of fear nipped at the back of his mind. What if he hurt her?

The tip of his blade dipped with the flash of indecision.

Anice flicked her sword against his and knocked it easily out of her path. She lunged, her attack going first left, then right, then left again. He blocked each blow but did not strike out at her.

She renewed her efforts with such vigor, James's full attention was required to ensure he didn't become her next fallen opponent. On her following attack, she ducked as she lunged, nearly catching him in the gut. While he evaded being struck, he hadn't anticipated her foot sweeping toward his legs. He flew backward and hit the ground with a hard crash.

Anice appeared over him with the dulled point of her blade hovering over his neck. "I told you." She removed her weapon and offered her hand instead. "I'm not delicate."

He clasped her hand but used his own body weight to stand lest he pull her down with him. Though in truth, the idea of having her on the ground with him held great appeal.

Mayhap the next battle could be hand-to-hand, a lot of rolling around together, bodies twisting against one another. The very thought made his blood to race hot.

She swept her long hair over her shoulder in a gesture far more like a lady than a soldier, and he found it equally appealing. Nay, she was not delicate, not in the ways that mattered, but there were parts of her that were fragile, vulnerable.

Like the secret she had tried to brush off and cover with lust. But he was a stubborn man and the more she tried to hide her secret, the more he wanted to know it. And he would find out.

∽

THE FOLLOWING days passed in a whirl of mock battle and stolen kisses. Anice enjoyed the time spent sparring with her future husband. Almost as much as the time spent alone in the dark corridor as she left him at his chamber each evening. Those intimate moments hadn't been anything like the night of the feast, much to Anice's disappointment, but they'd had the opportunity for several stolen kisses before James's guard arrived.

Preparations for their upcoming nuptials had been slow moving until after the third calling of the banns, when everything fired into chaos.

There was the feast to plan with Nan, the flowers and herbs for decorations to coordinate with her sisters, the fine details to smooth over with Bernard regarding the wedding mass. Honestly, it was all too much. She didn't want spectators there, casting their judgment on the union. Though she was marrying James to save her people, many saw the act of her wedding their greatest enemy as a betrayal.

It was all enough to make her head spin. She lay awake two nights prior to the wedding. Not with lust burning her thoughts as they had previously, but with the endless list of tasks. In truth, the only part of the marriage she anticipated had nothing to do with the vows said, or the finely sculpted marzipan flowers on a bit of pastry. It had everything to do with the consummation.

James still held back. She could sense it in the way his hands shook slightly when they kissed, in the restrained grip on the fabric of her dress. His kisses had stolen her breath and left her desperate for so much more.

*Soon.*

Desire swept away her other worries and replaced them with the steady pulse between her legs. Soon, James would peel away her gilded thread dress and she would enjoy the press of his body to hers, gloriously naked and aroused.

A scream sounded in the distance and obliterated all sense of lust. Anice leapt from her bed before her mind realized what she was doing. No sooner had she set foot in the hallway than the cry sounded again, pitched and mournful.

Anice spun in the direction it had come from and ran all the way to her sisters' room with Piquette close behind her. There they found Ella and Cat beside Leila in their large bed.

Ella smoothed Leila's dark hair from her face. "She won't wake."

"Leila," Cat called. "Sister, you must wake."

Leila jerked her head from Ella's touch and swept back away from them all, her eyes wide with terror. "Mama."

Anice flinched at the empty word. It had been used for their mother when she'd been alive. Leila, however, had never once spoken of her as 'Mama'.

Piquette issued a sharp whine and nudged at Leila's hand.

She did not so much as look down at the beloved dog. "Our Mama." She shook her head vigorously, sending the dark tendrils whipping around her shoulders. "I don't want to see. I don't want to see." She pushed her hands to her face and screamed. "Don't make me see it."

Anice lurched forward and caught Leila's small body in her arms. "Look at me," she said with force. "Now."

Leila obeyed, her pupils mere dots in the sea of wide, panicked blue. "They took her." Leila shook her head. "The Grahams. They took our Mama. She clawed the ground and her nails bent backward." Leila's hands curled in front of her face and she studied them with intensity. "They had no mercy."

Anice's heart slammed in her chest. She covered Leila's eyes, as though she could stop the vision, and pulled the child to her chest. "Don't, my sweet lamb. Don't."

"Is she well?" James's voice came from the doorway. He wore only his leine and a pair of trews.

Anice turned to him and shook her head. She'd meant it as a way of telling him to leave, but he quickly made his way to her side. "What's happened?"

Leila turned her frightened gaze up at James and began to

tremble forcefully in Anice's arms. "You remain in the company of men who commit vile offenses."

James straightened as though he'd been struck.

Leila broke free of Anice with a strength she didn't know the girl could possess. "I thought you were different. Better." She launched herself at James and pummeled him with her small fists.

At first, James did not move. Lines of exhaustion etched his face and his eyes were bright and unreadable. He swallowed and carefully caught Leila's hands, stilling her attack. They stared at each other for a long moment, both mute. It was as though something unsaid passed between them.

Leila's shoulders relaxed suddenly, and she buried herself into James's arms with a sob. He held her until the force of her tears ebbed, while the rest of them all looked on, helpless.

"It was so terrible." Leila's words were muffled against James's chest.

He closed his eyes, his expression crumpled with pain. "I know, lass. If I had been there, I would have stopped them. I would have…I would have done something."

Leila nodded against his chest. "Forgive me." Leila leaned back to regard James with a long glance. Her brow furrowed and her mouth tucked downward with chagrin. She put her hand to her lips to stifle a gasp. "It will be a failure," she whispered.

Graham or not, James had endured enough of Leila's dreams. "Come, sister," Anice said gently. "Getting some sleep will help."

She guided her youngest sister from James and back to the large bed, where Cat and Ella waited with concerned expressions. It was never easy sleeping with Leila. Anice remembered the times when she'd had to sleep with her. The poor thing was plagued with terrible dreams and often woke up screaming: sometimes of people who had long ago died, other times of things that might come to pass, and still others of a man she referred to only as the lion, while shuddering in fear.

Leila shook her head stubbornly, as she climbed into the large bed. Anice tucked the blankets around her youngest sister and wished she could as easily put a shield around the girl, to dispel the horror of her dreams.

"Shush now and sleep." Anice kissed Leila on the brow, then Cat and Ella, though they were both far too old for such endearments. The dreams had always left them rattled, regardless of their ages. Anice had taken over their mother's former chambers after Marin left for Kendal Castle. That space of time had still not been enough that Anice had forgotten how terrible the after-effects of such nightly interruptions.

Leila set her steady gaze on James who stood awkwardly in the middle of the room, wearing only his hastily donned leine and trews, then turned her large eyes up to Anice. Leila sighed, the huff of air somewhere between exasperation and sadness. "I mean, the marriage will be a failure."

## CHAPTER 14

Anice hadn't needed Leila to tell her that the marriage would fail. Of course it would. What marriage starting under such circumstances could possibly be successful?

Regardless, in the following two days, her youngest sister's warning carved their worry into Anice. They had affected James as well, though he didn't say as much. Worry etched lines across his brow that he tried to smooth away when he saw her.

It was the night prior to Anice's wedding and all she could do was stare at the gilt cloth dress. The thing was as heavy as it was costly. How fitting for a marriage that seemed to match those very traits.

A gentle knock sounded at her door. Her heart lurched with excitement as much as trepidation. But surely it was not James. They had not been alone together since the night of Leila's dreams, and her declaration of failure.

Her warning could encompass so many different outcomes. It could be as simple as Anice's inability to give James an heir, or it could be as great as the Grahams using the alliance to attack Werrick Castle. The latter thought sent an icy shiver down her back.

But Leila could not always elaborate on her visions, and so oftentimes, one was simply left with a warning.

"Anice, are you in there?" The warm voice curled around Anice's fears like a balm.

"Marin." Anice raced to the door, nearly tripping over Piquette, who leapt up with equal excitement.

Marin stood on the other side of the door, looking as regal as ever in a long, flowing blue dress and a wide, beautiful smile. She opened her arms and Anice flew into them like a child. The familiar comfort of her sister's embrace exacerbated all the anxiety of Anice's upcoming nuptials, and tears began to prickle her eyes.

The solid weight of Piquette laying his heavy body at their feet called her back to her senses and kept her emotions from overwhelming her. She pressed her head to Marin's shoulder and squeezed her eyes shut until the threat of crying abated. She was a woman who was old enough to marry, a woman who had saved her people with her decision to wed James. Tears were for whelps.

"Are you well, Sister?" Marin asked and drew back, her brows pinched with concern.

"Aye, of course." Anice waved off her sister. "Come in, we have so much to discuss."

Marin bent to scratch Piquette's ears and bestow a kiss on his broad head, but her expression still held skepticism and concern when she straightened. The woman was impossible with how much she seemed to inherently glean from others.

Anice rushed on before her sister could try to dig deeper. She wasn't ready. Yet. "Life at Kendal agrees with you, Marin. You're practically glowing." Anice lowered her voice. "Unless there is perchance another reason why you're glowing."

Marin's elated expression wilted slightly. "There is no child. Still." Her fingers swept over her flat stomach.

"Then it must be marriage that so agrees with you." Anice grabbed her sister's hands to draw them from her empty womb. "You look perfect."

The sparkle returned to Marin's eyes. "I am so happy. Far more than I ever thought I could be." Marin's hands tensed against Anice's. "I hope the same for you."

*It will be a failure.*

"I am certain it will be," Anice lied.

"And this is your dress." Marin released her hands and swept to the wedding gown. She bent to examine the detailed hand embroidery at the neck and sleeves. "It's lovely. You'll be the most beautiful bride to ever grace a chapel."

And just like that, with the power of Marin's approval, the heavy garment took on an airiness that made Anice want to glide into it and soar.

"You do know what will happen, don't you?" Marin asked the question in such a soft, low tone, Anice almost did not hear her.

"What will happen?" Anice asked slowly.

"Aye with, well, on the wedding night."

"The wedding night," Anice repeated.

Marin turned from the gown and made her way to the bed, dragging Anice with her. "Yes, the consummation." She sat primly on the edge of the mattress and patted the space beside her for Anice.

Piquette leapt up on the bed, thinking the command for him.

Anice sat beside the bulk of his body and regarded her sister with an intentional wide-eyed innocence. This would be amusing, if nothing else.

Marin hesitated and gave a little sigh. "Heavens, I would have thought that you would have read those same books as Ella."

"Which books?" Apparently, there was a stash of decadence Anice had missed.

"Medical texts."

Ah, that would explain why Anice had not read them. Medical texts were torturously uninteresting. All humors and balancing and bile and blood. She must have made a face because Marin gave a gentle laugh.

"Well, if you had, you would know this already, what goes on between a man and a woman. In bed. After, well, after marriage." Marin pressed her lips together, undoubtedly waiting for Anice to stop her.

She did not. This would be far too good to miss.

"Men have a sword, you see." Marin held up a forefinger.

"What if he has a battle axe?" Anice countered.

"He doesn't," Marin gasped in horror. "'Tis only a sword." She made a loose fist with her other hand and her cheeks warmed to a shade of pink. "And there's a sheath." She grimaced uncomfortably. "In women."

"There's a sheath in me?" Anice kept her tone bland.

Marin cleared her throat. "Aye. Betwixt your legs. And the man's, well, his sword—"

"Not a war hammer?"

"Nay! His *sword*." Marin strained her forefinger in the air. "Slides into your sheath." She took her forefinger and pushed it into the palm of her loose fist.

"Are they all so small?" Anice asked, unable to stop the smile pulling at her lips.

Marin's mating hands dropped from the air and she regarded her sister with incredulity. "You knew already, didn't you?"

A giggle burst from Anice. "Aye, but you did a fine job of explaining."

"You are so terribly wicked." Marin grabbed a pillow and

swung it at Anice, who grabbed another to counter the blow. Piquette leapt from the bed for the safety of the hearth, while the air filled with laughter and a fine cloud of feathers. Anice and Marin collapsed on the bed, breathless and smiling, neither one the victor, given the number of feathers loosely clinging in their golden hair.

Anice had forgotten Marin's playfulness. It had disappeared after their mother died, buried under the burden of all the eldest sister's newfound responsibilities.

"I like seeing this side of you again," Anice said aloud.

"I'm glad to have it back." Marin's expression turned tender. She sat up and helped Anice to do likewise. "You will be an excellent wife. I only hope he will be good to you."

Anice warmed under Marin's praise, basking in it the way one does the heat of the sun's brilliance.

"If he is not good to you, you will tell me?" A stark seriousness entered Marin's tone. "Aye?"

"If he is not good to me, I'll disarm his sword." Anice grinned.

"You mean his battle axe?" Marin asked.

And at that, they broke into giggles once more. On and on they talked, through three years' worth of lost time, until the candle sputtered out and then even longer still. Eventually Marin declared herself far too tired to stay awake another moment. She tucked Anice into bed and quietly slipped out without Piquette so much as lifting his head.

Though exhaustion pulled at Anice, she could not sleep. Not when the next day would bring her marriage to James.

And whatever failures that entailed.

∽

JAMES TOOK extra care on his appearance on the morning of his wedding. Not that it mattered much. A brushing of his beard and the smoothing of his hair only went so far. He would never be the kind of handsome man Anice's beauty warranted.

Not like Drake. Or the Master of the Horse.

He turned from the looking glass. The luxury was wasted on him. He had no desire to see himself. Lady Leila was correct in her assessment of the upcoming nuptials. They would be a failure. Her words hadn't surprised him. They'd merely echoed the expectation souring in the pit of his stomach.

He strode from his chamber, but the man standing outside his door did not appear to be a Werrick soldier.

This man was lanky and dark-haired with a serious expression made all the more so by his narrowed eyes. "Wedding day, eh?" His accent wasn't English, but Scots. He pushed off from the wall he leaned against and the little black cat at his feet stretched. "To my sister-in-law."

Ah, this was Bran, then. The one who had taken the castle and forced the eldest sister into marriage. Also the one who had killed many Graham soldiers.

Laird Graham would be greatly displeased with his presence.

"Aye." James strode past him and down the hall. The black cat appeared beside him and tried to wind its way between his feet, forcing him to slow.

Bran winked at him. "Ye know what they say about Bixby, aye?"

When James didn't answer, Bran went on. "I hope yer intentions in the marriage are honorable."

Yet again, James didn't bother to reply. Why should he? He owed no explanations to this man.

"If they're no'..." Bran continued in a threatening tone.

The implied warning demanded a response. James peered

down at the shorter man and flexed the powerful muscles of his back, knowing how much more intimidation it added to his already large frame. "Ye'll what?"

Bran grinned up at him, nonplussed, with a mouth full of perfect teeth. Did all the people of Werrick have to be so damnably attractive?

"I wouldna have to do a thing." Bran lifted one shoulder in a casual gesture. "Her sisters would handle ye."

James lifted a brow. "They're lasses, they canna be that bad."

Bran scoffed. "Ye'd regret any wrongdoing. Of that ye can be certain."

James relaxed his body and strode onward. "Is that experience talking?"

"Aye. And whatever is left of ye, I'd handle." The warning edge had returned to his tone.

James cast a glance down at the man he would soon be linked to through his marriage. "I'll assume the threat is derived from your own honorable intentions when ye were wed, aye?"

They arrived at the double doors of the chapel. Bran, who conveniently appeared to not have heard James's last statement, turned and offered his hand to shake. James accepted and was met with a vice-like grip.

"Treat her well." Bran opened his fingers.

James did not release the other man's grasp. He held on for one last moment, delivering his own menacing message. With a lingering look at Bran, James pushed through the chapel doors and abruptly froze.

An entire congregation stared back at him in anticipation, as though he was supposed to do something. The priest had told him exactly what that was the prior evening, except the nervous man's mousy blinks and constant flinching from him had been so distracting, James hadn't been able to focus.

A hand slapped against James's back.

"Good luck," Bran whispered, and slipped away with such deft haste, he surely did not see James's glare. The black cat trotted after him.

A slender woman with Werrick golden hair and flashing blue eyes approached, her manner as authoritative as it was kind. "You shouldn't be here yet," she whispered. "Follow me." She cast a chagrined look at Bran, who offered only a shrug in return. She led James from the chapel to yet another door, this one smaller and far less ornate.

"You have your bag of gold coins?" She asked.

James nodded. "Are ye Marin?"

Her smile was bright and immediate. "Aye, forgive me my lack of introduction. And you are James Graham."

He almost replied, but as soon as the simple door had been pushed open, all thought fled his mind. The small room of the chapel was crowded with the Earl of Werrick and his steward, William, as well as the twitchy priest. And Anice.

James swallowed hard and forced his feet forward.

"Isn't she lovely?" Marin cast a knowing glance at him.

"Lovely" was not adequate. Even "beautiful" was lacking. She was like an angel in a gown of glittering gold and white, her blonde hair in perfect waves with part of it pushed back over her shoulders to expose more of her face.

"You are both of age, and the match is not consanguineous." The priest looked up at him and blinked. "You are marrying of your own consent?"

"Aye," James replied without thought.

"The dowry is in order?" The priest asked.

"Aye," William said. "The coin is on its way to Carlisle as we speak, and the transfer of land will be complete as of this afternoon."

The priest looked up at James once more and took a step

back, as though realizing his own insignificant size beside the warrior. "The bag of gold?" he squeaked.

James pulled it from his pocket, grateful the bag was of quality leather rather than the aged ruddy one he'd carried his own coin about in for years. Anice unfurled her slender fingers and the weight of the bag settled into her white palm. Later, those coins would be handed out to the poor to ensure a blessing on their marriage.

"Thank you." She smiled at him and James's entire world melted away.

This woman, this exquisite creature whose beauty was such that it nearly hurt his eyes to gaze upon her, would be his wife. Today. In name, and...in bed.

He swallowed again.

"Let us proceed." The priest then instructed them to return to the chapel and make the proper entrances.

They did as they were told, with Anice leading due to her family's rank, and him following with only his father at his side. As their best swordsman, Drake stood by the church's entrance to ensure all would go accordingly and without interruption.

The ceremony was performed mostly in Latin, a language James's mother had forced him to learn. Regardless, he had never held affection for the language. It always felt like too many words jumbled into one's mouth and ears. It was a short ceremony, an overwhelming affair in which one's soul and eternity were quickly, and irrevocably, bound.

James drew the ring from the pouch at his belt, a slender gold band with a small blue gem. Keeping with custom, he placed it on the third finger of her right hand. With that token, they were wed, the deed needing only be sealed with a kiss.

In the years of James's life, he had fought many battles. He had reived his fair share of livestock, hidden from the law for his misdeeds, and been chased by more Armstrongs than he cared to count. Through it all, he had maintained his calm the way a good warrior ought to. Calm breathing, a clear mind, a steady heartbeat.

Until now.

There, in front of many curious faces staring in their direction, James's pulse thundered erratically. It continued as he gently tilted Anice's chin upward, and even still as he lowered his mouth to hers. The touch of their lips was tender, soft, painfully erotic in its innocence and its significance.

She was his.

## CHAPTER 15

A troubadour's voice rose up through the great hall and captured the attention of everyone in the great hall. Everyone except Anice.

How could she possibly concentrate? James sat beside her, his legs casually spread, one strong thigh nearly brushing hers. She could scarcely breathe, for the heat of his body so close to her own. It was a simple thing, she knew, but coupled with the memory of his kisses, with her entire body longing to burn with their shared passion, it was nearly unbearable.

She flicked a glance up to see if he watched her, and his gaze darted quickly from her to the troubadour. A smile tugged at her lips.

He *had* been observing her.

No doubt, he was the only one, with everyone else so enraptured in the troubadour's tale. Emboldened by this knowledge, she pushed her legs toward James, so her thigh pressed against his. He shifted his attention back to her. There was something in his stare, bright and eager. A shared desire.

Lust.

She took a hasty swallow of wine to wet her suddenly dry

throat. The aching heat between her thighs left her agitated, consumed with anticipation for the very powerful maleness of him.

He rested his hand on his knee in a casual gesture none would assume was amiss in any way. Beneath the cover of the table, his fingers slid over her skirt, brushing at her thigh. Her breath caught.

She settled her right hand on his where the ring tying their souls together sparkled alongside the ruby from her mother.

The troubadour finished his song and the hall erupted into applause. James withdrew his hand to clap along with the others.

The food was brought out then, heaps of quality meat with thick, savory sauces and fluffy baked bread. Nan had been working at preparations for the better part of the week and it truly showed.

Only, Anice could hardly taste a bite of it. How could she when she was consumed with the low-burning simmer in her stomach? Her sisters, her servants, her friends—they had all gone to such lengths to ensure her perfect wedding feast. Through it all, she could think of nothing more than James's hands and mouth on her, his sword and her sheath.

She had to swallow a giggle down on the last one.

After the feast she had not tasted, and the glass of wine she couldn't swallow, came the dancing. James and Anice were the first to grace the cleared area of the great hall, their movements stiff and formal beneath the gaze of all in attendance. But as other dancers began to join in, as they became more obstructed from view, James pulled her closer, letting his touch linger longer, until she could take no more.

She tilted her head toward his own. "Surely it is time for bed, is it not?"

"God, I hope so." His hands on her tightened, a possessive flex of his fingers.

After the music had drawn to a close, James held her hand aloft. "Ye all may drink and dine 'til morn, but I've a wife to see to now."

The rowdy calls and cheers answered his statement. That he would keep her up through the night, that they both might be thoroughly exhausted the next day, that she might ride him well.

Anice was inclined to agree with them. Except the latter, of which she was rather uncertain in its meaning, but she intended to find out.

Laird Graham pushed through the crowd. "We have to ensure the consummation happens." He narrowed his shrewd, glittering gaze. "We canna have ye backing out of the agreement with an annulment if it isna consummated."

*It will be a failure.*

Leila's words inserted themselves into Anice's thoughts once more, a loud cry of warning.

"Nay." James stepped in front of Anice. "The ceremony of putting us to bed willna happen."

"It happens," Laird Graham growled, "Or this marriage doesna exist."

"'Tis fine," Anice said quickly. The less arguing done, the more quickly they could be upstairs together. Alone. Naked.

If this marriage was truly doomed for failure, she would at least enjoy it for the pleasures she could reap. For too long, her body had hungered with curiosity at what transpired between a man and a woman, beyond swords and sheaths mimicked with fingers and hands.

Laird Graham rubbed his hands against one another and summoned the lot of the party. They walked them to Anice's chambers, which would act as the marital bed until they left for Carlisle. Except no one had the patience to stay to see them disrobed and put to bed, not with the free-flowing spirits and platters of remaining food remaining at the great hall.

Ella, however, did take a moment to pluck the blue ribbon from Anice's hair, hugging it to her chest. No doubt her heart was filled with dreams of marriage for love, a marriage of her choice.

Anice was beyond such girlish dreams. What she wanted now, she wanted as a woman.

Laird Graham lingered until Isla grabbed his arm and hauled him from the room, leaving James and Anice finally alone with the door closed and locked.

Anice had only to meet James's hot stare before he drew her into his arms and his mouth caught hers. He tasted of ale and wonderful spicy male. With one arm curled around her for support, he edged her back to the wall, pinning her there with his hard body.

Anice rose on tiptoe to kiss him, her face tilted upward. Her neck pinched at the angle, but the reward was well worth the effort. His lips, his tongue. Nipping, licking, kissing, sucking.

He grabbed her bottom with his hands and hoisted her up onto his waist, holding her aloft with the press of his pelvis to hers. She had to spread her legs to accommodate the new position. It left her center open beneath the layers of costly fabric, and the hard length of him jutting against her.

Pleasure tore through her like torrents of fire. Every nerve tingled and heated, wanting more and more and more. She'd fantasized of him here, like this, with her back against the wall and his hips thrusting against hers.

Why was he making her wait so long? Why did he not push up her skirts and extinguish the burning ache at her core?

"Please, James," she panted.

His mouth dragged up her neck and his reply rasped in her ear. "What do ye want?"

"You." She arched her hips to show how genuinely she did desire him, how frustrated she was with the drag of time.

That was when she sensed the subtle dam holding back his power splinter apart, and the tide of his strength breaking through.

~

JAMES'S BRAIN could barely form a thought. His body was fueled by pure desire. He stroked his tongue deeply into her mouth, his hands groping and teasing. All the while, his cock strained with ferocity into the soft heat buried beneath layers of Anice's gown.

She wanted him.

She wanted *him*.

He tugged her bodice down and pulled free one creamy, pink-tipped breast. Perfection. His mouth closed on it, pulling deep, while his tongue flicked against the hardening bud.

Anice cried out and clutched his head to her bosom. She was grinding her hips against his, an awkward motion against the wall to be sure, but the friction still nearly drove him mad.

He pushed up her skirt. Skirts, rather. And a damn lot of them, at that. Layer after layer, he peeled back, like a flower with too many bloody petals and the sweetest, *sweetest* nectar within. His palms brushed milky white thighs that trembled against his touch, and his fingertips grazed her center. Wet with wanting, swollen with need.

Anice buried her face against his neck and cried out.

He ran the length of his middle finger up and down her sex, never quite touching the engorged bud at the top. Energy raced in his veins like lightning, blazing a path into every muscle, heightening every sensation. Too much want. It threatened to overwhelm him.

Here. There. Now. Later. Naked. Different ways. Dress falling around his hips while she rode him. Here against the hard wall. Through the night. All of it.

Her hands roamed down his torso. There was no hesitation as she reached between their bodies and molded her hands to the outline of his cock. His bollocks tightened.

A growl tore from his throat. He grabbed her hands and pushed them gently, but firmly, to the wall, so she remained aloft only by his body pressed greedily to hers.

She clung to him with her thighs, squeezing, grinding, opening and flexing. It would be so easy to take her like this. To tug free the ties of his breeches and let his cock spring free from its brutal confines. One thrust.

He dragged his mouth down her flushed chest to one bared breast, tipped with a hardened nipple and desperate for suckling.

One thrust and he would sink into her wet heat, buried to the hilt. She panted in excited gasps. He released her hands and grasped her bottom, holding her in place while his right hand jerked at his ties. One thrust. She would be his. Here. Now.

His elbow knocked the table and something on its surface gave a wobbling rattle. A stone jar. The ointment the healer had sent up. To ease a virgin's first time, she'd claimed.

In an instant, that little pot of balm broke through the frenzy of his lust. He couldn't take her against a wall, or with a single lusty push. He needed to be gentle. No matter how much she begged for it, he would need to ease her through this.

With a harsh gasp, he carefully eased her to the ground and backed away. Her dress swept over her legs once more, the fabric crumpled.

She blinked and her reddened mouth fell open. "Did I do something wrong?"

"Nay, lass. I did."

"But you'll still—" She bit her lip.

"Ach, aye." He stroked a hand down her cheek, to her neck and cupped the silken weight of her bared breast in his hand. "I almost forgot myself for a moment there. I was too eager." He brushed a thumb over her nipple in a subtle sweep.

Her lashes fluttered downward. "I'm as eager as you."

"Ye're still a maiden, lass." He circled the hard, pink nub, while his other hand pulled free the ribbon at the back of her gown. "I need to be gentle with ye." One loop at a time slipped free and the bodice began to sag open.

"Not so gentle." She leaned her head back, exposing her long, graceful neck.

He licked a hot line up her neck and tenderly nipped the skin just under her ear. "No' too gentle. Just the right amount, aye?"

She shivered and tiny gooseflesh ripples rose over her skin. Apparently, she was in agreement.

James released her breast to pull away the bodice and push it into the crumpled fabric of her voluminous skirts below. A stiffened linen binding remained over her chemise, wrapping over her torso and restrained only half of her bosom. A quick slip of a bow released that as well, and it joined the cloud of fabric at their feet.

Anice regarded him with a hooded expression and pulled free the small tie at her chemise. Her fingers moved with coy grace, widening the neck until it fell over her smooth shoulders, past her firm breasts and dropped to reveal the tempting triangle of blonde curls.

James swallowed.

He reached for her with a trembling hand. Every part of her was as exquisite without clothing as she was with. More so.

Just as he was even more hideous without clothing than with.

She was like hot silk beneath his touch. Her breath came

faster as he stroked her flat belly and paid homage to the breast he had ignored, the one trapped in the linen binding she'd worn for the gown.

He kissed her again and traced the seam of her mouth with the tip of his tongue. When she parted her lips, he let her control the speed, the heat. He wanted her to be so desperate for relief that she would not feel pain.

Blindly, he grabbed the small stone pot and guided her to the bed amid the slanting, passionate kisses. She sank to the mattress, clinging to him, pulling him toward her.

He flicked the jar top free with the edge of his thumb. It clattered noisily to the ground and a sweet, herbal perfume filled the room. Meadowsweet and chamomile, and something he could not quite identify.

Regardless, it gave him an idea.

"Lay on yer stomach," his whispered.

Anice lifted a brow, her swollen mouth curling into a sensual smile. She obeyed. Her round bottom rose firm and tempting below the seductive dip in her lower back, while her breasts pressed out from beneath her. James swept away her thick golden hair, revealing her back to him. He dipped his fingers into the sweet-smelling ointment and smoothed it over her upper back, applying pressure as he did so.

Anice gave a hum of pleasure. Encouraged, he continued on, working over her upper back first, slowly making his way to her fine arse. At long last, his hands cupped each globe in his palms and squeezed. She arched, pushing into his touch.

He swept his hands over her arse and let his fingertips casually graze her center. She gasped with a sharp intake of breath and wriggled her bottom higher, her thighs straining to part.

He moved to her legs then, rubbing his fingers against the delicate curve of her calf, the back of her knee, up her inner thighs, which parted for him. Only one swift glance of his thumb over her sex and then he was massaging her bottom again, gripping it in his hands while his fingers teased closer to the inside of her thighs.

She squirmed under his ministrations. The scent of meadowsweet and chamomile rose around him like a drug, intoxicating in the most wonderful ways.

"Touch me," she whimpered. "Please."

He dipped his fingers into the pot once more and did exactly what she asked: he pressed his hand between her legs and stroked up the line of her sex.

She cried out and pushed her bottom more firmly in the air. One day he would take her thus, with her breasts cradled in his palms while he thrust into her from behind.

But for now, tonight, he would take his time and treat her with the greatest care. Though it might drive them both mad with wanting.

## CHAPTER 16

Anice could not arch her back any further. Already, she had her bottom in the air as high as it would go, her intimate place bared for James's touch. He cupped her sex in his palm and rubbed against her only once before massaging her thighs and bottom again.

The mattress shifted as he got onto the bed beside her. Warm breath caressed the sensitive dip between her neck and shoulder. "Turn over."

She complied immediately. She'd leap from a cliff right now, if it meant sating the pounding heat thundering between her thighs.

He scooped his fingers into the small jar and the sweet scent hovering in the air grew stronger. "Spread your legs, wife."

Her thighs parted immediately, eliciting a lopsided smile from him. And then his fingers were on her. *In* her. Stroking, spreading, filling. Her hips undulated with his careful rhythm as the tingling heat of the balm set her aflame.

"I can't take any more." She grabbed his hand.

Watching her, he circled his thumb upward and hit the most sensitive spot of all. He pushed inside her with the finger of one hand, while the other hand stroked that bud until her heart nearly rent from her chest.

He stopped abruptly and got to his feet. He turned his back to her and pushed down his trews, revealing a sculpted bottom and muscled legs. Next came his doublet, and finally his shirt.

Anice sucked in a breath. She knew James to be taller than most men, his shoulders broader. However, she had not anticipated all of him to be crafted from such raw power. Lines carved deep shadows and sensual valleys into his back, hard-won strength that glowed with good health. His body was magnificent, stacked with muscle and strength.

"James." She hadn't realized she'd spoken his name until he turned toward her.

Scarred flesh, rippled and mutilated, slashed across the expanse of his massive chest. Whatever he had endured to receive such a mark would have surely felled a lesser man.

Were she not in such a fevered state, she might have lost herself on the horror of such a scar. She slid her gaze down where his hardened muscles flexed and strained with each ragged breath, and even lower still.

Anice's mouth went dry.

A thick column of flesh jutted from a cloud of dark hair. Certainly far larger than Marin's slender finger in her sword-to-sheath display.

A battle axe, indeed.

Perhaps Anice ought to be frightened by such a display of masculinity, but the wet heat of her core was eager to be filled with every inch of it. He crawled onto the bed once more, positioning himself on top of her. *So close.*

Anice bent her legs at the knees to welcome his weight. Regardless, only half of his bulk settled on her, the other part braced on his elbow while his free hand shifted to his shaft to aim it toward her center. He ran his fist up and down his length, leaving it glistening with the balm he'd used on her.

*Now.*

Anice wriggled and tried to move higher to meet him. The blunt head of his arousal clumsily brushed her entrance. Her hips jerked upward.

"Slow," he gritted out.

But she didn't care for slow. Not when she had spent so long anticipating this moment.

His pelvis flexed forward, and he pushed inside of her. There was pleasure, and a low-lying burn. Anice remained in place, held thus by inexperience, by unknowing.

James pushed into her once more, but he did not go much deeper than his first attempt. "Relax, *mo leannan*."

The burr of his Scottish words melted over her, and the tension drained from her muscles. He moved in slow, careful thrusts, easing into her a fraction of an inch at a time.

Each shift brought him deeper into her, filling her more and more, rubbing at the swollen nub of her sex, pushing past the pinch of discomfort and creating a wave of pleasure.

Anice moved with him, awkward and clumsy at first, then slowly caught on to his rhythm. Their bodies rocked together; their breaths came in gasps.

She clasped her feet to the back of his buttocks and pulled him firmly toward her. "More," she gasped.

He pushed into her, so their pelvises met, his shaft buried fully within her. He caught her hips in his hands and plunged into her harder, faster, building speed. Her body tightened and everything splintered apart on the wings of her crises. The thrusts against her came in quick jerks before he shoved fully and completely into her, following with a low grunting groan.

They remained locked together, hearts racing, breaths coming heavy and fast. Anice glanced up with a shy look at her new husband, in body now as well as in name, and discovered him watching her with an unreadable expression.

"Did I hurt ye?" he asked.

She shook her head. "Nay." She rolled her hips and a little shiver of pleasure rippled through her. "I'd like to do it again."

"Now?" He gave her an incredulous stare.

The leisurely relaxation of her limbs and the giddiness tickling through her veins pulled a languid smile from her. "Mayhap a bit later..."

He smoothed the hair from her brow. "Ach, later for certes, *mo leannan.*" His mouth brushed against hers.

She parted her lips and swept her tongue against his. Her hands slid up the chiseled lines of his body. Had anyone ever been as powerful and impossibly strong as her husband?

She wanted to touch every part of him, savor the steely muscle beneath surprisingly soft skin.

James lifted his head from hers, breaking the kiss. "*Luath,*" he groaned.

*Later.*

He eased himself from between her thighs and pushed himself to his feet. He padded softly to the ewer and he swiftly washed himself. He then wet a second length of linen and carried it to the bed.

Anice merely laid in bed and observed James's body as he moved, the play and flex of muscles she had not known one could possess. He turned to make his way to the bed, and again she noted the massive scar marring his chest, though he held the linen in an obvious attempt to shield it.

This time, she was not so distracted. "What happened?"

"I'm going to clean ye." He settled on the bed beside her and let his fingertips trail over the sensitive line of her inner thigh.

A wonderful tingle followed in the wake of his touch. She widened her legs. "The scar on your chest." The cloth swept over the heat of her sex, cool and refreshing. She leaned her head back in pleasure as it stroked over her once more. "From battle?"

"Aye." His ministrations were gentle and done with obvious care.

"What happened?"

Another sweep of the linen. The soothing circular motion was pulling her attention back to the idea of coupling once more. Abruptly, James got to his feet and returned to the ewer.

"An injury," came his simple reply.

"Will you tell me about it?"

He pulled the covers back and first tucked her beneath them, then crawled onto the bed beside her. "It isna a story for lasses."

"I'm no ordinary lass." She glanced up at him with a grin.

He chuckled, a warm, deep sound that rumbled in his broad chest. "Nay, ye're no'." His expression turned serious and he pressed his lips together. "I generally dinna talk about it."

"Will you?" Anice danced her fingertips over one of his large shoulders, marveling at how firm his body was beneath. "With me? Please?"

He was quiet for a long moment. And she was on the edge of thinking he'd decline, when he finally nodded his head. "Aye." He stroked a hand down her face. "Then mayhap we can both truly know one another."

It was her turn to be hesitant. Her confession to him about no one ever truly knowing her had been foolish and dramatic. She had hoped he had forgotten it, but evidently it had stuck fast in his memory.

At least now, she would get to know him.

∽

JAMES HAD NEVER TOLD anyone what had happened the day death came for him. He'd mentioned part of it to his da, but it was not the whole story. Even now, the temptation was there to only regale Anice with what she was expecting. Except Leila's warning had stuck with him as surely as Anice's confession had that day he'd given her the dried venison.

This marriage could not be a failure, not for Anice's people, not for his people who wanted a better life, and not for James and Anice. Not when their souls were bound together for all eternity. They would not fail.

And honesty would be the first difficult step.

"We were reiving a castle, one of the ones in the Middle lands. Some nobleman's home with fat cows and so many well-fed soldiers, we assumed he wouldna notice a few head of cattle had gone missing."

Anice gave a skeptical lift of her brow. "They always notice."

He shrugged. "Aye, and they did. A fight broke out. I had an especially large cow on a line and was trying to tug the obdurate beast from its pen when I heard a voice telling me to stop. I swung about and saw a lad there, nay older than yer Leila. The sword in his hand shook, but he dinna back down from me."

James could still see the lad in his mind's eye, the scruff of blonde hair falling over either side of his small face, his glinting dark eyes narrowed with stoic resolve.

"One of our men saw him and ran at the lad in the haze of blood lust, as some men in battle are wont to do." As the words spilled from James's mouth, he hated the taste of them being spoken out loud. "I saw what my brethren was about to do, and I stood in front of the boy to protect him."

James shifted his gaze from Anice's upturned face and focused instead on the whorls of blue and white paint on the wooden underside of the bed's canopy. "I killed him. He was my father's own man, and I killed him. I dinna want to, but he wouldna back down. If I hadna done what I did, the lad would have died."

Anice said nothing, but her slender hand slipped into his and squeezed.

"I couldna believe what I'd done." James closed his eyes, but it only intensified the vision. His father's man pitching forward, face registering surprise, and one final fogged exhale as his face fell into the snow. "I was so stunned that I dropped my blade and staggered back. The lad was emboldened by my being disarmed and distracted. He lunged at me with his sword thrust in front of him like the warrior he would someday be."

James pointed to the heavy strip of scarred flesh on his chest. "He got me right here. I dinna fight back. It was daft, but all I could think was that he was only a lad, even as I fell." He smirked. "Of all the battles I've fought, and all the fierce warriors I've slain, it was a mere lad who finally brought me to ground."

Anice's graceful fingers swept over the pinkened skin of James's scar, and he did not stop her. What did it matter, when the most vulnerable part of him had been bared?

She lifted her hand to his face and gently turned him toward her once more. "You saved that boy. You did what was right; he was simply scared. It's why he attacked."

James nodded. "Aye, I realize that. I think it's what stayed my hand from defending myself."

Her touch returned to the scar in a delicate caress. "This is the kind of wound that could have ended a man."

"It almost did with me."

"Tell me," she whispered. "I want to know all of it."

With the worst of the awful tale already told, the rest came out with surprising ease. "I woke up in a feather bed with a heavy fur coverlet and a man in fine clothes sitting in a chair in the room. He told me I'd been struck down by his son for trying to steal the lad's favorite cow, and I'd nearly died from my wound, and then from a fever after that. I'd been there nearly three weeks and was only just beginning to rouse."

Anice's fingers stroked a gentle, soothing caress over the scar, as if doing so might erase it from his skin. "Though you attempted to steal from him, he still saved you?"

James nodded. "He saw good in me, he said." The familiar tightness ached in his chest, the one that came from being trusted so implicitly. "He'd been too far to aid his son as he'd been locked in battle himself, but he witnessed the entirety of... what I'd done. He kept me in his castle for the two months it took me to recover, to protect me from any who might have seen me kill my own man."

"He sounds very honorable." Anice's fingers stopped their thoughtful glide over his skin. "Who was he?"

"The Earl of Bastionbury. And, aye, he is a verra good man." James nodded. "He showed me that there are ways to live that dinna involve stealing or ransom. Land that could be tilled, the bounty sold. My people could have a life of honesty with hard work."

A smile whispered over Anice's lips in recognition. "Lord Bastionbury is a good man." The ghost of the smile disappeared. "That is why our betrothal was so attractive to you, then. For the land."

James caressed her face and tried to ignore the hurt shimmering deep in the blue depths of her crystal eyes. "Ye're more than just land and wealth to me, Anice." He cradled her cheek against his palm. "Ye're hope."

## CHAPTER 17

Anice's stomach dropped with James's declaration. If she was his hope, and Leila had declared their marriage would be a failure, then James's well-meaning intentions for his people would not hold promise.

Anice did not tell him as much while he held her in the protection of his large arms, nor did she bring it up again the following day as their belongings were packed into a waiting carriage. Most of their necessities had already been delivered to Caldrick Castle in Carlisle, and the Graham men would follow after Anice and James's arrival.

What lay only moments ahead was what she'd been dreading most: leaving her family. It had been easy to put from her mind over the past weeks, when her father and sisters were at her side—the same as they had always been. But now, with the cart loaded and the horses saddled, the time had come to face the most difficult part of her marriage.

James put a hand to her shoulder in a gesture both intimate and comforting. "We can come to visit any time ye like."

Anice nodded and tried to swallow the knot forming in her throat as she walked into the bailey where her family waited with strained expressions. She'd already said her goodbyes to the servants, and had received gifts of their affection upon doing so: a basket of honey pastries from Nan, a small Bible from Bernard, and a very large pot of the sweet-smelling balm from Isla, who gave a flash of a wicked grin with her white teeth when she handed it over.

Leila broke from the clustered line of their family and threw her small arms around Anice. As if knowing what was happening, Piquette broke from Anice's side and made his way to the sisters, bumping his large body against their legs.

"I didn't mean what I said." Leila's large eyes filled with tears.

Anice knelt, securing the embrace more tightly with her youngest sister.

"I thought I saw…" Leila shook her head. "I've made this wrong and it's not meant to be that way." She buried her head against Anice's shoulder and sobbed.

"Don't think on it any further, Lamb." Anice smoothed a hand down Leila's dark, glossy hair. "You can visit once we're settled, and James has already said we'll return to Werrick often."

"I'm sorry," Leila whimpered.

Anice pressed a kiss to Leila's warm brow. "Do not think on it again, my sweet sister. Shush now."

Leila clamped her lips together and nodded. She knew the false assurance for what it was, despite Anice's insistence. It was far too difficult to lie to the girl who always seemed to know better, even if it had been said for the child's own good. Anice got to her feet and touched Leila's solemn face. It was still as preciously soft as it had been when she was a babe.

Catriona was next, with Geordie at her back like a shadow, as the lad always was. Her bow was slung over her shoulder, as much a part of her as her windblown curls. What was usually a bright smile on her comely face was now grave, and her eyes sparkled not with joy, but with tears.

"I will come visit you any time you need me." Cat gave Anice a fierce hug, all her exuberance squeezed out into that one embrace. "Even if Papa says I can't go." This statement was followed by the mischievous grin Anice knew too well.

Anice tucked back a lock of Cat's golden hair into her braid. "Don't go getting into trouble on my account. You'll see me often enough. I'm not so very far away."

Cat nodded and the stubborn lock sprang free from where Anice had secured it.

"Geordie," Anice addressed the lad who had been squire to Sir Richard.

The boy leapt to attention like a soldier ready for battle.

"I wish you the best in finding a new charge to train you to knighthood," she said. "I know you will excel." And he would, with the ferocity of his determination. She gave him a hug, this boy who was nearly a man, who had been raised alongside her and her sisters. "Take good care of Cat."

"I swear it on my life." And he meant it too. Not only in the fortitude of his words, but in the tender, longing way he regarded Cat, whose sole attention was fixed on Anice.

Next came Ella with a small rabbit tucked in the palm of her hand, most likely an injured little beast she'd found in the forest. She cradled it against her body and embraced Anice with care so as not to crush it.

"Mind you stay safe," Anice cautioned.

Ella nodded, but Anice knew it wouldn't do any good. The girl would be up in a tree by sundown. The melancholy cast in her gaze said as much.

"I wish…" Ella blinked back tears. "I wish you could have married for love," she whispered.

Anice pulled her sister into another gentle embrace. "We are safe. That is what matters most."

Next came Marin. Bran removed the arm slung around his wife's waist and she came forward.

"I would offer my assistance with setting up the household, but I know you are already aware of what you are doing." Marin stroked a hand over Anice's hair. "You've done such a lovely job with Werrick Castle, and you were so brave in how you kept everyone safe. I'm so very proud of you."

The words washed over Anice and made her chest swell. She hugged her older sister close.

"You will do very well, Anice," Marin said softly in her sister's ear. "And if I may be so bold as to state, I do believe your husband may be in love."

Anice snapped her head up. "With me?"

"Of course, you." Marin laughed and glanced to James who lingered several steps away, his gaze fixed on them with a light smile curving one side of his mouth. Having been caught staring, he quickly jerked his attention away and turned to speak with his father.

Marin released Anice and returned to Bran. He nodded in her direction. "I'm glad Drake is coming with ye." His stare toward James was not as kind as Marin's had been. "I dinna trust a Graham with my life, and certainly no' with yers."

In truth, Anice was glad Drake would be joining them as well. If nothing else for a familiar face from home.

And last, finally, came Papa.

"My beautiful daughter." He opened his arms.

The endearment of him calling her beautiful did not rankle her, not when it was said with such obvious affection. She stepped into his arms, into the embrace of the familiar scent of her father, leather and horses and a subtle hint of clean herbs.

"You've made a great sacrifice on behalf of our family." He

said this quietly in her ear and then drew back. "I'm sorry I did not appreciate what you'd done before now."

Ah, so he had spoken with Marin. Or rather, Marin had most likely spoken with him.

"Thank you, Papa." Anice gave him a kiss on the cheek, as she'd always done since she was a girl.

The crinkles at her father's eyes deepened and concern showed in the deep blue depths. "Be safe, Anice."

"Of that you need not worry." Anice fingered the new throwing dagger at her belt. "You've seen us properly trained."

"Then I give you my blessing to go." He stepped back. "The door to Werrick Castle is always open to you, Daughter."

The tension returned to Anice's throat. This was it, then. The end of her life at Werrick Castle. Piquette was led into the back of a waiting cart where a soft bed of clean rushes awaited him. It had been decided that although Piquette had once belonged to all the daughters, he now had become solely Anice's.

James and his father were already waiting on their horses, having mounted them while Anice spoke with her father. Peter led her to her own steed and assisted her onto the palfrey's back.

"Best of luck to ye, my lady." The Master of the Horse lowered his head in respect and backed away.

James trotted to her side and narrowed his eyes in Drake's direction. "Are ye ready?"

Anice nodded and tried to swallow down the hard ball of emotion lodged in the back of her throat.

"Is he coming with us then?" James didn't need to specify that he was referring to Drake.

"I did marry our greatest enemy."

James grunted; his mood surlier than she'd seen as of yet. Any concerns, however, fell away as they made their way through the gates of Werrick Castle. She passed without turning back to look at those she loved, for she feared doing so would sap her strength to depart.

She was not only leaving behind her family and friends, she was leaving behind the girl she had been to become a wife, mistress of her own castle. Contrary to her reassurances to Leila, the girl's words echoed in Anice's mind.

*It will be a failure.*

She could only hope that in saving her people, she had not lost herself.

~

JAMES WAS familiar with Caldrick Castle and the rich land surrounding it. He'd done a raid or two to it in his day, but never had he dreamed he would be its lord.

Anice did not speak on the journey to Carlisle, her expression somber despite the smile she'd woken up with. How he'd loved having her in his arms when he woke, the quiet joy shining in her eyes, the sensual roll of her hips against his, hungry with lust.

The thought made his groin tighten. He shifted in his saddle and focused on the great castle rising in front of them. A cockstand wouldn't do now. Not when he was about to take ownership of the castle.

All it took was regarding Drake, who rode irritatingly close to Anice, to quell James's rising desire. The warrior sat straight and perfect in his saddle, his handsome face serious with his task of protection. The cur.

Of all the warriors in Werrick, of course it was Drake who had come.

Laird Graham edged his horse closer to James. "I see the bonny man came too, eh?"

James grunted.

"Ye watch yerself with such a fine wife, lad. Ye're no' as pretty as that man." His father gave a wheezing laugh. "That's the thing about the loveliest ladies. They're lusty. Eager to spread their legs for men to get what they want."

"That is my wife," James snarled in warning.

Laird Graham shrugged, nonplussed. "Mind her. Or he might do it for ye." He nodded his grizzled head in Drake's direction.

Were the old man not so frail, James would have been tempted to knock him hard enough to throw him from the horse. Damn the old goat for being so bloody weak.

James said nothing more to his father, but rode at a faster pace the aging laird could not match in his fragile condition.

The lingering warmth of James and Anice's wedding night cooled, as had the heat in his groin. He would not be a cuckold. He would not be subjected to what he had with Morna. Not again.

He gritted his teeth as he entered the courtyard and forced his thoughts from Drake. Instead, he pushed them to the castle. His castle. Powerful, imposing, the walls strong with stone gone dark with the passing of time. The servants waited in an anxious line to greet their new master.

James jumped from his horse and strode toward Anice to help her dismount. Drake had the good sense to step back and let James have the honor.

Anice's smile at his approach was small, barely a lift at either side of her lips, as though mayhap the ride had been difficult for her.

"Anice." He spoke in a gentle tone and lifted his hand, indicating his intent to assist her from her horse.

She placed her icy hand in his and allowed him to aid her from her horse. He tenderly touched her cheek. "Are ye well, lass?"

She drew in a hard, pained breath and nodded resolutely. "Aye."

He took her freezing hands between his and chafed them together several times to warm them, then offered his arm. She leaned heavier on him than ever before.

It struck him suddenly then, what she had given up that day for his dream. She had left her home and her family, her entire world upheaved. The marriage had bestowed James with great wealth and opportunity. But for Anice, the union had cost her everything.

He knew her to be strong, but in this moment, she seemed so very delicate that it pulled at his heart. This woman and what she did to him: a cockstand one moment, raging jealousy the next, and now intense tenderness and affection.

His wife might very well be the death of him.

A young man stepped forward. The lump in his skinny neck was overly pronounced and the legs jutting from the tunic were as thin as that of a stork. "Welcome to Caldrick Castle. I'm Engelbart, your steward." The lad looked like a hearty wind could take him off.

James hesitated. This was the part of castle ownership he had been dreading. The pomp of the wealthy and how he might best behave in such situations as handling servants and the like.

"Thank you, Engelbart," Anice said at his side. "We should like to meet the staff."

James tossed her a grateful look, which she answered with a light squeeze at his forearm. The color had somewhat returned to her cheeks. A good sign to be sure.

"Of course." Engelbart bowed from the waist and nearly bent in half.

The Englishman proceeded to recite a string of names James would have no hope of remembering at a later date. They were near the end when a sour-faced old man glared at them, drawing James's attention from Engelbart.

The corners of the man's mouth tucked down in an ugly sneer. "I won't offer my fealty to you."

Anger welled up like a flame within James, the quickly lit temper he'd struggled with for the better part of his life. It would be so easy to crush this man, both in body and spirit, to make an example of him. However, the lessons he learned from the Earl of Bastionbury entered James's mind like a splash of cool water, dousing the flames of his rage.

"Why is that?" James asked.

The man's head cocked back in surprise. "Well, you're a Scot."

"Aye." James lifted his hands in a helpless gesture. "There's no denying I'm Scottish. But I'm a fair Scot who intends to see the land well-tended and the people of Carlisle cared for."

Anice put a hand to the man's shoulder. The curmudgeon's bitter expression smoothed into one of awe as he gazed on Anice.

"The Earl of Werrick has entrusted James Graham with this land." Anice glanced at James and gave a shy smile. "I can vouch for my husband's character. You'd do well to give your new master the respect he is due. Better a Scot who is fair than an English lord who would have had you beaten for the sharpness of your tongue."

The words were said with gentleness, but there was an authoritative note that dismissed any opportunity for argument.

Anice removed her hand from the man's shoulder. "Are we understood?"

A slow, stupid smile spread over his weathered lips. "Aye, my lady."

While James appreciated Anice's intervention, he vowed

Anice would not fight his battles for him. This was his land to tend. He would see it well-run.

In a brief meeting with Engelbart later, James discovered his tasks to be great, indeed. The land was in disarray. Without the earl's ability to devote his full attention to Caldrick, it was overmuch for Engelbart to keep up with. It struck James that Engelbart most likely had not been fully forthright with Werrick in their communication on his ability to see to everything within Carlisle.

The lands were overrun with reivers, livestock was constantly being carted off, and the few bits of land being properly farmed were often destroyed. It was madness.

And it was a world James knew better than the back of his hand.

This was the opportunity he had wanted. Now he only needed to find the solution to put it all to rights.

## CHAPTER 18

Anice had seen to her duties within the keep upon arrival. James had suggested she rest first, but she knew laying down would not assuage the melancholy shrouding her; it would simply give it the space and solitude to smother her.

Once she started, she did not stop, working nonstop for the first sennight of their arrival, seeing to the servants and getting the household in order.

Much of her time was spent going about the halls of the large, dark castle with Piquette at her side. The massive dog drew many wary looks, but Piquette did not seem to notice as he loped faithfully in her shadow. He paused only to sniff about from time to time and once ate something wet that she'd promptly dug free from his clenched mouth.

The cook was a burly man named Dicken who rolled out dough with the same thick-handed heaviness he used to hack apart a leg of venison. She knew because she'd seen him do both tasks in the span of time she met with him. It was with great relief, however, that she noticed he washed his hands in between. His declaration that he would be making meat pasties for supper Wednesday, however, immediately caught at her heart and yanked it back to Werrick.

Nan always made the best meat pasties, thick with hearty gravy and meat so tender, it fell apart with the same ease as did the flaking, salty crust.

She'd hurriedly excused herself after that, followed by Piquette, who had required several callings to abandon the warm room full of wonderful smells. Next, she met with the chatelaine, an aging woman named Sarah, who spoke with a slow drawl. A painfully slow drawl. Each word was carefully rolled out in such a manner, Anice found herself biting her tongue to keep from finishing the woman's sentences.

It was a direct contrast to Werrick Castle's chatelaine, Rohesia, who ran the household with clipped efficiency. She had an authoritative stare that could make a cat leap to attention and her wiry body possessed strength only a warrior could rival.

After confirming the proper days for laundry and dusting and hearth sweeping, Anice went to inspect the garden. Being early spring, it should be primed with rich black soil, awaiting seeds. Possibly beginning to sprout soon if the seeds had already been planted, as the ones at Werrick had.

She pushed through the solid wooden door, noting the need for grease on the squealing hinges, and stopped short. A tangle of stems and various foliage showed bits of withered leaves where beans had once grown. Or possibly basil. Or mayhap peppers. It was impossible to tell for certain when not one plant was discernible from the next.

It would take at least a week to clear out the sprawling garden, let alone prepare it properly for planting. And if this was what the castle gardens looked like, what condition were the fields in?

Heat swept through her, prickling her brow and tingling at

her eyes. A familiar tension knotted in her throat. She would not cry. Not here. Not now.

She twisted the little ruby ring on her finger, her nail grazing the one beside it, the one James had given her. He had been similarly busy, and she had seen little of him. He came to bed long after she'd gone to sleep, rising before she roused.

She clenched her fists, as though she could similarly allay the storm of emotion threatening her control. A pathetic little whimper escaped her. Piquette edged closer and nudged her hand with his cold nose.

It wasn't the state of disrepair of the grounds that so affected her, but the emptiness of Caldrick Castle, when Werrick had been so full, of order, of people, of love.

She had not known the pain of missing her home would be so great.

She did not want to be at Caldrick Castle with its unfamiliar people and its choked garden. Her soul ached to be home, around the warm company of her sisters, in a world of organized perfection. She knew her life there, she fit perfectly. Here she was dislodged, like a broken pin set to tough fabric.

Piquette nudged her hard with his massive head, seeking confirmation that she was well.

"Not now," she choked out.

The liquid brown eyes gazing up at her remained locked in place, drinking in her sorrow and returning solace in its place, the way only a faithful companion could do. It was his need to offer such comfort that broke the dam.

In spite of her resolute control, tears ran down her cheeks and the sobs choked from her throat.

The door behind her sounded. Anice quickly put her back to it and scrubbed her hand over her cheeks.

"Lady Anice." The deep voice carried with it the familiarity of home and family. "Are ye well, my lady? Has someone hurt ye?"

"I'm well," she croaked.

"Forgive me, my lady, but it does not appear ye are." Drake appeared in front of her, but she did not look up at him. "Will ye tell me what's happened?"

She shook her head. "It's foolish, really. It's only that I...I just...things here are...it isn't..."

"It isna the same as Werrick Castle?" He surmised gently. "And ye miss yer family." He spoke with such understanding. And of course he did understand; after all, he'd been forced to leave home at an early age to provide an income for his mother and sisters.

Anice nodded miserably. "Will it always feel this way?"

"It will get better." His hands were folded across his chest. But the ache in her soul wanted the comfort of an embrace.

The very idea choked a sob from her throat again. "Forgive me, I—"

Drake hesitated and then slightly opened his arms, whether intentionally to her, or in preparation to move. Her body reacted before her mind could stop it. She practically ran into them as her tears fell.

He smelled like the leather from the stables that Peter cared for, and like hot bread Nan pulled from the ovens. Like home. She turned into him and buried her face into his chest to breathe it all in. It scorched and soothed her heart in one painful, wonderful inhale.

Drake, who was usually one to pull away from such an inappropriate embrace, put his arms around her and held her. He was strength when she needed it, and familiarity in a world that was foreign. "Ye're a strong woman, Lady Anice, a daughter of the Earl of Werrick, and yer heart is good. This isna anything ye canna handle."

He was right. She was a daughter of Werrick. She had gone out to the enemy, starving and vulnerable, and had come up with a way to end the siege. And now she was weeping at the sight of a ruined garden.

She pulled away and swiped the tears from her cheeks.

"Forgive me, my lady." He drew his arms from her, and a flush of color stained his face. "I shouldna have—" he pressed his lips to stop himself. "Ye're fully recovered?"

She nodded again. "Thank you. I'm much better now." And she was. She had needed only the reminder of her own strength to restore her mettle. "And I do believe I practically forced you to embrace me." She gave an embarrassed chuckle.

"I am here for anything my lady needs." Drake tucked his arms behind his back. "And if anyone hurts ye, I ask that ye tell me at once. Even if it's yer husband."

"James would never hurt me," she protested.

"Of course." He inclined his head, a servant agreeing unfailingly with their masters, rather than in a way that signified his belief of her words.

Heavy silence followed, one she hoped he would fill with words to express how he truly felt about his new location, especially after she had given in so violently to her own emotions. Soldier that he was, he remained quiet, his hard jaw locked with secrets.

"Thank you, Drake. I believe I should like to go to my chambers to rest now."

He snapped to attention, a warrior in need of a task. "I'll escort ye."

"I can manage," she reassured him. Though guilt pinched at her for having said it. He was doubtfully as alien in this new home as she. "Forgive me," she added as an afterthought.

"There is nothing to forgive, my lady." He pulled open the heavy door with ease and held it for her.

Anice put her hand to Piquette's warm back as they coursed through the snaking corridors of Caldrick Castle. In fact, they went through them several times. She became quite turned around and hopelessly lost in her own home.

∼

JAMES WOULD NOT HAVE BELIEVED it had he not seen it with his own eyes. Or mayhap he would have. If Morna had done it, why wouldn't Anice?

Deep in his heart, he knew the truth of it. He hadn't wanted to believe it. Not of Anice.

And yet, there they had been, in the tattered garden, Anice and Drake, locked in one another's arms. James stormed through the castle, set on finding his cuckolding wife and— and what? He couldn't ask for an annulment; his father had seen to that, crafty old goat that he was. He wouldn't beat her, of course. He would never be that physical no matter what a woman did to him. He certainly wouldn't beg for her fidelity.

Damn.

He turned the corner, and nearly tripped over a pony. Confused, he straightened to find not a pony, but Piquette tangled in his legs, and Anice fluttering about the two of them in a distracting attempt to help.

"Enough," James growled.

Beast and wife alike froze.

"What are ye doing here?" James asked Anice.

"If I'm being entirely honest." She swallowed and looked about. "I don't know where I am. This whole castle, it looks the same from the inside."

"Ye're rooms are down that way." He pointed in the opposite direction.

The tension melted from her face and a fragile smile

wavered at the corners of her mouth. "Can you take me, please? I'd rather not get lost again. Poor Piquette is past due for a nap." Her voice wavered somewhat.

Piquette gave a low grumble, as if confirming his mistress's words.

"Aye." Taking her to her room would give him the perfect opportunity to speak to her without a dozen ears straining toward their conversation. He would not have an audience for this discussion.

Regardless of his anger toward her, he offered her his arm. She was, after all, still his wife.

"Caldrick Castle is terribly confusing, don't you agree?" she asked conversationally.

But he was not of a mind for small talk and simply grunted in reply.

"There are many rooms, though," she offered. "When my sisters come to visit, they might each have their own room."

He did not bother with so much as a grunt this time.

Her attempts at chatter fell silent as they walked through the door to her chamber.

Ava, a redhead who upon their arrival had been hastily pulled from the kitchens to act as Anice's maid, bobbed a quick curtsey. "Good day, my lady. I—" the young woman cut off when James entered. "I can leave if ye like."

"Aye." James said this at the same time Anice answered, "Nay, that is not necessary."

The woman looked between the two, and then bolted for a hasty departure. She closed the door behind her, leaving Anice and James alone.

He faced Anice, the hurt in his chest welling into anger—a far easier emotion to accept. It was then he noticed her eyes were red-rimmed and her small nose tinged with pink.

She put her hand to her face and turned her head from him. "Oh, don't gaze at me so. I know I look a mess."

"What would cause ye to look a mess, wife?" The edge in his tone skimmed his censure.

She went to the ewer and splashed water on her face. "I didn't want you to find out."

"What dinna ye want me to find out?" he said through his teeth.

She lifted a linen towel for drying. "That I, ugh." She shook her head, clearly not wishing to divulge her admission. "That I was crying." She turned to him with a chagrined expression. "I cannot remember the last time I cried and now my head is achy, and my eyes hurt. And I'm puffy." She dabbed under her eyes with the bit of linen.

Suddenly the scene in the garden took on a different context. Not one of passion, but one of violence. "Are ye hurt? Did he hurt ye?"

"He?" Anice frowned and shook her head. "Nay, I'm unhurt. I feel so foolish confessing this to you. It's only that I've never been away from my sisters for so long. My father, aye, when he was away on campaigns for the king, but not my sisters. And certainly not in a place so foreign to me. I couldn't stop crying and poor Drake happened upon me. Doubtless, he wished he hadn't. He's so chivalrous and I all but fell into his arms in a weeping mess. I'm so embarrassed."

The turn of events had occurred with such speed, James's mind nearly snapped to keep pace. "Ye were upset because ye missed Werrick Castle?" he asked.

"Aye." Anice sniffed and stroked Piquette's head. The beast stared dotingly up at his mistress.

"And Drake comforted ye?"

Anice rolled her eyes. "Aye. I felt awful to have intruded upon his person. The poor man actually blushed."

James grunted. He was sure the man did not blush and was even more certain the cur did not at all mind the "intrusion upon his person."

"And ye dinna want me to find out?" James pressed. "Why?"

"I didn't wish to burden you." At this, Anice swept across the room toward him, her steps delicate and graceful, as every movement she made was. "You have much on your mind, I am sure. But I also did not wish to taint the start of our life together with my sorrow. It is but a longing for home and it will pass." She put her hand in his. "This is the beginning of our marriage and I want it to be happy."

The final word she spoke struck him. *Happy.*

Had he ever known happiness? Mayhap when he'd been a boy, when his mother was still alive. Or possibly in the quiet reconciliation of his time at Lord Bastionbury's castle. But truly happy? Had he ever known such a thing?

"Oh, I forgot." She turned away and went to a small trunk at the base of her bed. "This was already packed, and I could not give it to you with—well, I know you have been busy." She gave him a shy, sensual look that heated his blood.

She knelt at the chest and sifted through a neat stack of contents. "I have a wedding present for you."

"I dinna think the bride gives the groom a present." Regardless, he stepped closer, drawn in by curiosity and her loveliness.

"Oh, but they do, and I had the perfect one purchased for you." She drew out a book and lifted it to him.

He gazed at the smooth, leather binding of the costly tome as she got to her feet. "What do you think?" She beamed proudly at him. "'Tis a book on harvesting. I thought you might have it for reference."

He ran his fingers over the gilt letters, their meaning incompressible. English, no doubt. He knew well how to read and write in Gaelic, but his mother had died before she could teach him English. His da had never cared to learn it for himself.

Anice watched him brightly, awaiting his response.

"This is the finest gift I've ever been given," he said earnestly. And certainly it was. Books were costly, far beyond anything a reiver might ever consider owning when food and clothing were of more import. "Thank ye."

"I'm so glad you like it." She clasped the book and drew it from his hands, her movements slow and sensual, her expression coy.

His blood went hot.

"I've been..." His throat clogged and he had to clear it gruffly. "Busy. We havena had much time together since our arrival."

She set the book aside and sauntered toward him. "Mmmhmm..."

The air had gone thinner and it was suddenly harder to draw breath.

She took his hands in hers and guided him to hold her waist. "There are better things to think about than what I've been dwelling on."

The fabric of her gown was slippery under his palms. His caress glided up her body to the gentle swell of her breasts. "Oh?"

"Like you," she breathed. "And me."

His hands smoothed down this time to the sweet curve of her arse where his cupped hold fitted as though she'd been made for him. "Oh?"

She pressed her sensual curves to him. "Love me, James." Her fingers worked under his shirt and ran cool, tingling lines over his abdomen.

"There is much to do about the castle." Even as he said the words, his mouth lowered to hers. The saltiness of her tears lingered on her lips, and he kissed them away, as if he could do the same with her hurt.

"You will need an heir." She guided his hand once more to the heat between her legs.

James groaned. There were tenants to visit, the steward and his list of ledgers, and—

Her fingers curled around the column of his cock.

And there was happiness to be had. For now, at least. And damn the consequences, for surely how bad could they be?

## CHAPTER 19

As it turned out, being absent for an hour had its consequences, and came in the form of a cluster of agitated tenants. The crowd of them hushed as he approached, scowling their disapproval.

The grumpy man from the day of their arrival was in the crowd, his mutterings causing those around him to bob their heads in agreement.

Engelbart made haste to James's side. "The people have been waiting, Mr. Graham."

"I've a favor to ask ye." James leaned down to the lad's height. "Will ye teach me how to read in English?"

Engelbart cocked his head in an inquisitive bird-like fashion. "Aye, of course."

James nodded, pleased. He couldn't read Anice's book now, but he certainly would be able to later. How much harder could it possibly be than Gaelic?

The grumpy man threw his arms in the air and several women nearby shook their heads and tsked with what he'd said.

"Who is that man?" James nodded in the direction of the one riling up the crowd.

Engelbart clutched a parchment to his chest like a shield and regarded the man with a discreet side glance. "Tall Tam. He used to head the raids across the border."

"Used to?" James regarded Tall Tam. His head rose above those around him, but not above James's.

"Aye," Engelbart confirmed. "He got nipped by an arrow in the arse on his last run and hasn't been able to ride comfortably since. Now he works the fields."

James strode through the crowd and ignored Engelbart's squawk of protest. Tall Tam was so consumed by his own grousing, he did not see James approach, not until it was too late.

James stood over him, looking down at the shorter man. If there was anyone James knew how to manage, it was a reiver. "They say ye're Tall Tam."

The man looked up and squinted his eyes. "Aye. And ye're our new master. Guess neither one of us lives up to our names, eh?"

"That remains to be seen in one of us." James cupped the fingers of his right hand in the palm of his left and pressed them together. The knuckles popped audibly in the suddenly quiet room. The action also flexed James's massive arms. "My wife isna here to protect ye this time."

He took a step forward, and Tall Tam jerked one back.

"Ye're going to regret yer obstinance." James took another step and loomed over the man. "Go to the back of the line."

The man blinked. "What?"

"I'll resolve yer troubles last and ye best pray my temper calms by then."

Tall Tam's mouth fell open, revealing several missing molars. "But I've got complaints about the miller's boy—"

"If any of ye lift a finger to help him," James said to the waiting crowd. "I will force ye to the back of the line with him."

The people waiting immediately stiffened and threw hostile

glares in Tall Tam's direction. With a lord once more established in Caldrick Castle, they did not want to ruin their opportunity for their grievances to be heard.

And hear them, James did. A thatch roof that had fallen in on an old widow's cottage in need of repair, a man who swore his neighbors were stealing eggs, followed by the panicked neighbors who swore the missing eggs were due to a fox. On and on the list went, with several he had to tuck away to bring to the Earl of Werrick for the next Truce Day between the March Wardens.

As it was, the line did not finish within the time allotted and the remainder of the people, Tall Tam included, would need to return the following day.

The remainder of the daylight would need to be spent with the Graham reivers who had arrived on James's heels. They waited for him in the fields outside the castle, restless and moving about with impatience. At their head was James's father and Anice.

The full sun overhead warmed over Anice's golden hair and made her eyes sparkle. Or perhaps it was the way she smiled at him that did it. Either way, she was lovely. And she was there to offer her support.

Piquette bounded over to James and stuck fast to his side, there to support him as well. Which was much appreciated when his father glowered at him with distaste, obviously opposed to the plan, regardless of his hand in making it happen.

The opportunity had been offered to all of the clan, but it appeared only half were interested, based on the number of people in front of him. The rest most likely remained in the pele towers in the Debatable Lands, content with reiving and not willing to sacrifice such a life.

The crowd of people in front of him, clustered with children and women, gazed at him with open skepticism.

"I'm glad so many of ye came," James said. He hadn't anticipated such a number. "Our timing is good, as crops are needing to be planted now."

"So, ye expect us to work the land, and then we pay ye for the right to do so?" A heavyset man asked from the front.

"Aye, Gilly." James nodded. "Ye have the harvest to feed yer family with and to sell for coin."

"And we owe ye a portion of our harvest as well?" Another man's voice asked in the back.

"Aye." James put up his hands to stay the questions lest they be hurtled at him too quickly. "The land is good, verra fertile. Ye can make a home here, one that willna be burned down, and ye can feed yer family with food ye grew with yer own hands. Ye will always have enough food to eat and ye willna need to risk yer lives to get it. Ye came here for an opportunity, one of peace and prosperity. And I mean to give it to ye."

An approving murmur hummed through the clan.

Laird Graham folded his arms over his chest and cast a smirking grin in James's direction. "Now how are ye going to teach these reivers how to farm?"

"I'd already thought of that." James turned to Engelbart. "When is the farmer going to arrive?"

The knob in Engelbart's neck bobbed with his hard swallow. "I do not believe he will be coming today, Mr. Graham."

James stared hard at the skinny steward. "Why would he no' come?"

Engelbart began to quake. "Be-because you didn't see him to hear his grievances."

James fought his rising irritation with as much patience as he could muster. "Why dinna ye tell me he was there? I'd have heard his first."

"I was going to." Engelbart's fear faded in light of his apparent exasperation. "But you told him to get to the back of the line and I wasn't about to speak against you in front of your people."

James closed his eyes against the realization of who the assisting farmer was. "Do ye mean...?"

"Aye." Engelbart gave an apologetic smile. "He is Tall Tam."

∽

THE UNREST in the Graham clan made itself known with several squabbles between the masses, boredom quickly leading to fighting. While Anice was not near enough to hear the conversation between James and the young steward, she could sense it would not possess a positive outcome. Especially in light of the delayed farmer.

She faced her husband's clan. "While we wait on the farmer, I'll explain how it will all work."

They ignored her at first; mostly the wives, rather than the husbands, who were content to simply stare at her. She tamped down her ire. If they gaped at her for her appearance, hopefully some of what she said might get in as well.

She began first with the basics, explaining how the plough would be dragged over the soil by oxen to turn the strips of land for planting. As she spoke, more and more of the clan began to regard her with interest, some even appearing to actually listen. She went on to detail how some of the fields would be used for dredge, a combination of oats and barley, while some would be used for peas and beans.

"The peas and beans take a bit of work," Anice admitted. "But the effects are worth the effort as the food stocks will store well throughout winter and will provide hearty fare."

"How do you do it?" A woman with a long dark braid asked.

Anice knelt to the basket at her feet and withdrew a stick that had been whittled smooth by Leila some months back. She had deemed it too long and so had given it to Anice, who was now grateful for the bit of wood.

Anice held it out for everyone to see. "This is a dibbler." She scooped up a handful of small hard peas and approached the group of several dozen men, women and children. "First you poke it into the ground, not too deep, but not too shallow." She jabbed at the firm earth. "It will be softer once it's turned."

After a sufficient hole was dented into the ground, Anice held the hand clutching the hard peas over the crevice. "Then you drop in several peas. Not too many or the plants will all lose their battle to take root, but not too few, or you won't have a sufficient harvest."

"How many then?" the woman with the braid asked.

"In Werrick, we often did four." Anice let four peas roll out of her hand and into the soil, which she then patted over to seal them within.

"And ye helped with planting?" a red-haired woman asked, brows raised with skepticism.

"Not always," Anice admitted. "But we all helped a bit every year. Father insisted we all know the land." She glanced to a little girl whose red curls matched her mother's. "Would you like to try?"

The little girl slid a wary glance at Piquette, who had left James's side to see what was being put in the earth and if it was worth digging back up.

"He won't hurt you." Anice rubbed a hand over Piquette's head and the great dog tried to lick her face. She laughed and drew her head away.

"May I pet him?" the girl asked.

"Aye." Anice waved the child over.

Without bothering to look up at her mother for approval, the girl raced over and patted Piquette on the head in rough bounces. Poor Piquette handled the assault with quiet endurance.

"What's your name?" Anice took the girl's hand gently and showed her how to properly pet the dog. Piquette's tail swung back and forth with appreciation.

"Mairi." The girl spoke without bothering to look up from the dog.

"See?" Anice rubbed her hand over Piquette's ears. "He's not at all frightening."

Mairi smiled brightly.

Anice held the dibbling stick to her and knelt down so they were eye level. "Would you like to try?"

Mairi nodded shyly and took the stick.

"Jab it into the ground now." Anice made a stabbing motion.

The girl did as she was bade.

"Perfect. Now put your finger in it to determine if it's deep enough." Anice demonstrated with her own pinky. Mairi followed suit.

"Is that deep enough?" Anice asked.

The girl nodded with a proud smile.

"It is," Anice confirmed. "Now take these peas."

"Four!"

"Aye, four." Anice doled out the peas. "And put them in the ground."

The girl did it with all the clan watching on. Her fingers, still dimpled with youth, patted down the earth to cover the planted seeds.

"I want to do it again." She poked the earth, stuck her finger in the hole, nodded with authority and held out her hand for peas.

Anice handed her the remainder of the seeds in her hand. "Last one. The rest we must save for sowing, as these will be turned up when the land is ploughed."

Mairi gave her a long, considering look, then knelt by the little hole she'd covered up previously and dug. With deft fingers, she plucked out not only her own four peas planted, but the ones Anice had sown.

She handed them to Anice with a solemn expression. "We should save these for harvest. Food shouldna be wasted."

"That's very prudent of you." Anice closed her hand around the gift. It always softened her heart how children, who had gone without for so long, had to possess such a profound understanding of how important it was to conserve.

Mairi ignored the praise and instead tenderly pet Piquette once more. The dog took advantage and lapped at her face, much to Mairi's giggling delight.

Anice got to her feet and addressed the clan. "The work can be done. The children can help, not only with the planting, but also when the shoots come up to keep birds and animals away." She turned to James.

He watched her with a curious expression on his face, his brow furrowed. Suddenly she was self-conscious of the dirt dusting her knees from having knelt, and how it hardened into dry grit in the creases of her hands. She swept at an errant hair tickling her cheek in her discomfort, and immediately regretted the act, as it no doubt left dirt streaking her skin.

He had married a lady, and she was not acting like one.

"Aye, it can be done." James strode forward and stood at Anice's side. "And if ye need any help figuring it out, ye need only ask Mairi."

The little girl straightened with pride and beamed out at her clan.

They all nodded to one another, agreeing the work did not appear complicated. Once it was determined the plowing would start the following day, the parceling out of land was completed, assigned by Engelbart who knew the lay of it better than most.

Some plots had thatch homes still on them from the previous tenants, and others would need to be built.

Those whose dwellings had not yet been built returned to the keep to stay until they had their own shelter.

All the while, Anice cast anxious glances in James's direction, curious at the way he'd looked at her, and hoped she had not compromised his authority by taking the lead.

# CHAPTER 20

James could scarce take his eyes off Anice. This woman, bonny beyond words, elegant without compare, had sunk into the dirt like a peasant and dug into the earth to plant peas. Not only had she performed the task to educate his people, but she'd done it in such a clever way in showing the child so that no adult could possibly complain about the difficulty of the task without coming across as a dullard.

He had not been the only one impressed with his wife's lack of concern in settling in the dirt. The women of the crowd had been heard protesting among themselves at Mistress Graham for having ruined so fine a gown, but there had been pride in their eyes. Their mistress was as comfortable in the dirt as they. It brought her to a real level they could understand and appreciate.

In one singular act, Anice had paved the way for his dream to become a reality. She glanced shyly up at him now. A smudge of soil showed on her cheek. He stretched a hand out to wipe it away and she swept her lashes down to hide her expression.

"Forgive me if I embarrassed you." She flicked a cautious

glimpse up at him. "Or if I perchance stepped over your authority."

"I'm no' embarrassed, *mo leannan*. I'm impressed."

A pretty flush spread over her cheeks. He liked that about her, how his flattering words made her blush. Morna hadn't been like that. She'd drunk in compliments like strong wine. They intoxicated her, emboldened her. They made her brash and uncaring. The heartless wench.

But not James's Anice. His compliments never ceased to warm her fair skin, and he relished every shade of pink he could inspire.

"I knew ye had a bit of knowledge about planting, but I thought that was gardening. I dinna know ye were aware of how to work the land." He put a hand to her lower back, the move as protective as it was intimate, and led her through the wide castle entrance. "'Tis not the work of a lady."

"Nor is battle, but many have been won with the addition of women." She tilted her head in a coy gesture. "And ladies."

"After seeing the way ye fight, I believe ye."

She ducked her head, but not before he saw that he'd made her blush again.

He grinned.

"Tell me how ye came to learn how to tend the land." He guided her down the long corridor of the castle, being careful not to get lost himself. She was right. Every bit of the interior was nearly identical. It was all too easy to get turned about.

Her answer did not come swiftly. In fact, it came after a great, hesitant pause. "The same way I learned to fight."

The dullness of her words dropped a heavy pit into the depths of his stomach. He didn't think he would like the response, but he had to know.

"How?" he pressed.

"The attack from yer clan." She paused and glanced at a door.

"Two more down," he noted.

She continued walking, albeit faster. Evidently wanting to be done with this conversation.

"Many of our vassals were slain in the attack," she said. "There were not enough left to complete the planting on their own. Every able-bodied man, woman and child needed to help. I was an able-bodied child, as were my sisters." She shrugged, as if it were no big thing she'd done. "We've aided in the following years as well, to keep it tucked into our minds how to perform the task should we have need again. You know there is little peace of mind on the border."

He stopped in front of her door. "And ye learned to fight because of my clan as well?"

"Papa wanted to send us away, but we'd just lost our mother. Leaving Papa made us feel as though we were being orphaned." Anice worked at a speck of dirt clinging to her cuticle, a mote barely visible in the low light of the hall. "Our father insisted if we were to stay, we had to learn to protect ourselves. And so we did."

"I'm glad he did. Ye should have known as much from the first."

"We were children," she said. "And most women, especially ladies, do not know how to lift a weapon with skill."

"Ye're extraordinary."

"I'm not." She lowered her head, but he caught her chin between his thumb and forefinger and gently guided her to look back up at him.

"Ye are." He stroked her cheek, so supple and sweet, as all of her was. And he knew well exactly how much so. "Thank ye for what ye did today."

He curled his fingers to the back of her neck and her mouth

softened, parted. His lips came down on hers. He'd meant only a simple kiss, but the silkiness of her tongue darted out and swept against his. With a groan, he'd pulled her more firmly against him and deepened their kiss. She leaned against the door and it rattled on its hinges.

"My lady, I'm so glad ye've come back." A voice spoke on the other side, oblivious to the passion simmering between the two in the hall.

James had just enough time to pull back from his wife as the maid opened the door, a smile on her face.

"I've got just the gown for ye to wear to—" Ava froze mid-word and bobbed a curtsey. "Mr. Graham, forgive me." Her bright blue gaze darted between the two, red-lipped and flushed. "Shall I leave ye, my lady?"

"Nay." Anice put a hand to her chest. "Nay, I must ready for supper and I'd love to see the gown you've chosen. I wouldn't have such consideration go to waste."

"I hope you'll be pleased." Ava glanced down at the ground and twisted her hands together. "I'm afraid I'm none too good at all this, Mistress."

She had confided to Anice earlier that morning that she missed her place in the kitchens, the task she'd been familiar with.

"I'm sure it will be perfect," Anice said. "You always pick out such lovely gowns."

The smile returned to Ava's face. "By your leave, Mr. Graham."

James nodded and allowed a door to be placed between himself and his wife. A hollow ache rang out in him at her disappearance. A curious thing, that. He'd only felt it once previously, and to a woman far less deserving, and only a shadow of what he currently was experiencing. This time was so much brighter, more vibrant, powerful. The sensation was entirely undeniable.

Despite his efforts to avoid it, and no matter how many times he'd told himself he would not feel such, it appeared his stubbornness was all in vain. Regardless of how James weighed it, he was keenly aware of the ultimate truth. Somewhere between the bravery to save her family and the unique skills she possessed, in addition to the genuine kindness shown to all, James was falling swiftly in love with his wife.

∽

It was the sound of shouting that drew Anice to the great hall the following day. The people of Carlisle had come to bring their grievances to James, to remedy as only the master of the land could.

Anice recognized the sour-faced man at once, the very source of all the roaring commotion. A nagging voice in the back of her mind insisted she stalk up to him and demand to know what he was carrying on about. Her more logical, however, was simply curious to see how it all might be handled. She summoned Piquette to her side behind a column to allow James to handle his people.

"Tall Tam, ye again." James's voice echoed from the stone walls. "What is the meaning of this?"

"I tell you, I've come to complain about the miller's boy." Tall Tam's voice growled with rage. "You're lucky I've not killed the bastard yet. But I'll not hang for a crime he committed."

"Verra well, I'll see to ye first today so long as ye're respectful."

While the tension did not relax from his shoulders, he nodded in acquiescence. "This is my daughter, Ingrith."

Anice peered around the column to see a comely blonde-haired woman beside Tall Tam.

"Tell him what happened." He nudged her and she gave a swift curtsey.

The young woman pursed her lips and shook her head vigorously. "I don't want to say it, Papa."

"The miller's boy had his way with my Ingrith." Tall Tam huffed out an angry exhale. "Now the lass is with child."

"It was not willingly," Ingrith protested. Her cheeks went red. "Gilbert forced himself on me. I tried to fight him off, but I...I wasn't strong enough." She choked on a sob and the heart-wrenching sound of it echoed around them.

James leaned forward in his seat to peer at the gathered people. "Where is he?"

Tall Tam jerked his thumb to the line behind him. "He's waiting to air his grievances on me for insisting he marry Ingrith."

Ingrith erupted into tears and cowered closer to her father. Anice's heart flinched with the girl's misery.

A beefy boy with thick forearms and ruddy cheeks stepped forward. "I'll not marry that slattern. I'm a miller's son. I can do far better than the likes of her."

James got to his feet slowly. The hum of errant conversation fell away, and the hall went perfectly silent. Piquette shifted at Anice's side, uneasy about the sudden quiet.

For her part, Anice's body tensed with anticipation. Part of her, a very large part, wanted James to take the miller's son to task and use his beaten body as an example to others. But all her experience as an earl's daughter knew such punishments were not welcome among the people, especially when the master was newly seated in his power.

James came to stand in front of the young woman, who sniveled her tears into muted snuffles and cast a frightened stare up at him. Her hands settled protectively over her lower stomach. Unwanted though the child may be, maternal instincts were already setting in.

"Ye said the miller's son took ye by force." James spoke quietly, in the careful way he did when he'd first met Anice. A gentle contrast to minimize the intimidation of his size.

Ingrith nodded again. "Aye. Gilbert Miller. I tried to fight him off as best I could. It's how he got that scar on his cheek."

The attention in the room swept to Gilbert and the angry red scar running up from his jaw, cutting through his close-cropped beard.

Gilbert shrugged indifferently. "She'd been flirting with me enough—"

"That's not true," Ingrith protested.

James held up his hand to still her argument and she immediately clamped her mouth closed. He stalked to Gilbert. "Did ye rape this lass?"

Gilbert scoffed. "She enjoyed it. It's obvious she did, or she wouldn't have ended up with child. Everyone knows that. So, nay, it was not rape."

To Anice's horror, a murmur of agreement rippled through the surrounding witnesses.

Anger surged through her, but before she could acknowledge her fury, James's fist shot out and slammed into the young man's face. Gilbert staggered back, holding his cheek. At first, he bristled, as though he intended to return the blow, but then eased back as he thought better of it.

"He needs to wed my Ingrith for what he did." Tall Tam folded his arms over his chest.

James looked at Tall Tam's daughter, who had fallen once more into a pitiful weeping that made Piquette whine with empathy on each exhale.

"Do ye want to marry this man?" James indicated Gilbert.

The young woman furiously shook her head.

"How do you expect to care for the babe without a man to see you both fed and clothed?" Tall Tam demanded. "I'll not be doing it. I already saw you grown and won't do the same for your bastards."

"She can work here." Anice swept in from her hiding place. "I needed a lady's maid anyway, and she'll do nicely. Once the babe is born, it will be safe in the castle and she'll be nearby."

James smiled at her and everything inside her went warm and fluttery.

Was there ever a man such as that of her husband? One who fought for what was right, who defended the weak with his undeniable strength and newfound power. He was good and just, everything she'd never expected from a Graham.

And he was hers.

James faced the culprit once more. "Gilbert, son of the miller, ye are henceforth excommunicated from Carlisle."

Those in the great hall drew a collective gasp. In a world where one's survival was based off their trade, off the protection of one's family and the fabric of the community to whom they belonged, excommunication could well mean a bitter and lonely death.

The color drained from Gilbert's face. "What will I do? Without a home, without a trade?"

"Ye can do what it is ye expected her to do with a babe and no man to see her cared for." James turned his back to the man, indicating he had no intention of discussing the matter further.

"This isn't right," Gilbert bellowed.

James flicked his hand toward the reivers standing menacingly on either side of him. "See him out and get him off our land. Let it be known rape will not be tolerated in Carlisle."

"This is your fault." Gilbert lunged at Ingrith and launched one meaty fist toward her stomach.

Without thought, Anice delivered two blows of her own. The first to block Gilbert's path from striking Ingrith's tender stomach, the second smashing with a satisfying crunch into the cur's face. Ingrith gaped at her in shock.

In fact, every person had gone silent as the dead in their surprise as many regarded her with wide eyes.

Anice resisted the urge to shake free the pain in her fingers from the assault. "Come." She casually took Ingrith's arm and led her from the great hall. "Let's leave the men to their handlings. I'll show you to my room." She gave an apologetic smile. "If I can find it."

Ingrith was a small-faced woman with fair blonde hair and bright, clear blue eyes, albeit rimmed with the misery of her tears. "I can help you with that, Mistress Graham, but it is all I can offer in regard to my assistance." She bowed her head and stared hard at her scuffed shoes as they walked. "I know naught of hair or clothing."

Anice waved her off. "I can show it all to you. I had no lady's maid at Werrick Castle. I have four sisters and the lot of us would help one another every morning and night." She smiled at the memory of so many giggles and stories shared between them.

A fresh chasm of pain opened in her chest. How had it been only a sennight since she'd last seen them? It felt as though a lifetime had passed.

"I'll try my best, Mistress." Ingrith stopped and regarded Anice with a wide, honest gaze. "Thank you for what you did, for saving me." She pressed her lips together, but it did not quell her growing smile. "When you landed a blow on his nose. That was marvelous."

Anice flushed. "I'll show you how to do it so you're never in such a position again."

"I would like that very much." Ingrith's face set with determination. "And I appreciate Mr. Graham for what he did in sending Gilbert away. Your husband is a good man."

"Aye, he is." There went the warmth inside her again, growing and swelling, as though she was glowing from within.

It was then Anice understood something she could never have anticipated with this marriage, something already beginning to blossom in the time she'd spent with James at Werrick, and what they'd experienced in Caldrick Castle: Love.

Perhaps Leila had been wrong after all when she'd predicted the marriage would be a failure.

With everything going so right, what could possibly go wrong?

## CHAPTER 21

The next month in the castle flew by in a series of ploughed fields and planted beans, with James settling into his role of master of the land in Carlisle. The days were filled with doing what he could to set his people's wrongs to right, and the nights were spent with his lovely wife, warm beneath sheets as they learned every sensual inch of one another's bodies.

In only that short amount of time, the crops had begun to take root and grow. Dirty-kneed Graham children ran about together with the English-born children of Caldrick, armed with stones to throw at birds and animals who threatened the tender shoots. Thus far, they'd done a good job. Very little was lost and day by day, the fields filled in with green.

Cottages were freshly thatched and the construction of new ones had begun. The large amount of coin included with Anice's dowry afforded enough food for the whole of Carlisle while they waited on their growing crops. The following years could sustain on what would be harvested.

And James had begun to learn to read in English, bit by bit, and had already begun to implement what he'd gleaned from the book Anice had given him.

The Graham reivers were adjusting well, and a sense of peace had settled between the Scottish and the English. Anice's new maid was coming along nicely in her duties, spurred on to learn by her desire to repay the kindness bestowed upon her. Ava was pleased to return to her duties assisting the cook, and certainly, her pastries reflected as much. Even Drake had been satisfyingly out of the way for the better part of the month. Or at least from what James had seen.

Everything was going according to plan. *Better* than planned. James opened the shutters to let in the crisp spring air and stared out the window of his solar to where the neat rows of new, pale green plants grew. Peas and beans and wheat and oats and barley. They were planting life. Honor. Freedom.

Lord Bastionbury would be proud. Mayhap James would invite the older man to join them for the Lammas Day celebration in early August when the first wheat was harvested.

The murmur of male voices sounded just below James's window where a patch of ivy grew over an alcove on the battlements. That the place was ideal for clandestine meetings and private discussions and located in such close proximity to the solar window was surely not a mistake, but the work of a crafty and clever lord.

"Do ye think it can be done?" a male voice asked.

"Ach, aye, I know it can." The rattling voice was more familiar than James could ignore. His father.

The other man spoke again. "Ye were no' there so verra long."

"I assure ye, nearly a month was plenty long enough," Laird Graham said. "I know every way in and out of Werrick, as well as any potential weakness. Do ye think you can round up the men?"

James strained to listen. Surely his father did not mean to try to take back Werrick after the forced marriage. It had been he who had secured this land. He'd even had his own tryst with Werrick's healer.

His father's fellow conspirator did not reply at first. "The men are happy here. They like working the land. They especially like a bellyful of hot food in their gullet every night. No' just for them, but also for their wives and bairns."

Laird Graham scoffed. The crass sound morphed into a great, wracking cough. He continued to do poorly despite the clean air at Carlisle and the onset of warmer weather blowing in. It wasn't just the wheezing and persistent hacking, but also the sallow tinge to his face and the lines around his mouth that bespoke of an unmentioned pain. Isla had sent some bundled herbs for his father to burn, but James doubted the old man had gone through the effort.

"The men are content now," Laird Graham agreed. "But what happens in several years when wielding a plough and scythe aren't enough? When their souls crave adventure?"

"'Tis a quiet life," the man said simply. "I like it."

"Ye dinna miss reiving? Ye dinna miss *plundering*?" James's father emphasized the last word.

The man didn't reply this time, or if he did, James could not hear.

"How would ye feel if a sudden raid were to raze the lot of yer hard work to the ground?" The low menace in Laird Graham's voice prickled James's spine.

There was an unmistakable threat there, one that could put the whole of Carlisle in danger. This needed to stop. Now. And James would have to tread lightly with the topic, lest his father take it upon himself to enact his vengeance.

"I'll speak to the men," the nameless man said at last.

"Aye, see that ye do. I'll have an answer from ye in three days' time, aye?"

A grumble sounded in return.

"Think on it, lad," Laird Graham said emphatically. "The purloined spoils of Werrick Castle, ours again."

With that, the conversation ceased and the departure of footsteps crunching over the stone battlements moved in opposite directions. James dragged a hand through his hair. The quiet peace of his current life could not last forever. He knew that well enough, but he'd expected at least more than a month.

However, James now understood what the marital negotiations, the insistence that they remain at Werrick Castle until the nuptials, had truly been. A ploy, a way to learn the layout so that Laird Graham might relive the glorious plunder of Werrick one last time. And he'd exploited James's desire for a more peaceful life to get him to comply. James's stomach turned at how easily he'd been fooled.

He should have known better. A lifetime with his father's perfidy and all-consuming egoism should have taught him better than to trust.

Now it was James's people who would pay the price.

He tapped his finger on the stone sill and stared at the several options facing him. He could confront his da, but that ran the risk of his father making good on his promise to destroy the newly farmed land. Doubtless, the half of their clan in the Debatable Lands would leap at the opportunity. James could confide in Anice, except that if she told her family, they would have another war on their hands, and he was heartily done with war.

Or he could play into his father's hands, pretend to aid him when really, he intended to thwart the old man's efforts. Aye, this way, no one got hurt and everyone stayed safe.

The only one at risk would be James.

~

ANICE SUSPECTED something was amiss with James. He was always an attentive husband, but the prior two days, he had been distracted and forgetful.

She pointed to a pot of balm, the one tinted a soft red, for Ingrith to use in application. The young woman had learned quickly with her tasks and had become a far better lady's maid than any of Anice's sisters. The very thought of her sisters still knocked hard at her tender heart.

She shoved away the image of them that threatened to rise. It was far easier to stuff the hurt of missing them into a dark corner of her mind rather than give in to its suffocating ache. Thus far, setting herself to other tasks had been successful.

Ingrith lightly touched the balm and rubbed a perfect amount on Anice's cheeks with her soothing, cool fingers. Just enough to give her a hint of a flushed appearance.

"You're so lovely, my lady." Ingrith's praise was given with apparent pride. "Everyone says Mr. Graham is by far the luckiest man in all six of the Marches."

Anice's cheeks warmed with a genuine blush. "That is kind of you to say, Ingrith." She bit her lip, debating whether to confide in her new maid or not. "I confess I fear he has been acting strange of late. It's why I asked you to apply the rouge to my cheeks."

She forced herself not to squirm in her seat after the foolish admission. In hindsight, she ought to have kept her words to herself. But she'd been so long without a confidante, other than James. It threatened to drag her back into the pit of loneliness once more.

No doubt the color she'd had Ingrith add to her cheeks was just as foolish of an idea. In the time of their engagement and now through the first month of their marriage, James had never once told her she was beautiful. She knew he found her comely. His ministrations at night, the way his mouth and hands drew toward her as soon as the door to her chambers was closed and how he stayed with her through the night. All his actions bespoke of strong attraction.

He did praise her. For her skills in managing the castle, her fighting abilities as she instructed the ladies of Caldrick how to protect themselves, the ease with which she'd overseen the ploughing and planting. He noticed every small thing about her.

Except her appearance.

James was perhaps the only man in her life to have not praised her beauty, and he was the only man she'd ever wanted to impress.

"The people of the village have been acting a bit off as well, my lady." Ingrith's words broke into Anice's thoughts. "Only the Grahams, if you pardon my saying as much."

Anice tilted her head in consideration. "Only the Grahams," she murmured, more to herself than to Ingrith.

Ingrith shifted her attention to Anice's hair, smoothing and weaving the long blonde locks into a plait to coil atop her head. "I hadn't thought to mention it to you. But after you'd said as much about Mr. Graham, I thought it best to make you aware of my observations."

"I'm grateful you did." Anice smiled at her through the small mirror. "I have a suspicion they may be all linked."

"I will inform you if I hear anything, my lady." Ingrith carefully laid a gauzy veil over Anice's hair and secured it into place with a gold circlet.

"Thank you, Ingrith." Anice studied her reflection.

Life in Carlisle had been kind to her. She'd gained back the weight lost during the siege and radiated with good health. Between that and Ingrith's newly discovered skills, Anice was more attractive than ever. Mayhap enough to encourage a compliment from her husband.

"You will be all right with Piquette?" Anice asked.

Finding himself the source of discussion, the large dog lifted his head, his brow furrowed as he listened intently for his favorite words: walk, come, food, good boy.

"Aye, my lady." Ingrith winked at Piquette. "We'll find a sweetmeat, won't we?"

Piquette cocked his head and lifted his ears.

"Thank you." Anice knelt beside her beloved pet. "You cannot come into the village because I'm afraid you cannot keep up with the horses, and I do not want you to injure yourself."

Piquette whimpered and gave a nervous lick at the air near Anice's face.

"Don't worry, Piquette." Ingrith joined Anice beside the great dog. "We're going to go for a nice long walk."

He leapt and both women laughed. Anice quickly made her departure without having to pry the large dog from her side.

She made her way to the courtyard to meet James so that they might attend the market together. He did not show. After several minutes of waiting, Anice went to ask after him with the stable master, who apologetically informed her that Mr. Graham had already left for the village nearly an hour ago.

Truly strange behavior. And vexing. She twisted at her ruby ring and made up her mind on what to do.

Irritated and determined, she had the lanky man saddle her horse, and tried not to judge how he did it compared to Peter's swift efficiency. As with all the other thoughts of her old home, she pushed them away and focused only on what lay in front her. Or at least, what she could control.

A touch to her belt confirmed the dagger Sir Richard had given her hung at the ready to be grabbed in a moment's notice, should it be needed. She set off to the village on her own with the great wide spring sky open overhead and the green fields full of life sprawling on either side of her.

On a typical market day, people crowded vendors, snapping up pastries with honey glossed currants, eyeing buckets of nails for the straightest ones, patting at tufts of wool for spinning. All looked as Anice had expected, at least for the people of Carlisle. The Grahams, however, hung about in clumps, idly fingering wares while they engaged in quiet discussion amongst themselves.

Anice tethered her horse to a pole in front of the Flying Goose Tavern. A gust of wind swept down the row of aging cottages and sent the wooden signs swinging noisily on their rusted hinges. Were this a market day as any other, the sound would never have been heard above the din.

Anice stroked her hand over her horse's velvety nose and left to find her husband. It was a feat easily done as James stood so much taller, so much prouder and more powerful than any other man. He glanced in her direction and then swiveled around to fully regard her properly.

She approached him with a smirk, waiting for him to apologize for having forgotten her.

"Anice, what are ye doing here?" His smile was one of delight, while his brow bespoke of genuine confusion.

She leaned closer to him and spoke in a low tone, mindful of the two men he'd been speaking to being within earshot. "I believe we were supposed to come together."

His eyes widened.

There. Now he remembered.

"Ach, Anice." He shook his head. "It must have slipped my mind. Forgive me, *mo leannan*."

*Mo leannan.* That endearment was said in the intimate moments between them, when her heart did not feel tethered to her body and threatened to float away. It was not meant to be said in a moment of half-hearted apology amid people who glared their annoyance at her interruption.

She extended her hands to indicate the ground she stood upon. "I found my way."

"So ye did." He winked at her. His attention turned to the two men and he hesitated as though unsure what to say. "Eh, we were...that is to say I..."

"I can see to some of the items I was going to look for," Anice said in a rush. It was a lie. She didn't need anything, with the exception of escaping the terribly awkward scene where she had been an unwelcome participant.

If she were quick-witted like Ella, or perpetually optimistic like Catriona, she'd have had a more convincing statement to offer. As it was, she was simply the beautiful daughter whose falsehood came out sounding as flat as it was untruthful.

James rubbed the back of his neck. "That isna necessary." He flicked his attention to the men again.

She held her smile as regret at her decision for having come soured in the pit of her stomach. She had given James an opportunity to let her flee, why was he not taking it?

Suddenly, from around the corner came a wonderfully familiar face.

"You really needn't worry about me," Anice said with a more convincing air. Or rather, she hoped it was a more convincing. "I can look about with Drake."

Before James could offer a halting excuse or pathetic protest, she swept away from the messy intrusion and into the comfort of the familiar.

Drake, ever the chivalrous one, bowed and immediately

offered her his arm. She accepted and allowed herself to be spirited away. But even her escape did not allay the ache in the hollow of her chest.

Not only had James not noticed the effort taken with her appearance, he didn't appear to want her there at all.

## CHAPTER 22

James wanted to smash Drake's perfect jaw. The bastard wouldn't look so very fine with his mouth gone lopsided.

"James," Hamish hissed at him. "Are ye listening?"

James grunted and turned from where his wife had slipped her delicate creamy hand against Drake's rippling forearm.

"Are ye sure ye can betray her?" Seamus cast him a dubious look.

"Bedding a lass and betraying her are two verra different things." James forced a casual shrug. The words on his tongue were bitter, but they needed to be said. Laird Graham may be a nefarious cur, but he was a careful nefarious cur.

James knew that if he went to his father and asked to be part of the raid, the old man would realize the offer stank of duplicity. Instead, James would continue along with the Graham reivers and feign ignorance of his father's hand in it.

James had invested two days of discreet conversations and perfectly worded compliance. Surely, it would not be long until Laird Graham approached him.

"I never got to sample Werrick." Hamish leaned causally against the clapboard wall of a booth, which creaked in protest at his weight. "I hear the bounty is plentiful. Enough to feed a man for years."

James swallowed his disgust. "Nor have I."

"That's shite." Seamus knocked James's arm with his sharp elbow. "Ye sample Werrick every night."

The two reivers laughed and barely escaped being pounded into nothing by James's fist. Instead, his gaze slid to Anice as she selected an apple from a vendor, her arm still affixed to Drake's arm. James narrowed his eyes, as though doing so could break the perfection of the other man.

A hand extended from the shadows of the alley to James's right and curled a finger at him, beckoning.

Speaking of the old goat, there his father was now.

James gave a nod to the two men and strode toward the alley. In doing so, he passed Anice and Drake and envisioned sweeping his wife from Drake's arms and kissing her until she gazed up at him in the way that made his soul melt.

Anice caught his eye and cast him such an affectionate look, it nearly pushed him to make the fantasy a reality. That is, until he shifted directions toward the alley and her expression took on a look of confused suspicion. Or maybe it was simply confusion, and the suspicion came from James's own guilt.

Regardless, someday he could explain this all to her, and then she would understand. No doubt she'd be grateful. He brightened at what that gratitude might entail from his alluring, lusty wife and strode into an open doorway in the alley.

"What's got ye grinning like a fool?" Laird Graham snapped.

All elation faded at the gravelly voice. James's entire life had been surrounded by hope for praise from this surly man. Even now, even in the face of the old man's betrayal, there was a desperate part of James clinging to the cliff of acceptance from his father.

The alley stank of rot and refuse, and the small square room beyond the doorway offered no reprieve from its assault. The space offered little with only a table, a sputtering candle for passable light, an empty hearth scarred black from years of use and two wooden chairs that looked like they wouldn't support a flea.

James clasped his father's forearm in a greeting of unity and affectionate familiarity.

Laird Graham gazed at his son. Bits of white whiskers thick as fish bones stood out against the old man's sagging jaw and breath rattled in his chest louder than a cat's purr. Still, his eyes held a quiet pride James could not deny wanting.

Laird Graham tapped his temple with a yellowed fingernail. "I know ye've heard what it is I've got in my head."

"Mayhap." James folded himself into the better of the two chairs and prayed it held. The rickety thing teetered but held. "If ye're the one behind it…"

In truth, James hated to sit during conversations such as these. It put one at a disadvantage to be so much lower than their opponent. However, he needed to appear relaxed, at ease.

His father held onto the back of the other chair, but did not sit, clearly taking the advantage to remain standing. As expected, the old man made a competition out of even that and smirked down at James with his victory.

"Ye'd betray yer wife?" Laird Graham asked.

James paused as if considering. "Will ye allow the men to come back to Carlisle after to resume their efforts with the harvest?"

"So ye can see yer precious oath fulfilled?" Laird Graham wrinkled his nose.

His father's disgust at the Earl of Bastionbury had rankled James initially. Especially as James had tried to convince his father to be a better man, to consider the condition of his soul once he departed this world.

Now though, the vehement reaction held a different perspective. One of jealousy, of wanting. Mayhap for the affection and respect James once held for him, but James was no longer the eager-to-please lad of his youth. Or at least, not as overtly so.

"Aye," James agreed.

James father gave a wheezing chuckle. "Ye knew I was behind this all along, aye?"

"I was well trained." James presented the flattery toward his father with a grin.

Laird Graham eagerly accepted the offering. "What do ye hope to gain? I know ye care no' for plunder."

"That ye get ye what ye want with one last raid of Werrick, my people vanquish the last bits of reiving from their blood, and ye give me what I want."

"Yer land and yer peace?" Laird Graham scoffed.

"Yer understanding." James put his elbow to his knee and leaned forward. "Ye turning to a life of good, while there's still time to make amends."

Laird Graham shook his head, his gaze purposefully averted. "Ye know there's no' a hope for me, lad." He released the chair, stepped forward and put a gnarled hand to James's shoulder, the way he did when James was small enough to have to look up to see him. It'd been a good many years since either of those actions had occurred.

"So, ye're in then?" James's father squinted his eyes and got the dogged, intense look he'd possessed when living in his prime. "To betray yer wife and take Werrick Castle."

James did not flinch outwardly from the question, purposefully worded to dig into any perceived tender spots. He met his father's gaze with matched determination. "Aye."

Anice never had been good at pretending all was well when it so apparently was not. After James disappeared into the alley, her stomach had begun churning with acid.

She and Drake had stopped at several booths while her fingers danced dispassionately over ware upon ware. She didn't need a wooden bucket, or twine for dry tinder. Except that she felt compelled to see them all as she waited for James to reemerge.

Her hand stroked over smooth white feathers. "These chickens are lovely," she said with absentminded attention. Her gaze flicked to the empty alley. How long was James going to be in there?

"Lady Anice, forgive me. I believe they're dead." Drake spoke carefully and with his usual chivalric softness, as if not wanting to offend.

Anice jerked her hand back and regarded the befeathered form laid out in a stiff line across the counter of a booth. "So they are." Her body grew warm with mortification. "Should we bring several home to cook?"

"I believe they already arrive at the castle with efficient regularity, my lady." Drake lifted his brows to the shopkeeper.

The man nodded. "Aye, Mistress Graham. They were delivered this morning past."

Anice smiled. "And they are always of good quality. Thank you."

The shopkeeper gave her a toothy grin from beneath the tangle of his brown beard. "God bless you, Mistress."

Anice moved on to the next stall and examined several strips of rough leather laid out for purchase.

"My lady." Drake looked directly at her, his dark eyes reflecting his concern. "What troubles ye?"

Anice glanced toward the empty alley once more and drew

Drake from the seller's stall. "Something is amiss," she whispered. "Not only with the Grahams, but also with James."

Drake nodded once. "I've noticed as much myself. Thus far, I have no' been able to uncover what is the source. Forgive me for saying so, but I dinna think it is anything good."

Anice's stomach sank as he voiced her own concerns. "I am of a similar mind. Do you presume the people of Carlisle are safe?"

"I will ensure they are." The resolve in Drake's voice was meant to convince her, but she did not need it. She knew him well enough after years of their acquaintance.

More than his drive to become the knight his father had been, there was something in him that was moral and just, the kind of man who would lay down his life in the aid of an innocent.

James reappeared in the alley and Anice's pulse leapt to life. She pulled her arm from Drake's. "I'll discover what is afoot."

"Nay, my lady." The finality of Drake's tone stopped her for only a brief pause. "I canna have ye risking yer life."

She didn't bother to argue with him. She'd learned long ago a staunch chivalric code of honor was not open for a challenge. Instead she simply inclined her head in a way that might pass off as being agreeable and left to rejoin her husband.

James approached her even as she closed the distance between them. His jaw was tight, and he appeared weary.

"What is it?" Anice asked.

James shook his head and gave her an easy, lopsided grin. "It isna anything. I'm hungry enough to buy the lot of those pastries and devour them all. Let us return to Caldrick for supper, aye?"

And while Anice agreed, she was not convinced all was as well as James tried to portray. Something was amiss, and she would find exactly what it was.

For the next three nights, James slipped from their bed as

soon as Anice fell asleep. She knew this because once the bulk of his warmth and weight eased from her side, she immediately woke. The first two nights he'd returned quickly enough that it did not stir her concern.

The third night, however, he was gone so long, she wondered if he meant to return at all. It was near dawn when he finally came to her, icy cold and exhausted.

The fourth night, she was determined to follow him. The subtle queries she'd made on her own had done no good. Ingrith had reported that the Grahams also kept from the villagers and left their secrets blanketed. With the exception of the maid's claims that they continued to behave in a strange fashion, there was nothing further to add.

In accordance with the prior nights, James slipped from Anice's side once she was asleep. Except she was not truly sleeping. She'd merely altered her breathing to make it appear as though she was.

She remained still until the door closed with a barely audible *click*, then quickly roused herself from the bed and slid on a waiting robe. Piquette, who typically did not stir when James left, lifted his large head sharply.

"Nay, Piquette." Anice whispered the words and made a lowering motion with her hand to instruct him to lay down. "Sleep."

She'd walked him throughout the castle and surrounding lands that day in the hopes of tiring out the aging dog. Piquette uttered a grumbling groan, obviously torn with indecision.

"Sleep," Anice repeated. "I'll be back soon." She gave a soft shushing noise and Piquette lowered his head, eyes drooping shut.

After over a month at Caldrick, she'd finally learned the layout of the halls and did not bother with a lit candle as she made her way from her room. She closed the door quietly behind her to prevent Piquette from following.

As anticipated, James's steps on the stone floor of the silent castle echoed with enough sound for her to follow. Silent in her leather slippers, she whispered along the corridors far enough behind him so as not to rouse suspicion.

The clop of James's large feet on the stairs alerted her to follow him down the narrow spiral of stone steps. She moved quickly, silently, when a door slammed closed. She waited only a moment, then pushed it open to ensure she did not lose sight of her husband.

There were no more footsteps, but there was the soft click of a door that was limned in light. She crept toward it.

"How much longer?" The voice was thin and gravelly. Anice knew it at once to belong to Laird Graham.

"A sennight," James replied.

A growl of aggravation sounded followed by a wracking cough. "That's longer than I'd anticipated."

"Patience," James said. "Ye'll have what ye want."

Laird Graham spoke again, but it was far too soft for her to make out. She shifted closer and strained.

"Patience, Da." James spoke in a quiet tone Anice had always thought pleasing.

But it was not pleasing now. Rather, it sent a chill of ice rippling down her spine.

"Whatever it takes, we leave in a sennight, aye?" Laird Graham groused. "I've waited far too long to reclaim Werrick Castle."

Anice pushed her hand to her mouth to keep from crying out.

"Once the remainder of our clan arrives," James said by way of reply. Calm. He was far too calm for what had just been spoken. Which only meant one thing: he was involved.

James, who knew the torment Anice and her family had suffered after her mother's rape, at the fatal violence of Leila's birth, at the near death they had faced from starvation only two months prior due to the Graham reivers. James, who she had thought so above it all.

James, who at his core, was still a lying, thieving, murderous Graham.

## CHAPTER 23

Anice did not know how she made her way back to her chamber. Her legs were numb and her entire body trembled. She was only half aware of trying to keep silent on her return journey, though her thoughts were surely clattering about loud enough for everyone to hear.

She opened the door and was leapt upon by Piquette, who had not appreciated being left behind, if the scratches gouged deep into the bottom half of the wood door were any indication.

But she did not chide him. She fell to her knees and embraced her beloved dog. The warm fur of his wriggling body and the cold nose rooting about her cheek brought her comfort when she was surrounded by strangers. Especially when the man who should have earned her trust had just delivered the worst betrayal.

Logic flooded back once more. She needed to hurry; to hang her robe, return the shoes to the chest and climb back in bed.

In a flurry of activity, she cleaned up the proof of her clandestine actions, and dropped onto the mattress. No sooner had she pulled the covers up to her chest than the door swept open and James's heavy footsteps entered the room.

"'Tis just me, lad." James spoke softly. The same as he'd done with his father.

The memory turned her stomach.

A rustling sound filled the room. "Go on back to sleep, Piquette."

The dog's nails clicked over the floorboards and muted against his bed, which he flopped onto with a great sigh. James slid into bed beside Anice and pulled her against him. She did not stir.

He traced a circular pattern over her bare shoulder where her chemise had fallen aside in her haste. Anice had to force herself to lie still rather than jerk her loosened garment back over the exposed skin.

"*Mo leannan,*" he whispered. His mouth replaced his fingers on her shoulder. Even his lips were cold, his beard prickly as it met her flesh.

Anice squeezed her eyes shut. How could he say such tender things to her when he was planning to assist his father in an attack on Werrick? She pushed past her distress and kept her breathing smooth, as if she were in too deep a sleep to notice his affection.

Within minutes, James's body relaxed and rolled heavily against hers as sleep claimed him.

Anice, however, had no rest. How could she, when her mind churned with the ache of such treachery? When at last the graying light of dawn showed at the cracks of the shutters, she slipped from the bed, and put on her men's trews and tunic to join Drake for sword practice. Every morning he was out before the sun rose, going through the motions of battle, training his body to be the perfect knight in the hope that someday he could follow his father's noble path.

He'd invited her to join him and she had, twice. Now her acceptance of his invitation would serve twofold: to keep her battle skills from getting soft and allow her sufficient privacy for discussion. Piquette did not so much as lift his head as she eased silently from the room. Poor thing was exhausted from the excitement of James and Anice both coming and going throughout the night.

Anice exited from the main door of the castle, already unlocked by the servants who roused ahead of the sun to see to their daily tasks. Silent as a shadow, she slipped her dulled blade from its sheath and sprinted toward Drake.

Though her leather-clad feet were silent on the cobblestones, Drake spun about to face her. He swept his blade up and stopped hers to keep it from slamming into the back of his head. A grin flashed on his face and he dropped into a bow. "Good morrow, my lady."

"Good morrow, Drake. May I join you?"

He straightened. "'Tis always better to practice with another skilled soldier." He flipped his blade with his wrist and eased back to allow Anice time to ready herself for the attack.

She tightened her grip on the pommel of her blade. "I am here with purpose, Drake."

He lifted his own weapon and crouched in preparation for her attack. "I am always at yer service."

Anice lunged forward and swung her sword. Drake blocked it and they remained face-to-face for a long moment. "The Grahams are planning an attack on Werrick." She pushed off him.

Drake's jaw clenched. "Do they know ye know?"

"Nay." She feinted left, then attacked right.

The blow was swiftly blocked. "When will the attack occur?"

"In a sennight. Though Laird Graham wishes it to be sooner." Anice pulled a dulled dagger from her belt and jabbed it toward Drake's ribs.

He deftly avoided the strike. "How did ye learn of this? Did yer husband tell ye?"

Anice faltered, a move that could have easily won Drake the duel. Instead, he cocked his brow and gave her a moment to recover. A man on the battlefield would not give her such chivalrous courtesy.

"I overheard him speaking to his father." She ran at Drake.

He spun away from the attack. "We must leave."

"Now?"

"Aye." His blade swung toward her, but she knocked it away.

Above them, the sun was rising like a ball of glowing embers from between the low-lying hills. Already, the sky had lightened to shades of pink and gold.

Anice dropped in a crouch and swept her legs against the back of Drake's knees. "It's dawn," she hissed. "We can't go now, not with everyone watching."

Drake caught himself. "They're no' paying attention. We could leave."

"And if they did notice?" She whipped around, putting momentum into the force of her blade. "We'd never make it out."

He knelt, avoiding the strike, while thrusting his sword at her. "Tonight then."

She leapt to a safe distance. "Aye, long after everyone has fallen asleep."

After James would return to their bed, following yet another secret meeting with his father. But Anice couldn't voice such a thing out loud. It was far too intimate.

Drake bowed. "I'll be prepared." He straightened and clasped her hand as warriors do with one another. "We will need to plan today. Piquette—"

"Will join us." Anice did not leave room for him to deny bringing her dog.

A line of concern creased his brow.

"They may hurt Piquette." The very idea twisted Anice's gut like a blade. "If they are vengeful."

Drake's mouth thinned. "We'll devise a way to bring him as well."

"Tonight, then." Anice released Drake's arm. "I'll come to you when I'm free."

He nodded once and turned to leave as she made her way in the opposite direction.

Yet the decision did not fill her with the relief she had hoped for. There was a hollow ache in her chest, one which James had filled in the short month they had been married. She had hoped what they had shared was real and long-lasting.

She ought to have known better. Leila had predicted it, and now the warning was coming to pass. The pact had failed. Anice's marriage had failed.

Perhaps if she had been wise enough to have anticipated it, the reality of such loss would not have been so painful.

∽

THE PLANS for the raid on Werrick were happening too quickly, and everything that could have gone wrong had gone perfectly right. James ran a hand through his hair. The day prior, he had sent the missive to Lord Bastionbury through a reiver he trusted. His hope was that if Bastionbury was there to side with Werrick, the combination of the two wardens would be too powerful a force for the Grahams to take on.

James wouldn't get a reply for at least several days. At the rate things were moving, the Grahams might be well underway with the attack before he heard back from Bastionbury.

Dejected, exhausted and frustrated beyond measure, James made his way to the great hall to break his fast. Piquette loped along beside him, abandoned by Anice. It was not surprising for James to wake and find his wife no longer in bed. It was unusual, however, to find she'd gone without Piquette.

In his sorrow, the poor beast had scraped up the lower part of the door. James reached a hand to rub Piquette's great floppy ears. "We'll get ye some hearty fare to make up for it, aye?"

Piquette's forehead crinkled and his large, liquid brown eyes brightened.

The two walked into the great hall amid the hum of conversation and savory scents of sizzling ham and freshly baked bread. It should have left James's mouth watering, but his stomach had been in knots these last several days.

What if Bastionbury couldn't come to James's aid?

Was there a way to resolve this without causing a war?

Did lives have to be wasted on this venture?

Those questions and so many more crowded in James's mind, leaving room for little else. Surely, there had to be a way to stop this without fighting.

Laird Graham was already sitting when James approached the raised table, in the seat directly beside James's.

"Ye may get the whole of my meal this morning," he muttered to Piquette.

Laird Graham gave him a seedy smirk and kicked out the chair meant for James in silent invitation.

"I dinna need yer permission to sit where I like," James said in a surly tone.

"Ach, so then ye already knew." His father tsked softly. "And here I was hoping I'd get to be the one to tell ye."

James grabbed a roll from the wooden platter in front of him and cut off a chunk of ham. He tossed the ham to Piquette, who had settled like a sleeping bear beneath the table. The meat disappeared without ever hitting the floor.

"About yer wife and that warrior of hers." Laird Graham licked his lips.

James narrowed his eyes. "What are ye talking about?"

"Then ye dinna know?" His father rubbed his hands together with barely contained eagerness. "She was up early this morning, training at swords with her protector."

The roll lost its scant appeal. James lobbed it under the table and heard a wet snap as Piquette caught it.

"They've been spending a lot of time together, the two of them." Laird Graham bit into a thick slab of pink ham.

James shrugged with indifference.

"Ye're making the right decision, lad." Laird Graham wiped his mouth with the back of his sleeve. "It's good to have ye at my side again, ready to fight."

He continued to prattle through the meal in his low, gravelly tone, though James had a difficult time listening. He could think of nothing other than Anice and Drake. Neither of whom he saw come down to the great hall for food.

In fact, James did not see his wife until much later, when he purposefully went to her chamber to look for her. Ingrith was there with her, plaiting Anice's golden hair into a thick rope of a braid down her back. The sweet scent of jasmine water hung in the air and stabbed at James's heart.

He hated his jealousy toward Drake. And he hated the lies he'd have to tell to Anice.

"James." Though Anice turned toward him with a bright smile, the way she'd said his name wasn't the same. Flat. Lackluster. Without the heady excitement of which he'd grown accustomed. Her gaze was much the same—gone was the sparkle he'd come to anticipate.

"I heard ye were practicing with Drake this morning." The words did not sound casually as intended, but hard with accusation.

The realization of this was echoed in Ingrith's curious glance and Anice's pinched brows.

"I cannot lose my ability to fight simply because I'm a wife," Anice replied slowly. "One never knows when an unexpected attack may occur."

The last statement came out hard and pointed, a dagger of words. Aye, there was a coldness to her demeanor to be sure.

"I would protect ye no matter what." The pressure in James's chest squeezed.

He would protect her; die for her if necessary. Even his betrayal now was to keep her safe. Hiding the truth of the attack, planning a way to stop it before men could be killed—it was for her, as much as it was for her people.

A voice nagged him, begging him to tell her. However, he knew doing so would push her into danger. She would sacrifice anything to save her family, and he could not allow that.

"Ye left Piquette," he said, intentionally changing the topic of conversation.

"He was tired." Her gaze swept to her lap, masking her emotions. "You both were."

Ingrith rubbed a light rouge on Anice's lips and cheeks.

"Anice." James said only her name, but it was enough to draw his wife's face up. He hadn't known why he'd said it, only that he wanted her gaze upon him.

He needed her close to him, so that he might touch her, caress the sweetness of her. He stepped closer and ran a finger down her soft cheek. She continued to watch him without expression.

"Ye're so verra lovely, *mo leannan*."

She blinked suddenly, and her eyes filled with tears.

"Anice, are ye unwell?" He knelt at her side and took her slender hand in his large ones. "Has someone hurt ye?"

Ingrith immediately backed away and busied herself with

the trunk of clothes on the opposite side of the room. Anice shook her head and waved James off. "I'm simply thinking of Werrick Castle."

"Ye have me."

A tear ran down her cheek, and she nodded. She didn't understand exactly how much she had him, but she would. When the mess of this was behind him; when she realized what he had done. She would understand.

## CHAPTER 24

Finally, Anice knew James truly did find her lovely. And yet it had hit her with an empty pang.

He left the room after delivering such a stunning piece of flattery, and it haunted her as she set upon her tasks in order to leave him. The work had consumed her thoughts, for which she was grateful. Food was smuggled from the kitchen, a large sling was fashioned for Drake to wear across his chest to help secure Piquette in his lap as he rode the horse, and they'd planned how best to ease the horses from the stalls without arousing suspicion.

Throughout it all, James's words had come back to her again and again.

*Ye're so verra lovely.*

She tried to push the compliment away, but it was a stubborn thing that refused to be set aside. Instead, it curled around her heart like a thorny vine, squeezing and pricking deep.

Initially she had thought to beg off from a night of intimacy with her husband. She could cite an aching head, or her monthly courses. Doing so might arouse suspicion. But there was more to it. After dawn, she might never see James again. She would certainly never be held by him again, or loved by him again, never have him whisper "*mo leannan*" in her ear again.

A knot of emotion lodged in her throat, as it had throughout the day.

Nay, she wanted this last night with him. To pretend he was still the man she had thought him to be and make her peace with her decision to leave.

Ingrith kept Piquette for the first part of the night, as was usual. Not only did it allow Anice and James time alone, but Ingrith told Anice having the large beast at her side helped her feel safe enough to sleep.

When James came to her chamber later that night, it was only the two of them. Anice's heart pounded at the sight of him, racing with too many emotions to name.

He drew her into his strong arms and surrounded her with his clean, cedar scent. "Are ye better?"

She was not but could not trust herself to say so. Instead, she simply nodded against his chest. He drew back slightly and held her face in his hands. "I know ye miss yer family. I think mayhap I havena told ye enough how verra much I care for ye."

*Nay. Not this. Not now.*

Anice opened her mouth to protest, but James lowered his head and kissed away her words. His lips moved over hers with such tenderness that her knees seemed to melt away from her legs.

"I never told ye how lovely ye are." He caught her chin between his thumb and forefinger, tilting her face upward. His gaze swept over her features like a savoring caress.

"You were the one person I wanted to find me beautiful," she whispered. "I've been trying—"

"I hope I still am that one person," he said playfully.

Her insides shrank in horror at her slip.

"I havena ever said it on purpose." He brushed his thumb

over her lower lip and left a slow, pleasant burn in its wake. His fingers slid down her neck, grazed over the swell of her breasts and gently pulled at the ties of her gown. "Everyone tells ye ye're bonny."

One by one, he slipped free the binding of her kirtle.

"It isn't their opinions I seek," Anice replied.

"Nay, but ye hear them nonetheless." He pushed the loosened garment from her shoulders, so she stood only in her shift. "Ye know ye're lovely." He drew the feather light fabric off her and let it float to the ground.

She was naked, bared for his viewing. James gazed at her, slowly up and then back down. "Ye're so verra beautiful," he murmured. "But ye're more than yer appearance, Anice. It's why I never said it to ye."

Her breath caught. "What do you mean?"

His fingers moved to his doublet, working free the toggles as he spoke. "Ye once told me no one has ever truly known ye."

Her cheeks went hot at the memory. She had been so dramatic, so hungry, so ready to offer anything for food. "It was a foolish thing to say."

The doublet slipped off and he tugged his leine over his head. It was her turn to allow her gaze to feast upon him with appreciation. God's teeth, he was a powerful man. Solid muscle and strength. Her core pulsed with desire for the weight of him between her thighs and the stroke of his length inside her.

"It was an honest thing to say." Next came his trews, tugged slowly from his muscular thighs. "But I dinna think even ye truly knew yerself."

Fully naked, fully aroused, he came to her. He stroked a hand down her arm and then let it lazily sweep back up from hip to waist to breast. Anice drew in a shaky breath. "Of course I know myself."

"Nay." He shook his head. "I've listened since I've met ye, and I disagree."

Anice lifted her face toward his, her mouth desperate for the sensual, masculine taste of him. One last time. Everything had to be enough, this one last time.

"It's all in what ye've said, *mo leannan*." He did not kiss her. Instead he stroked her face and her neck and shoulders and breasts. His fingers moved in tantalizing, teasing caresses over her entire body. Slowly, gently, he eased her back to the bed. "Ella dances better than ye, Marin fights better than ye, Leila plants better than ye."

Anice stared at him in surprise. Had she said all those things?

"It's why I dinna tell ye how beautiful ye are." He crawled over the top of her and brought his hands back to her face, cradling her in his palms. He stared down at her as if she were the only woman in the world to ever have mattered. "I've seen how ye dance, and my body has burned from it." He grinned his approval. "I've watched ye teach a clan to sow crops in the course of an afternoon with yer kindness, yer skill and yer wit. And I've fought with ye myself." He nodded approvingly. "Ye're so, so much more than simply an attractive woman."

His mouth came down on hers then, sweet and tender. Sensual and loving. Anice clung to him as his kisses trickled downward to her nipples, to the dip of her navel, to the ache between her legs.

She clutched the bedclothes as his hot tongue licked at her center. This had to be enough. *This had to be enough.*

However, she knew it would not be. Despite the knowledge of his betrayal, despite her need to save her family, and despite the knowledge she would never forget this night, or the impact of his words, it would never be enough.

A greater part of her would always want James. Forever. Not

only because of how he made her feel, or because he was the only person in the entire world who understood her better than even herself, but because...because she loved him.

∼

JAMES HAD WAITED FAR TOO long to say what had been in his heart for so long. He ought to have told her earlier how he felt, but he had stubbornly pushed it away. Foolish rationale that if he let her know how beautiful she was, how deeply he cared for her, he would be giving her power over him.

The same as with Morna.

Except Anice was not Morna.

He loved her with his words, and now he loved her with his mouth, basking in the sighs and moans of Anice's pleasure. Her breath hitched and she cried out with her release. He continued to taste her, to lick and tease until her body relaxed once more.

His cock was swollen with desire for his bonny wife, eager to sate them both. He got to his feet and crawled on the mattress over her, the taste of her sweetness on his lips.

He nuzzled her cheek with his nose and pressed a kiss to the spot under her ear that always made small bumps of delight rise on her skin.

She arched her hips up, fitting their pelvises together so the sweet sensuality of her curves pressed to him. "I need you, James." Her arms curled up his back and she clung to him as though her life depended on it. "Please. I need you."

It was a request she didn't need to ask for again. Holding her to him, he shifted her underneath him and positioned himself between her legs. The cries of her crises only moments ago had left him hard for her. Hell, some days just looking at her left him hard.

He eased himself against her and thrust inside the grip of

her heat. She gave a breathy gasp by his ear. Her legs locked around him with the same determined grip as her arms, bringing them as close as they could possibly be.

They had not been intimate like this, locked against one another as though every part of them touched. James cupped her bottom with both hands and flexed his hips, deep and fast into her.

*Anice.* His lovely wife. So much more than she gave herself credit for. There was one final thing he hadn't told her yet.

His mouth caught hers and she kissed with a hungry, blind passion while their bodies joined again and again and again. He broke off the kiss and rested his brow to hers.

"Anice, I've never told ye." He released one hand from her bottom and braced himself over her, so he might look at her as he said it. "I lov—"

"Nay." She shook her head. "Don't." Her hips raised to his with more determination.

James grabbed her to him again, mind swirling with a distracted inability to understand her reaction. He thrust into her with renewed vigor, desperate for release, expelling his frustration, wanting to possess her completely.

She buried her face in his neck and loosed a muffled scream as her release took her. James was not far behind, his smooth pumps becoming shorter as the rushing swell of his climax overtook him.

Once their breathing had calmed and her clutching grip on him had loosened under the languidness of post-coital bliss, he rose to clean them both. When he was done, he pulled Anice into his arms, snuggling her back to his chest and cradling her with the whole of his body.

In those moments after pleasure, with heat still humming in their veins and cradled in the comfort of a shared bed, life was completely perfect.

Except that in reality, life was completely imperfect. And his father would no doubt be waiting for him.

James kissed Anice's smooth, naked shoulder. "Ye've always been bonny to me, *mo leannan*." She did not reply, clearly asleep as her deep, rhythmic breathing indicated.

He roused himself with much regret. He longed to be back at her side, in the warm comfort of her bed. With her.

Damn his father and this whole bloody scheme. James pulled on his leine and trews and quietly slipped from the room. But as he left, he caught a soft sniffling coming from the bed. He immediately said a prayer for his wife, in the hopes she was not falling prey to any illness and made his way to his father's room. Surely, they had enough planned out that their meeting would be brief, and James could return to Anice before his side of the bed cooled.

Lord Bastionbury had most likely gotten his letter by now. The thought invigorated James. With luck, he would have a reply soon. Preferably a favorable reply.

He pushed open the door to his father's room and saw not only the old man, but several of his reivers with him. A grim set to Laird Graham's face bespoke of plans gone awry. Finally.

Relief relaxed James's shoulders.

"How could ye?" Laird Graham growled. "I trusted ye."

A knot of apprehension coiled in James's stomach. The first rule of being interrogated was to never assume the person knew the truth.

"What in God's name are ye talking about, old man?" James stalked deeper into the room and stood in front of his father.

"I think ye know." Laird Graham's lips curled back to reveal his yellowed teeth. "I should've gone with my gut and kept ye out of this."

James crossed his arms over his chest. "I'll have my crimes told to me if I'm to be judged."

"Betrayal," his father squawked. "Telling that lass of yers all about our plans."

James regarded the old man with a genuinely furrowed brow. "Ye mean Anice?"

"Aye, unless ye got a different lass ye're no' telling me about." Laird Graham cast a grim scowl at him. "And if that be the case, I hope ye've not told her as well."

"I didn't tell Anice anything. What are ye going on about?"

Laird Graham's lower jaw thrust forward in a stubborn scowl. "Why else would she be leaving the castle tonight with her man?"

"With her man?" James muttered. "Ye dinna mean Drake?"

"Ach, aye, what other man would I mean?" James's father rolled his eyes. "They're always going together, whispering, the two of 'em."

James didn't need to hear this. His father was just trying to push a wedge between them, to keep James for himself. It wouldn't be the first time. James narrowed his eyes. "What are ye saying?"

"Yer wife plans to sneak out of the castle tonight with Drake," his father spoke slowly, as he would with someone who was hard of hearing. "Because ye told her our plans."

The old man was mad. Or had false information. Or both. Anice would never leave him. She would never do that to him. Just tonight, she had clung to him as they joined bodies. She was *not* Morna.

"I told her nothing." James unfolded his arms and leaned over his father. "And I dinna care for yer accusations toward my wife."

"Ye dinna know. Ye really dinna know?" Laird Graham stared at him for a long moment and then gave a wheezing laugh. "The stable lad saw Drake messing about within one of the stalls and later uncovered everything needed for saddling the horses quickly buried under the hay. So, why would they need to saddle their horses quickly, if they were planning to stay?" He turned to the other reivers. "Take him with ye when ye go. James needs to see this with his own eyes, then mayhap he'll believe me: his wife is leaving by cover of night." His father stared pointedly at James and added, "with Drake."

## CHAPTER 25

Anice hurried down the hall to the soldiers' sleeping quarters. When she passed the entrance, Piquette at her heels, Drake appeared at her side—so silent she had not detected the rustle of his clothing as he moved. He put a hand to his lips to ensure she remained silent.

Together they rushed toward the side exit of the castle, the one scarcely guarded at night, due to the treacherous terrain limiting its accessibility. It would be easy enough to use, so long as they stayed on the path.

As they made their way to the door, Anice gazed down the hall behind them, under the pretense of looking out for any who might have followed them. In truth, she was looking back at the corridors that had finally become familiar, at the life she had begun to love. She would be leaving James. Forever. After what they had shared that night, after what he had confessed... There would be no recovery of what they had after such deception. On either of their parts.

She looked away lest she change her mind. This was for Werrick, for her sisters. This was to save her family.

And contrary to James's tender words, he had betrayed her.

Drake held up his hand for her to wait as he eased the door open. He scanned the area and paused. His eyes narrowed.

Something was wrong.

He drew back suddenly, but it was too late.

A shout came from outside. Drake pulled at the door to jerk it closed, but someone grabbed at his gambeson and dragged him out. In a final effort to keep her safe, he left himself vulnerable to an assault, and shoved the heavy door closed.

The hall fell silent for only a moment, then the door was flung open again. Piquette snarled in a savage way she'd only heard a few times in her life, each of them rife with danger. A net shot out, its weights clattering to the ground, locking Piquette beneath. The dog howled in outrage, thrashing uselessly against the tangle of netting.

Anice shrieked her outrage and attacked. She grabbed the dagger sheathed at her side, and launched herself at the men surrounding her, kicking, punching, slicing. Any impacting harm she could exact, she did—all in an effort to save her sweet, innocent Piquette. Someone caught her around the waist and tugged her outside into the moonlit night. Cold air washed over her hot face and filled her lungs.

Her wrist was twisted, gently but firmly, and the strength bled away from her hand. The dagger dropped harmlessly to the ground. Not that it mattered. She didn't need any weapons to escape this ambush. A solid kick to the man in front of her caught him under the chin and knocked his head sharply to the side. He staggered back, revealing a disarmed Drake fighting with the same determination.

Someone grabbed Anice from behind. She squatted down, forcing her weight to the ground, then kicked her heel upward into the man's groin. He gave a choking sound and pitched forward. Anice did not wait for another to attack before she moved on to her next opponent.

She drew her arm back and smashed the meaty part of her forearm into the next man's face. His nose crunched beneath the savage blow. She turned to the next one, crouched, and swept his feet from underneath him. Once he was on the ground, Anice fell on top of him to lock him in place. She could break his neck.

A glint of silver caught her eye. Her blade.

She grabbed the dagger from the cold, wet grass and drew it up.

"Anice, stop." The voice was softly spoken, dejected. Familiar.

Her hands dropped, and so too did her heart. A figure stood over her, blotting out the moon, but she did not lift her face to see who it was. There was only one man who was large enough to block out the moon.

*James.*

She could not bring herself to look up at him, to witness the pain of her deception. Only an hour ago, he had held her with such gentle affection, understanding her in a way no one else ever had. He had been about to tell her he loved her.

She was grabbed and hauled to her feet. Still she did not look up. She did, however, glance to the side, in time to see Drake roughly manacled and poor Piquette struggling against the net just inside the open door.

That forced her to lift her head and face her husband. His body was tense, arms folded over his chest, massive and impenetrable. His eyes though, his eyes glittered in the moonlight with every emotion he could not mask. Disappointment. Hurt. "Ye betrayed me," he spoke so quietly, his words were nearly lost in the wind.

She glared up at him, trying to force anger to burn away the awful grip of guilt wringing her heart. "You betrayed me first."

"Take them to the dungeon." James turned his back to her. "Leave the dog."

*Not Piquette.* Anice jerked free of her captor and spun around to plant a punch to his jaw. Strong arms captured her and held her fast in a grip. It wasn't the hold that stopped her from fighting. She'd gotten out of worse.

It was the scent.

That scent of cedar, masculinity, intimate moments, a man she once thought she loved. It disabled her senses and left her sagging against the hard body she knew better than her own.

"If I were to hurt anyone this night, it wouldna be him," James growled in her ear. "Get the manacles on her and take her to the dungeon." He released her and several men caught her.

The clank of the heavy metal sounded as the cold weight of the iron bonds were clapped over her wrists behind her back. As the reivers did this, James knelt to Piquette and gently stroked the dog's head. The low murmur of his voice carried toward her, indiscernible, but obviously meant to be soothing.

"Go on with ye." The man behind her nudged her forward.

As Anice was led inside, Drake was already being walked back into the castle.

James settled beside Piquette and gently stroked his head while speaking in soothing tones. The dog ceased his struggling and whined as Anice passed by, staring up at her with liquid brown eyes.

"'Tis fine, Piquette," she said in a reassuring voice to the old dog. "All will be well."

It was a lie, of course. But Piquette took comfort, as she'd hoped, and ceased his whimpers.

She tried to shove the scene from her mind. She tried not to think of how James had looked at her. Instead, she considered what she had lost: the opportunity to warn her family.

They descended the stone stairs into the dungeon. The air was icy and thick with the odor of wet dirt and mold. A shiver prickled down her back.

She had let emotions cloud her actions. When she could have continued to fight and push on, she had allowed her heart to dictate rather than using her head.

As the door to her cell swung closed with an echoing finality, all she could think of was Werrick Castle, and how greatly she had failed.

∼

IT HAD TAKEN NEARLY the entire night for James to calm down enough to go to the dungeon. In that time, he had refused to see his father. The old man would gloat and goad.

It was impossible to say what James might have done in such circumstances, especially when his blood already ran hot with rage. Memories of Morna dredged from the dark areas of his mind and tangled with thoughts of Anice, procured images of her lithe, fair body stretched over Drake.

James stalked down to the dungeon. It had been in his mind to see Drake first. To smash that pretty face of his into something no one would want to look upon again.

But it was not the way Lord Bastionbury had taught him. James balled his ire into his fists and made his way to the wooden door barring him from the second woman to have broken his heart.

The guard unlocked the cell and stepped back while James entered.

"Go." James nodded to the man.

"But it should be locked—"

"She willna leave." Of that, James was certain. His heart hammered in his chest so hard, he could scarcely hear. He bristled with impatience.

The man obeyed the order with no more protest and quickly made his way up the stone stairs.

Dread and anxiety mixed into a noxious brew in James's gut. It churned so violently that it left his hands shaking. A deep breath in, and a deep breath out, and finally he was ready to face Anice.

He pushed through the door and found her beside the open doorway with a length of wood clenched in her fists like a club. A disassembled chair lay only a foot behind her.

James shut the door and glared at her. "First ye betray me, and now ye intend to beat me?"

She did not lower her weapon. "You betrayed me first. I only did what I had to."

"Ach, pray tell what I could have possibly done that forced ye into Drake's arms?" James could not quell the bitterness rising in his voice. "I did everything for ye, Anice. I stood up against my da for ye; I've cared for ye. I learned to read in English for ye, so ye wouldna think me too ignorant to read the book ye gifted me."

The chair leg in her hands drifted downward slightly. "You learned to read English for me?"

"Aye, and none of it was enough." James dragged a hand through his hair and rubbed the back of his neck. "Why? Because I'm no' as bonny as yer Drake? Because I'm too ugly and no' good enough for ye?"

Anice blinked. "Drake? Nay, he—"

"Just like Morna." James raked a hand through his hair again. "Ye're just like Morna."

Anice threw down the leg of the chair. It thunked onto the

cold, wet earth below. "Damn it, James. I don't understand what you're going on about. What I do know is that you are conspiring with your father to reclaim Werrick. To benefit from the fall of my family." She closed the distance between them and glared up at him. "I did trust you. I did everything I could to be a good wife. And *you* betrayed *me*."

James stared at her in shock. Was it true? Of course, it had to be true. She couldn't have known such information had she not discovered the plot. *How* had she found out? "Why Drake?" he demanded. "Why did ye leave with him?"

"What would have happened to him if I left him behind?" Anice put her hands to her hips. "He'd be strung up on the gallows at best. I would never leave my father's man behind to face such a fate."

"I wouldna have done that. Ye should know that."

"I thought I did." Anice's brow tightened in concentration. "But not now. Not when you've betrayed my family. Me."

James glanced toward the door to ensure the guard had not returned. Still, he lowered his voice. "I'm no' working with my da. I'm only making him think I am."

Anice folded her arms over her chest, appearing to not believe him any more than he believed her.

"It was the only way, Anice." A door closed somewhere in the distance and echoed down the dank dungeon passage. James froze and listened, straining for the heavy fall of a guard's steps. Hearing nothing, he continued on, almost in a whisper now.

"If I tried to oppose my father, he would go around me, enlist the reivers who dinna join us to raze the new fields," he said. "I worried he would hurt ye to spite me. This way, I kept ye safe. It was the only solution I could manage."

"And why didn't you tell me?" Anice demanded. "I would have helped."

"Nay," James replied sadly. "Ye would have tried to warn yer family."

She glanced down, not bothering to counter the claim.

"If ye were caught, we would be found out," he continued. "I had to do this on my own, aye? Ye know I've wanted peace for my people, that I want them to lead honest lives."

"I only know what you've said." Her gaze shot back up to him, hard with wariness.

"Aye, and I only know what ye've said." He drew in a breath around the painful ache in his chest. "Ye and Drake have been close since I've known ye. It's obvious he's in love with ye, Anice. If ye dinna see it, ye're blind."

Her mouth fell open. "That's preposterous. He treats all my sisters with the same level of respect."

"Respect, aye, but no' the same affection." The anger was returning, pumping heat through his body and filling his mind with images of Anice and Drake, entwined and naked. "Do ye deny lusting after him as well?"

"Aye, I deny it." She glared up at him.

"Do ye deny leaving me to be with him?"

Her glare turned incredulous. "To be with him?"

"Ye knew leaving would betray me," he said. "Ye knew ye'd never see me again if ye succeeded."

To his surprise, her eyes filled with tears. She nodded. She pressed her lips together and swallowed. "It was a risk I had to take. But I...I hated that I had to leave you. You lied to me, James. You put my family in danger."

Before he could stop himself—before he let himself want to stop himself—he reached out for her and drew her to his chest. Anice put her face against him and her back shuddered with a sob.

"This month has been one of so much joy, and I've been so

happy." She looked up at him, her lashes spiked from her tears. "I trusted you completely."

"And now?" He brushed his thumb over her cheek to wipe away a tear. "Will ye trust me now?"

She continued to stare up at him, not speaking for long enough that he doubted that she ever could truly trust him again.

## CHAPTER 26

Anice hesitated in replying only because she knew that a ready answer would make her look like the fool. After such an incredible betrayal, she ought to be wary of his explanation about siding with his father rather than her. Except that everything in her drew toward trusting him again, reclaiming what had been briefly enjoyed and rapidly shattered.

"Tell me about Morna," she said.

James shifted further from Anice. "Why?"

"Because what happened between you was impactful." Anice reached for him. "My scars have been laid bare for you and it's helped you to understand who I truly am."

"Ye want to see my scars?"

Anice frowned. She hadn't meant it like that. "I want to avoid accidentally prodding them."

He nodded. "Aye, I thought I was in love once. It was a good while back, when I was barely older than a lad, back when I was too young to separate passion from love." He shrugged casting a nonchalance to what was obviously a painful memory. "We were to be married. My da told me she was wrong for me, but I dinna listen. To be fair, my da doesna always have good advice."

James winked at Anice. "Except when it comes to marriage."

She couldn't help the heat creeping over her cheeks. Even as she ought to appear cautious of trusting him again, she could not stymy her affection.

"What happened?" Anice asked.

James paced the short length of the cell. "I walked in on her in the stables with one of my da's reivers."

Anice winced. "With? Do you mean—"

"Aye." James stopped and a muscle worked in his jaw.

"You said I was like Morna." Anice went to James. "How?"

He slid her a side glance. "Because ye're beautiful," he said quietly.

Anice shook her head, not understanding.

"Morna was the most beautiful woman I'd ever seen," he replied.

A stab of jealousy plunged deep into Anice's chest.

"I was young." He began to pace again. "My experience with beautiful women was limited." He gave her another wink.

Small though the gesture was, it eased the prick of hurt in Anice's chest.

"But she was far too lovely for me." James smirked. "I know I'm no' a handsome man. Certainly no' fine enough looking to warrant having such a bonny wife. It dinna bother me, though, no matter how many people told me."

Anice opened her mouth to protest, but James shook his head.

"It dinna bother me until I realized Morna would flirt with other good-looking men."

"And the man she was with was one of them?" Anice asked.

James nodded. "And now I'm married to ye." He turned and faced her, his brows furrowed. "The most beautiful woman in the whole of England and Scotland combined. A woman far beyond me in all things: title, wealth, talent, and appearance."

Anice sucked in a breath. "James, nay."

He shook his head. "Ye are above me in every way, Anice."

"I have never once thought that." She stepped toward him. "I find you to be the most handsome man in all the world." She glided her hand over the powerful lines of his arm. "So strong."

"More so than Drake?" James prompted. "And Lord Clarion?"

Anice stepped back at the name of her departed betrothed.

James shook his head. "Forgive me. I shouldna have said that."

"I love Drake as one loves a brother," Anice answered truthfully. "And nothing more. We have been friends since Marin's husband first took Werrick. And Timothy..." She bit her lip and focused on the external pain rather than that within.

James's stare intensified and she realized he was bracing himself for her reply.

"I never loved Timothy." The awful truth of it burst forth from Anice. "He loved me. Fiercely. But I could never bring myself to return the sentiment. I agreed to his proposal of marriage to benefit my family. I used his affection."

Any anticipation at feeling lighter with the admission crashed into hard reality. The confession was as gentle as ripping a scab from a fresh wound.

"Women dinna have a choice in yer position, Anice," James said, his voice once softer in the way he often used with her.

"I did have a choice. Father would never make me marry someone. But I had nothing to offer my family, except a profitable match." Anice slid her gaze away, unable to look at James as she told him the ugliness of it all. "Marin did not wish to wed and instead ran the castle, seeing to us all. Ella is wonderfully smart and entertaining; Catriona's skill with the bow is unrivaled; and Leila has the sight, in addition to being a fierce warrior at such a young age. I have only ever had my beauty to offer my family and used it most advantageously."

"Including with me," James said.

Anice slowly regarded her husband. "Aye, including with you, although I'm sure your father would have made you marry me even if I had a second nose."

James scoffed in apparent agreement.

"It's strange, isn't it?" she asked. "How you have been working so very hard to prove I am more than my attractiveness, all while centering your focus on your own appearance. Do you think a man should be at my side only if he is fine-looking?"

He grinned at that. "Ach, if ye wanted me at yer side to be fine-looking, I'd disappoint ye to be sure."

"Nay." Anice closed the distance between them once more. "You would not." She ran her hands up his broad chest, her palms tracing the ridges and swells of powerful muscle. A shiver of delight ran through her.

"Anice." His voice was low and intimate and made warmth pool in her stomach.

She looked up slowly, infusing the glance with sensuality. "Hmmm?"

His large hand cradled her face while his other secured her about the waist. "Will ye trust me?"

"Aye, James." She searched his hot gaze and saw only earnestness there. Earnestness and desire. "Aye, I will trust you."

"I was hoping ye'd say that," he murmured. Then his mouth came down on hers, sealing their arrangement with a searing kiss.

Anice returned his kiss with equal passion, needing this man she had almost lost. There was a wild hunger between them, drawn to near madness with a desperation to be close.

While their previous joining hours ago had been tender and loving, now their hands shook with eagerness, their need so great they did not bother to undress. Skirts lifted, trews untied, a cold stone wall at Anice's back and the heat of her lover thrusting hard and fast between her thighs.

She clung to him as though she might lose him again and reveled in his warm familiar smell, the groan of his pleasure in her ear. It was over quickly and left their knees shaking with the aftereffects of such overwhelming desire.

James put his damp forehead to hers. "I love ye, *mo leannan*."

Anice's throat clogged with emotion. He said the words she had been feeling herself, and too afraid to say. Words she had been too heartbroken to hear earlier that eve. Now, at the cusp of war and death and loss, these words were being unveiled.

"I love you too, James." Anice nuzzled against the pleasant rasp of his whiskered jaw.

He tightened his hold on her and the thud of his heart tapped harder against her palm where her hand rested. "We can prevent this war," he said with finality. "But first, we'll need a plan."

~

JAMES WOULD HAVE LINGERED in the dungeon with Anice for a lifetime, had the reiver not returned and informed him Laird Graham wanted to see him.

Leaving Anice in the dank cell had been as difficult as prying one's own heart from their chest. Every step further echoed the injustice of it. Wrong, wrong, wrong.

At least they'd had enough time for James to share the details of the Graham attack on Werrick, as well as his missive to Lord Bastionbury. As he'd not yet heard from Bastionbury, James had finally conceded that it would be best to help Drake to escape. While James still didn't like the man, Drake was loyal and could warn Lord Werrick of the impending attack.

If nothing else, Werrick could prepare.

All too soon, James stood in front of the door to his father's room. He pushed it open and found the old man slumped in a chair by the fire. Ill health left his face gray and slack, his eyes dull.

In all of James's life, he had never disobeyed his father; certainly, he had never betrayed him. Not when Laird Graham had knocked him around a bit as a boy, not when James had been berated time and time again in front of his fellow reivers to ensure all knew he was inferior to his father. Nor even when the laird had cackled over Morna's betrayal and claimed to have already had her himself. Throughout a lifetime of cruelty and belittling, James had always been loyal.

The idea of defying him had not rankled James in the least. Or rather, not until now, when the old man appeared so weak and fragile, mortality clawing at his back.

Laird Graham lifted his head and belatedly regarded James with narrowed eyes. "Visiting with yer little slut, eh?"

Any niggling guilt quickly evaporated on a wave of ire. Ill or no, James wanted to plant one firm blow right in the old man's crinkled face.

But it wouldn't aid in the overall plan. Nay, James needed to act as though he'd been betrayed.

Instead of punching his father, James slid into the chair opposite him and scoffed. "No' mine. No' anymore."

"The bonny ones always get ye, lad." His father slapped James's knee and laughed. Something in the old man's skinny chest rattled. "Should we give her to the soldiers for a bit of sport? Fine lass like that..." His dull eyes went bright with lust.

In James's youth, he would never have been able to swallow down the rage building inside him. Now though, as an adult, after Bastionbury's instruction and tutelage, James was able to do just that. A deep breath and the violent hammering of his pulse slowed to a manageable rhythm.

"We can use her to get into Werrick," James offered in a casual tone.

Laird Graham curled his lips from his yellowing teeth. "Go on."

"Ye know the inside of Werrick, aye, but ye still canna penetrate its walls. If we use Anice as a prisoner and offer her in exchange for their gates opening, it'll work."

Laird Graham grinned. "Dinna the bastard who married Werrick's eldest daughter do exactly that?"

James shrugged. "It worked for him."

In truth, the suggestion had come from Anice. James loathed the idea of her being involved, especially being used against her family. However, with Drake getting away early and informing Werrick of the plan, they would be ready. Anice would be safe. James would see to it himself.

They would then implore the people following James's father to return to Carlisle. Those who did would keep their cottages and land; those who did not would be forever banished. As a majority of the men had women and children at Carlisle, James was certain many would join him.

It was not perhaps the strongest plan, but it was all they had.

"I dinna like to use the same strategy as others." Laird Graham rubbed the pad of his thumb over his grizzled chin. "But in this case, it may work verra well. Using his children against him to get what I want..." He nodded. "I like it."

Some of the tension eased from James's shoulders. At least his father would be sensible and not throw Anice to his soldiers. Peers of the realm had no need for broken daughters, and Laird Graham was too daft to realize Lord Werrick was a father who would take his daughter back regardless.

If only James had a more reliable army at his back, one that wasn't full of his father's clan members. If only he could get over the guilt that held him back from killing his own father.

So many regretful thoughts, and not one helped the situation.

"And her lover…" Laird Graham leaned forward in the chair and lifted his bushy brows. "I say we kill him."

The idea certainly held appeal—James wouldn't deny that. Anice might not be in love with the young man, but he certainly was in love with her. That alone ought to be enough to hang him by the neck.

Not that it mattered since Drake would already be at Werrick once the reivers arrived at the castle.

"Bring him along," James said. "Then kill him as the first warning to Werrick."

James's father nodded slowly. "Another fine idea from ye. For a lad wanting to poke about in the fields, ye've gotten damn good at strategy."

*Indeed, he had.*

Laird Graham looked directly into James's eyes. "I'm proud of ye, lad."

Words James had waited his entire life to hear. Except while once it would have plucked a chord deep in his soul, the praise now fell dull and unwanted after the years of disappointment.

His father was unaware of James's reaction and lifted his chin, quite pleased with himself on having bestowed such a rare compliment on his son. "Go on." Laird Graham jerked his head to the door, a clan chief dismissing his subject.

James rose from the chair and strode from the room. Once night fell again, he would see to freeing Drake from the dungeon. In the meantime, James needed to get a new missive off to Lord Bastionbury with the change of plans.

Through it all, he had to take the utmost care not to be caught, for he knew if he did, Anice would pay with her life.

## CHAPTER 27

James wasted no time making his way to the dungeon once more. While he tried not to think of Anice, his mind constantly wandered back to her, recalling the dank, dark room.

He stopped in front of the cell, the only one filled on the eastern side of the dungeon. Its western side stood opposite a massive stone staircase that bisected the great dungeon into two large chambers of cells.

The reiver in front of the heavy iron-bound door eyed James.

"Move," James stated simply.

The man complied.

James pulled a coin from his pocket and pushed it into the man's hand. "I require some time alone with the prisoner."

The reiver grinned in understanding and melted into the darkness. James waited until the heavy fall of his wooden-soled shoes faded with him. Only then did he open the door.

He pushed a candle into the darkness ahead of him. Drake squinted his eyes against the brilliance of the single flickering flame. Even as he flinched from the light, he swung a fist at James, who easily ducked away from the wild attack.

James slammed the door shut behind him and locked it. "Enough."

"Where is she?" Drake lunged again.

James evaded the attack.

"What have ye done with her?" Drake demanded. "If ye've harmed her in any way, I'll kill ye."

"Enough." James spoke with the authority of a man who would someday be laird, a man who owned his own land and was doing all he could to protect the woman he loved. "Stop and I'll tell ye."

Drake fell silent, though his vengeful glare glittered in the meager light.

"I know what ye think," James said.

"That ye're every bit the traitor we anticipated ye'd be?" Drake squared his shoulders. "If ye were an honorable man, I'd challenge ye to a duel."

Irritation tightened the muscles at James's back. "I was working against Laird Graham the entire time."

"I dinna believe ye. Why would ye no' tell Anice? Or me, for that matter?"

James shook his head. "Anice would have wanted to warn her family and wouldna have been able to quietly follow the plan. Her sudden disappearance would be suspect, and if she were caught, we'd all have been killed. And ye..." James cast a disgusted look at the other man. "Ye're in love with my wife."

The malice drained from Drake's face. No doubt the color did as well, but it was too dark to be certain. "I have sworn to protect all the daughters of the Earl of Werrick."

"Had I no' come about and taken her as my wife, ye'd have pursued her for yer own." The candle flame flickered under the vehemence of James's accusation.

"Lady Anice is far above my station." Drake's face tightened with resolve. "I would never be worthy of her."

"She's far above my station as well," James goaded. He was being petty, he knew, but he wanted to dig the blade of his claim deep into Drake's heart. Deep enough to score it with a constant reminder of one very important fact: Anice belonged to him.

A slight tightening of the skin around Drake's eyes was the only indication James had rankled the other man. "Did ye get Lady Anice to fall for these lies of yers? That ye claim to be working against yer father?"

"She saw it as the truth it is." James was sorely tempted to divulge the moments that had transpired after, but it was far too uncouth a thing to do. Not for a Graham, but for James. He would never disrespect Anice in such a way.

"Let me see her," Drake demanded. "Once I have ascertained her well-being with my own eyes and hear from her own lips that ye're to be trusted, then I'll believe ye."

"That's no' an option." James folded his arms over his chest. "And unfortunately, we have need of ye."

Drake merely lifted his square chin in silent question.

"Ye have to escape," James said in a low voice. He hadn't heard the reiver return but wouldn't take any chances. "We need ye to warn the Earl of Werrick of the impending attack, so they'll be ready."

He proceeded to explain the entire plan as devised by himself and Anice. How she would be used as bait to get Werrick to open its doors. It would look dark within, and safe. The first of the attackers would go in and promptly be slain by the waiting army. James would be at the rear of the battle, imploring the men to forego the attack and return to the safety of their fields and families. With luck, the reivers would be soundly defeated, many without injury, and return to Caldrick and the Debatable Lands.

The wariness did not abate from Drake's hard stare.

"If I gave ye a dagger, do ye think ye could escape?" James asked.

"Aye," Drake answered without hesitation.

It was as James had expected. No warrior worth his pottage would need more than a simple dagger to break out of a dungeon.

"Verra well." James withdrew a dagger from his belt and handed it hilt-first to Drake. "Take it."

Drake's gaze flicked between the weapon and James. "I could kill ye."

"Aye, ye could try." James tilted his head in consideration. "But if ye actually succeeded, ye'd be hung and Werrick Castle would never know of my father's plot. If ye take it and escape, however, ye'll save them all."

Drake reached for the blade, wrapped his fingers around the hilt and slowly accepted the weapon. "Ye'll need to hit me." He angled his sharp jaw in James's direction. "The guard thinks ye came in here to beat me. If ye leave with me looking unharmed, it will arouse suspicion."

It was tempting, of course. Especially when it was so obvious Drake was in love with Anice. Still, there was something about hitting a man he was trusting that did not sit right with James. Instead he grabbed Drake by the shirt and jerked him closer. The fabric of the man's doublet tore beneath James's grip. "Get on the ground and roll about, so ye look dirty." James released Drake with a little shove.

Drake did as instructed and popped up, sufficiently filthy. "Ye still need to hit me. At least twice where it can be seen."

James clenched his hand. "I'm no' going to hit ye."

"I can take a hit." Drake's body tensed for the impact. "This is necessary."

James hesitated. It would feel so damn good to crash his fist into that bonny face.

"I'd do anything for the people of Werrick." Drake's gaze softened. "I'd do anything for Anice."

That was all it took. James's body launched into action at the sound of his wife's name on the other man's lips. His blow struck Drake hard on the cheekbone. It left James's hand blazing with the agonizing pain of the impact. He struck again with his left hand, catching Drake in the eye.

For his part, the younger man held his braced stance and gave only a grunt with each hit. James did not strike again. Even with Drake's words resounding in his mind, the idea of hitting a man who did not hit back was without appeal.

Drake nodded. "Good. One more."

Already the flesh at his cheekbone and eye were reddening. James shook his head. "I'm no' going to pummel ye senseless. Ye need yer wits about ye to escape."

"Once this is done," Drake said. "I'd like to spar with ye. Ye've got a solid hit on ye."

"Keep the people of Werrick Castle safe and I'll gladly spar with ye." James departed from the cell, summoned the reiver to return to his post and went to find Tall Tam.

The former reiver had become James's most trusted ally after Anice had taken on Ingrith as her lady's maid. Through him, James would send another missive to Lord Bastionbury informing him of the changes to the plan.

It would all work out.

It had to, or Werrick would fall and James would lose everything.

∼

THREE DAYS in a dungeon was an interminable stretch of time. Or at least Anice thought it had been three days. It was nearly impossible to tell for certain.

It wasn't so much the damp cold seeping into her bones that nearly drove her to madness, though that was miserable for certs. Nay, it was the endless nothing.

Night and day blurred into one in her black world, and times of day were only gleaned from the groan of the floorboards above her head from people walking about. Only when everything went completely quiet did she assume it to be night. The meals were all the same—a thick, gray pottage with barely any flavor. The stuff was nearly inedible, but Anice forced herself to choke it down. She would need her strength.

James had not come to visit again. The risk was far too great. But it had not stopped her from thinking of him, dreaming of him.

At long last, after the mind-numbing passing of time, the day had arrived for the attack on Werrick. It was the footfalls above that first alerted her. They were no longer the careful treads of servants and castle inhabitants, but the wooden-soled leather shoes of warriors, thundering about in their preparations. Had she not heard them, she would still have known from the charge hanging in the air, seasoned with the pitch of excitement brought on only by war. The tang of it hummed through her and made her pulse quicken with anticipation.

And so it was that when her door was thrown open and the blinding light of a candle thrust in, she was prepared. After all, she was a daughter of the Earl of Werrick. She straightened her spine and stared at the empty black beyond the candle to the unseen person carrying it. Whatever the outcome that day, whatever her fate, she would face it without fear.

The small, flickering flame lowered for a breath of a moment and revealed the exact face she'd summoned in her mind the last three days: James.

It was only for an instant, but that one swift glance was all she needed. His eyes met hers, tightened with emotion, with sadness and love and longing. Her heart crumpled at the power of that holding stare.

"Drake?" she mouthed.

"Escaped," he replied in kind. The candle went up. "Get out of yer cell." His voice was louder now, with an authoritative gruffness he had never once used with her.

Though she knew his hardness was all merely show, she could not help the stab of hurt at his tone. After the cold, the darkness and the pressing solitude, she wanted nothing more than to curl her arms around him and breathe in the comfort of his familiar cedar scent.

"Get on with ye," he growled.

But the hand that reached for her was absent a similar malice. Rather than grab her, he put his fingers to the small of her back, much as he'd done in that first happy month of their marriage, and gently guided her forward.

"Wait," he whispered.

Quickly, he knelt and pushed something cool into the ankle of her leather shoes. She'd glanced down as he did this and caught the telltale glint of a blade.

He rose and took her arm in his. His squeeze on her was one of reassurance. "Keep going." He swung her forward and nodded his chin in silent indication of direction.

Anice allowed herself to be propelled into the hallway and staggered to a stop.

Several reivers stood by, a rope in their hands, their eyes fixed on the ground. They all knew her, just as she knew them. She had been by their cottages to offer bread when they had none and tinctures when they were ill. She'd cared for their children, for their wives, and in some cases, she'd cared also for them.

"You've come here for a purpose," she said in her best lady-of-the-manor voice. "I suggest you get on with it."

A fair-haired man she recognized as little Mairi's father, a man named Gregor, lifted a chastened gaze in her direction. "Forgive me, Mistress."

She held out her arms and leveled her gaze on him. "I know you mean to sack Werrick and destroy all the lives within for the sake of plunder." She looked between the two others who had still not raised their eyes. "Only God could forgive such deeds."

Gregor's large hands shook as he bound the rope around her wrists, his concentration intensely focused on his task rather than fixing on her again. When he was done, the knot was sloppy and the bounds around her wrists were loose.

It was a restraint she would be able to easily free herself from.

They led her from the dungeon like a band of naughty children who had already been caught and thoroughly reprimanded for their deeds. If she wished to, surely, she could easily flee the morose group of reivers.

"Where is Piquette?" she asked suddenly.

"Ye needn't worry about him," James snapped.

Anice clenched her fists. She didn't like this charade, not when she couldn't see Piquette to ensure herself of his safety. James would never let anything happen to him, of course. But such awareness could not stop the emptiness in her chest from yearning to see her beloved dog.

The reivers led her from the castle and into the bailey. The sky was so bright, Anice jerked back, blinking and unable to see. Her eyes teared no matter how much she squinted against the sun's radiance.

Her vision hadn't fully adjusted as rough hands grabbed her. "Take her to the back for her to be watched properly." Laird Graham's voice rasped through the air.

Finally the overwhelming light in her eyes normalized and her vision returned, just in time for her to be pulled from

James's side. His expression remained impassive as she was dragged away, watching for only a brief moment before putting his back to her, seemingly uncaring.

And though it shouldn't have affected her, the coldness of his apathetic attitude struck her to the core. The loneliness from the prior days, the inability to see Piquette, the indifference in the face of the man she loved.

"I'll take her." Gregor gingerly took her from the reiver she did not recognize, doubtless one of the many who had arrived from the Debatable Lands.

"Forgive me." Gregor cast a glance over his shoulder as he settled her on the pony. "Did ye love him? The laird's son, I mean."

"Aye," Anice said through a tight throat. "And I still do."

Within minutes, the remainder of the troops were assembled, an overwhelming number even for the Grahams. News of Laird Graham's desire to take Werrick must have inspired the larger part of the population in the wild Debatable Lands to join them. Though the Earl of Werrick would have forewarning, he would still have a difficult time fending off so many men.

The steady beat of a drum began and matched the worried thud of her own heart. The lines of stocky horses made their way forward for the ride to Werrick Castle. All too soon, Anice was swept among them in a sea of faces and horseflesh, dragged in the direction of her former home.

She only hoped her plan with James would work, so she would not have to watch Werrick fall and those she loved die. For with such a mass of soldiers at Laird Graham's command, Anice was truly worried.

A familiar face caught the corner of Anice's eye. *Drake?*

She spun about in her seat, but the man was lost in the shifting crowd once more. Surely, it had not been him. James had confirmed with her that Drake had escaped.

And though she did not see the man again, one who could well have been a mere conjuring of her imagination, an uneasy knot began to form in her stomach.

## CHAPTER 28

James rode at his father's side and tried to keep from glancing back at Anice. The entire journey, he'd been tortured by her absence, by the not knowing. He wanted to spin about in his saddle and confirm she was still safe.

As it was, he could not arouse suspicion. Not now. Not here. The army Laird Graham led was far too large for James's liking, and the separation between James and Anice weighed thoroughly on his thoughts.

"Are ye prepared to strike down the inhabitants of Werrick Castle?" His father leered at him.

"Aye. I've heard ye talk of it long enough," James replied. But the words could only be uttered with half enthusiasm. He fixed his gaze on his father to solidify his resolve not to look back.

"I had my doubts about ye, lad." Laird Graham narrowed his gaze at a distant shadow.

Werrick Castle.

The pace of the large party increased as they drew closer. James's blood roared in his veins, but not with the excitement of an impending battle as it had years ago. Now it thundered with apprehension. For Anice. His wife. The woman he loved.

She was absent any armor, lacking a sufficient weapon, save the dagger he'd tucked in her boot. If battle broke out, she would be in the melee. Vulnerable.

And he was too far to reach her to come to her aid.

"Ye're worried about yer wife, eh?" Laird Graham smirked.

James gritted his teeth. "Why would I care about that slattern?"

The Graham laird gave a wheezing laugh. "Because it's obvious ye're still in love with her, ye foolish whelp."

The walls of Werrick's outer curtain were in full view now, a dark band that stretched protectively around the castle within. James did not reply. There was no good answer to offer, not when his lie might come out too wooden.

"I actually believed ye at first," Laird Graham said.

*At first.* James's stomach slid down into his toes. He cast his father a wary glance.

"Ye put up a good show of it." His father nodded approvingly. "Speaking with the Grahams, acting with keen interest in the raid. Until I intercepted that missive ye wrote to that bastard, Lord Bastionbury."

A chill touched James's spine. "What missive do ye think I wrote?" he asked through numb lips.

"The missive I know ye wrote." Laird Graham shifted his gaze from the figure appearing on the battlements to James. "Ye'd always liked that bloody lord, looked up to him like he was yer da. Like ye wished he was yer da instead of the one ye got."

James didn't bother to protest his father's words. His father had always clung to his own interests and had used James to get what he desired.

"I know ye went to the dungeon to see yer wife." Laird Graham spat. "And I know ye freed that protector of hers. I tried to give ye the opportunity to tell me the truth, but ye only lied more."

James was grateful for his betrayal now. If nothing else, Drake's freedom would give the people of Werrick Castle a fighting chance.

Laird Graham grinned at him. "But I know much that ye dinna." He snapped his reins and his horse flew forward.

Before James could give chase, before he could process what his father was trying to say, something jerked at his leg, swift and strong, so he was pulled from his saddle and flung to the ground.

James struck the hard earth with such force that it knocked the wind from his lungs. His legs thrashed in an attempt to find purchase, but rather than grass and dirt, his heel planted into something soft. A body.

Men fell on him in a heap, hands grappling, weight pressing, locking him into place. James kicked and punched and writhed, but none of it did him any good. Within seconds, he was fully restrained, his wrists bound behind his back with a rough rope.

"Lord Werrick," Laird Graham's voice cried out in the cool spring air and echoed off the thick stone walls. "Cede yer castle, or yer man will suffer the consequences of yer refusal."

A scuffling came from the outskirts of the party and Drake was dragged forward. The tear at the collar of his shirt had been ripped to his navel and his bonny face was mottled with bruises and dried blood. The Graham reiver behind him knotted a rope into a noose and slung the loose end over the high branch of a tree. Drake tensed but did not attempt to run. Not that it would have helped. Instead, his gaze darted over the surrounding crowd. No doubt in search of Anice.

Forever her protector.

The reiver draped the loop over Drake's head and fitted it snugly around his throat. After the long production of preparing Drake to hang, Laird Graham shouted up at the battlements once more. "He isna all ye'll be sacrificing. We also have yer daughter."

Anice was pushed from the massive band of reivers toward the tree. Her blue dress was streaked with dirt, but she appeared unharmed. More than unharmed, in fact. She was defiant, her eyes flashing and her back straight and proud. James's chest constricted.

Within seconds, it became clear why he had been restrained, for a second noose was knotted. They meant to put the scratching rope around Anice's slender neck and—

His body erupted with rage.

One elbow caught a reiver in the gut while the top of his forehead smashed into another's nose. There was no pain with any of his strikes, only the overwhelming need to get to Anice. To save her.

James lurched forward, hands still bound, with her name on his lips and in his heart. A cold hand clasped over his face, stifling his cry. Grit from his attacker's palm ground harshly against his mouth, the pressure clamping off her name and muffling it to something she would never hear.

Many hands restrained him, and still he fought, helpless as the noose was placed over Anice's head and roughly tightened.

Laird Graham grinned at his handiwork. He faced the castle once more. "Well?" he demanded. "Will ye cede yer castle?"

"Nay," Anice cried out. The man beside her attempted to restrain her, but she shoved him away. "Don't do it, Papa!"

"Ye dinna have long to make yer decision." Laird Graham nodded to the reivers near Anice and Drake. "Slow, lads. Ye dinna want to break their necks."

To James's horror, the men obediently pulled on the ropes, arm over arm, until Anice's feet lifted off the ground. He struggled and fought against his captors to no avail. His father would get Werrick Castle, even if it meant that Anice would have to die.

James knew that now, and he was entirely helpless to stop it.

∼

ANICE HAD EXPECTED her fate as soon as the noose slipped around her neck and immediately formed a plan.

The loose-bound ropes on her wrists were made more so by subtle wriggling during the journey. Her bindings had slackened so much that she had to hold her fingers just so to keep the rope from slipping off. Then there was the blade James had slipped her.

*James. Where was he?*

Her gaze skimmed the crowd of faces with desperation, but he was not to be seen. She gritted her teeth. She couldn't think about him now, not when she needed to focus, to survive.

The dagger was in her boot. She would need to cut her own rope first, then Drake's.

The intention had been laid out and was ready to be acted on. But that was before the rope was pulled taut and her body weight was hung by the frailty of her neck.

*Pain.*

There was so much pain.

Even having been raised gently, the ache at her throat was stunning. Her feet kicked to find solid ground but met only air, and each shift in movement caused the rope to tighten around her neck, squeezing, digging. So much pain.

Tears blurred her vision and panic swept through her mind, threatening to wipe away her carefully thought-out strategy. Her hands jerked and the ropes slipped free, an action done in her body's desperate attempt to live. But it was the reminder she needed.

To save herself. To save Drake.

She drew up her right leg, plunged her hand into the side of her boot and withdrew the sheathed dagger. The world began to grow dim and shouting echoed around her. Shouting.

She could be caught.

Panic consumed everything else and pushed her further into action. She ripped the sheath from the dagger and yanked on the rope around her neck. It hardly gave at all with her weight pulling it snug, but it was enough for a blade to fit between. She shoved the dagger with the blade toward the rope and sliced outward.

The pressure on her neck abated and she fell hard to the ground. She wanted to gasp breath into her burning throat, to taste the sweetness of fresh air filling her lungs once more. But there was no time for even that. Her captors were already leaping toward her and Drake—

Choking, she lurched to her feet and sliced at the rope stretched in front of her from which Drake hung. He dropped like a sack of grain.

"The horse," she rasped. The two simple words were like fire to her raw throat. Drake quickly staggered to his feet as Anice had, and together they ran toward a nearby horse.

The reivers were nearly on top of them now, swords brandished. Drake grabbed her and threw her onto the horse. A man raised his blade. Drake's back was to them, vulnerable to attack in his desperation to escape, to save her. Anice aimed her dagger and let it fly as the man began to bring down his weapon.

Her blow struck first. The blade plunged into the reiver's throat and he dropped at Drake's feet just as the warrior leapt onto the horse behind her. Anice dug her hands into the mane and the beast galloped in the direction of Werrick Castle.

Already men were at their side on horseback, trying to run them off the straight path to the castle.

It was the first time she had truly looked at her family's castle since being strung up in the tree. Now, with a moment to spare as they raced to outrun the Grahams, she saw that the portcullis had, in fact, been opened.

"Nay!" The protest croaked weakly from her throat. Certainly nothing could be heard over the two armies preparing for battle. If anyone could actually hear, it was far too late. The portcullis could not be closed in time.

A man to their right edged closer and forced his horse to knock into theirs. Their mount staggered but caught its footing and continued on. An arrow whizzed past and the man fell from his horse, with a white-fletched arrow jutting from his eye.

*Catriona.*

A glance at the battlements revealed a slender blonde-haired woman armed with only a bow and quiver of arrows. She drew back an arrow and the man to Anice's left fell. One by one, Anice's sister cleared the path for them to get to the castle, even as the remainder of the army stormed behind them, rushing forward with the same purpose.

When the shadow of the entryway fell over her and Drake at last, they finally met with hope. They leapt from the horse on trembling legs and were greeted by soldiers pushing them deeper into the depths of Werrick Castle's bailey as men closed around them in a protective circle.

Catriona's voice rang out from above, calling to her archers on the battlements to ready their arrows.

"You were not set free?" Anice asked Drake.

"I was." His words were as roughly spoken as her own from having been hanged. "But the reivers were waiting for me just outside the walls. As if they knew." He slid her a glance, saying everything his words did not.

He suspected they had been betrayed.

The silent accusation slipped into her gut like a blade. Surely James had not betrayed her. "He gave me the dagger which saved both our lives," Anice reminded Drake.

His jaw flexed.

"Say your piece," Anice demanded.

"He did not stop the reivers when ye were hanged." The skin around Drake's eyes tightened. "He betrayed us."

Her heart slammed painfully inside her chest to hear such words aloud. She could not believe them. Not when James had given her the dagger, when they had spent so much time carefully laying out their plan, when he'd told her how he loved her. "Nay." Her response was determined and resolute.

James would not have betrayed her. But then, where was he? Fear trickled down her spine. She turned back abruptly to the soldiers racing toward the portcullis, once more seeking his face.

"Anice." Her father's voice pulled her attention away.

Lord Werrick looked every bit the same as he had when she had left, albeit in his armor. The slender face with hollowed cheekbones, the gentle smile, the kind eyes that were now filling with tears.

"My daughter." His voice choked off and he rushed to her, arms open.

Anice ran to him as she had when she'd been a girl, eager for his comfort and the safety only a father's embrace could give.

He held her to him and gave a shuddering exhale. "My girl, I thought I would lose you on this day."

"You raised us to be stronger than that, Papa," she said into his chest.

Her father drew back and took her face between his hands. His palms were cool and eased the blazing heat of her face. "I've never been gladder for it." He turned to Drake and nodded. "I am indebted to you yet again. Get you both inside where it is safe. Isla is at the ready for the wounded and can tend to you with haste."

At the front of the bailey, shouting rose and the unmistakable clatter of armed men slamming into one another shattered the still air. The battle had begun.

Drake's shoulders fell at the command. He glanced back to the melee with apparent regret, but dutifully nodded his assent.

"Nay," Anice said forcefully. "Laird Graham lied to us all."

*And James was somewhere in that mass of men.*

She could *feel* him, sense him in that crush of reivers as surely as she could sense her own heartbeat. "Bring us swords," she said. "For we will fight."

## CHAPTER 29

The arms restraining James released him suddenly. But it was too late. Anice was in the castle and the reivers were already breaking inside.

The departure from Caldrick Castle had been too abrupt for James to know if Tall Tam had been able to successfully deliver the message to Lord Bastionbury. It would be impossible to know until James was inside. And he *would* get inside.

He shoved free of his captors and sprinted toward the castle, toward Anice. Men rushed on either side of him, driven by avarice and anticipation for plundering.

"Go back to yer farms," James shouted at the men as he ran. "Yer wives and children are waiting for ye, for a life of peace."

But they did not hear him, or if they did, they did not care for what he said, for on they ran.

Surely Anice would know he hadn't betrayed her. After all, he'd given her the dagger. And thank God he had, or she would have been surely killed on this day. The very idea sent a shiver of fear rippling over his skin.

Ahead, the entry to the castle was jammed full of men

engaged in close quarter combat. Blades flashed in the afternoon sun, glinting red with blood.

James shoved his weight into the wall of men. His weapon had been taken, but he did not need it. Nay, he relied on his fists, refusing to take the lives of either a soldier of Werrick Castle or a Graham reiver. Both his brethren—by blood or by marriage—but brethren all the same.

His armor was good, and his instincts were better still. A blade flew in his direction, but he ducked to avoid its strike. The man beside him cried out and fell hard against him. James caught the reiver and held him upright. Not that he could do anything to save the man. Blood gushed from a wound in his throat and splashed hot and wet against James's gambeson, staining it with death.

The light dimmed from the reiver's pale blue eyes and the gripping hold he kept on James's sleeves slackened. Slowly, he slid to the ground, leaving James covered in gore from having borne witness to the man's final moments of life.

Regret and rage burned in James's chest. This was what he'd striven to prevent. Lives senselessly taken for no purpose but purloined treasure. It was disgusting, this greed.

He'd finally given peace to his men, but they wanted treasure more.

James roared with anger, with anguish, and shoved into the melee once more. Something hard and heavy slammed into his back. Searing pain cracked through him and robbed him of his breath. He staggered, held upright only by the pressing wall of others around him. Were it not for the armor in his gambeson, no doubt that blow would have felled him.

A massive battle axe came down from above, but James jerked hard to the right, through the agony it cost him to do so, and narrowly avoided the impact. He had to get through the melee and into the castle, to Anice. To do what he could to protect her. To do what he could to stop this battle.

All around him were faces he recognized, men from his youth and men from his weeks spent at Werrick Castle.

"Anice," he cried out. "I need to get to my wife."

The man in front of him, a Werrick soldier, shifted back slightly. Whether the move had been intentional, or by accident, James shoved past and slipped between the soldiers. Now he was on the side of battle with Werrick Castle's soldiers, an area far more dangerous.

Battle was confusing; it always had been with the cacophony of melee and screams and death. Fear ran high, as well as confidence and the heart-rattling energy pumping hot through every man's veins. James used that confusion to his advantage. He darted and dove through the men, pushing his way further into the bailey.

His awareness tingled. Something moved in his direction from the side. Something fast. He spun around and was immediately struck by a hurtling body. James dropped to the ground, the man still standing over him. He swept his leg out with all the strength he could muster. The man fell beside him.

Not just any man. Drake.

The younger man stared at him through the slits of his helm.

James held his hands at his side, trying not to appear as a threat. "Drake, I—"

Drake's right leg curled in as he moved to stand.

"Forgive me," James muttered. He shoved hard on Drake's chest, using the weight of the younger man's armor against him, and sent Drake crashing to his back once more. The weight of his helm crashed into the hard cobblestones and Drake went still.

The pain at James's back had abated some, but his breath still came like heavy fire in his lungs. He turned from Drake before the man regained his senses and regarded the castle once more.

Anice stood at the entrance only feet away, her eyes wide with horror.

"Anice—" He reached out for her. It was then he noticed his fingers, covered in blood. All of him, covered in blood. In that instant, he realized how it must look with him approaching her thus. He'd come through the battle still standing and smeared with gore.

He doubted he looked like a man set on reclaiming his wife, but instead a reiver set on pillaging.

"Anice, wait, I—"

She held her sword aloft between them, preparing to fight.

Persuading her of his innocence would not be as easy as it had in the dungeon. Judging from the raw anger flushing her cheeks, he would need to convince her soon, or she just might kill him.

∼

THE ACHE in Anice's heart threatened to cave in her chest. Drake lay still on the ground and James covered in blood. Surely, he had not...

"James." She choked out his name and stepped forward with more confidence than she felt. The blade trembled in her hand, belying the torrent of hurt and sorrow rushing through her. "What have you done?"

"He's no' dead." James regarded first the tip of her sword pointed at his throat and then her. "This isna his blood. Anice, please believe me."

"Drake was captured after you released him." She kept the tremble from her voice. She could not bring herself to ask if he had betrayed her, for she feared the answer. If he had, surely it would shatter her heart.

"My da knew I had lied to him." He shook his head. "Anice, I dinna betray ye."

She lifted the sword higher lest she give into the temptation to let it fall away. She wanted to believe him, with every piece of her soul.

"I'm no' armed," he said.

She drew a dagger from her belt, similar to the one he'd given to her, and tossed it on the ground at his feet. It skittered over the uneven cobblestones and came to a rest in front of his boots.

She did not wish to fight him, but if it came down to it, she would not battle an unarmed man. "How do I know I can believe you?"

He didn't look at the dagger on the ground, but kept his stare fixed on her, his expression solemn. The background sounds of war were loud and invasive. The clang of metal on metal, the cries of the dying.

"I gave ye a similar dagger for protection," he said. "Because I am on yer side. I always have been." He finally looked down at the dagger, untouched, at his feet. "I willna fight ye."

Her throat went tight, and her eyes grew hot with emotion. Hope blazed through her, a flame she realized had never fully extinguished. Hope that his words were true. "Then you did not betray me?" she asked slowly.

The clatter of weapons and men became louder, closer. They were running out of time.

His face softened. "Nay, *mo leanan*."

The endearment tore at her heart and her sword tip lowered slightly. So much was at risk if she was wrong. Her people, her home, her family, everything.

"My father intercepted my message to Lord Bastionbury,"

James continued. "He knew early on I was against him. When he —" His voice broke. "When he hung ye from that tree..." He lowered his head and sniffled.

"Where were you?" Anice asked, desperate to know what had happened to keep him from coming to her aid.

"They bound me." James's voice was thick and when he looked up, his eyes were glossy with tears. "They held me down and all I could do was watch. Helpless."

He knelt at her feet. Her powerful husband, who towered over every man, whose body was carved with raw strength, gazed up at her. "I thought they would kill ye. That I would lose ye forever." He pulled in a ragged breath. "My God, Anice, I would move the earth for ye."

It was too much. He was too much. An anguished cry released unbidden from her throat and the sword tip drooped to the ground.

No sooner had the weapon dipped away from him, his expression shifted from tenderness to determination. He snatched up the dagger and leapt at her, fist pulled back with the dagger in it ready to attack.

Instinct kicked in. The limp hold on the weapon in Anice's hand tightened as she drew it up once more and swung.

# CHAPTER 30

James had caught sight of his father coming up behind Anice at exactly the right time. The old man's sword raised, his eyes bright with the effects of bloodlust. James hadn't thought, he had only acted, lunging toward his father with his weapon drawn to protect the woman he loved.

Gaze fixed on his father, he flew through the air with all the strength he possessed. Something struck him in the side, a nudge he barely noticed, but enough to knock him slightly off his aim.

"Ye turned my son against me." Laird Graham brought the blade down toward Anice.

Though James held only a dagger, he leapt in front of Anice with the paltry weapon held aloft to block the blow. The old man still had strength in him, wiry and determined, and the sword came down with more force than James could stop and sliced his chest.

James staggered back. For that one moment, the entire world slowed, the same as it had when he'd been struck at Lord Bastionbury's castle. Anice spun around in surprise, then directed her attention from the danger of Laird Graham to

James, her expression crumpling. Laird Graham angrily shifted his gaze from James to Anice and lifted his weapon once more. The army of reivers at Anice's back rushed forward to aid him in killing her. In killing all the people of Werrick, no doubt.

James's chest and his side blazed. "Nay." He tried to run forward, cry out, anything that might stop them. But the ground was too slick, his body too tired, his voice only a whisper.

"James," Anice cried. Seemingly oblivious of the danger behind her, she tried to go to him, but Laird Graham caught her by a fistful of hair and yanked her toward him with such force, the sword fell from her hand.

The momentum pitched her backward and she threw her elbow into the old man's face. He staggered away, nose gushing with a spurt of blood. An arrow flew from somewhere unseen and sank deep into the aging laird's throat. The old man hadn't even had a chance to cry out before falling.

James's own weight crushed down on legs that could no longer support him and he fell to his knees. Anice reclaimed her sword as several Werrick soldiers broke off from the melee in the courtyard entrance and stood at her back. Ready to defend her as well as their home.

"More men are coming from the east." The masculine voice echoing down from the battlements was pitched with tension.

James's mind reeled. More men? How could there be more reivers coming? Hadn't they all arrived?

He looked to his father's prone form where he lay face down in a growing puddle of blood. Were there more men joining them that Laird Graham hadn't told him about?

"Nay." James's voice was too weak. He drew himself up, though it cost him dearly to do so. Every part of his body was leaden, and each breath he drew was like fire. Regardless, he filled his lungs and said more forcefully: "Nay."

The word boomed out over the bailey, echoing over the

warfare. He tensed the muscles of his legs to remain upright and straightened his back, though it made his entire body scream in agony.

"As new Laird of the Grahams, I command ye to cease." The last word rang with authority.

The reivers opposite Anice regarded him warily, even as their dead laird lay at their feet.

"I'm yer laird," he roared. "And I declare this battle finished." The intake of breath to speak once more was like inhaling flames, but he continued. "On pain of death, all reivers will cease this fight and leave the inhabitants of Werrick Castle in peace. With my father's death, so too dies the years of reiving and pillaging."

As he spoke, the clatter of weapons began to quiet, and the courtyard went still.

"I want peace." James's voice was beginning to fail. So too was his energy. He stepped toward Anice, but then faltered, fading.

Anice cried out and ran to him.

"Forgive me." Her arms came around him, enveloping the haze of pain in her sweet floral scent, easing his suffering with her beauty, her love and her incredible strength. A whimper caught in her throat. A sob.

"Forgive me, my love," she whispered. Her cool hands stroked over his face. "Do not go to sleep." There was a bright intensity to her gaze, as though she could will him to comply with her request. "For you may never wake if you do." Her voice choked off.

"The reivers who are coming." James gasped through the pain of his wounds. He had to tell her to act in his stead. As his wife, his consort, Lady of Caldrick Castle and a member of the Graham clan. He had to keep her and all their people safe.

Except he could speak no more. His tongue would not form

the words and the strength of his neck couldn't support the weight of his head. As darkness closed around on him, he clung to one very important thought: he must stay alive.

For if he were to die, Werrick would fall.

～

ANICE HAD STABBED JAMES. She had been part of the reason he had collapsed, why he might possibly die.

This last thought burrowed in her brain and left her frozen as she cradled James in her arms. His legs jutted out on the bloody cobblestones before them. He needed to be taken to Isla, and quickly. Werrick was still not safe. And yet she could not bring herself to move.

As though hearing her concern and putting it to voice, a soldier on the battlements cried out, "The army is descending upon us!"

Drake squatted opposite Anice and grabbed hold of James's ankles. "I'll help ye carry him inside."

Two soldiers came forward, one wearing the fierce black hawk of the Werrick crest, and one reiver. Together, the four of them hefted James's massive body into the expansive great hall where Isla had the floor prepared with makeshift beds for the wounded. Already men were strewn about, their blood bright against the freshly laid rushes.

Isla darted toward them, a basket of bottles clinking at her arm as she did so. "Set him there." She waved toward a dining trestle that had been covered with a blanket. "As is fitting for a laird."

Her somber tone shook Anice's memory of the brief affair between Isla and James's father.

"I'm sorry, Isla," Anice offered softly.

Isla shook her head as though the matter was of little import.

"Just because a man is good at warming a bed doesna mean he is a man worth living. I imagine yers is, though." The older woman offered a knowing smile with her brilliantly white teeth and went to James.

She yanked open his gambeson to reveal his gore-soaked leine. Anice's mind spun at the visible wounds, at so much blood

The air was coppery with it, the metallic odor filling her nostrils and causing bile to rise in her throat. Bile and panic. For this was too similar to Mama when she had died.

Anice's world wavered around her. She shifted her gaze to James's eyes, which had slid closed. Like Mama's had.

*Mama's skin had gone waxy. She didn't cry out anymore; she didn't grip the sheets or push. She was asleep, amid the sea of white sheets and blood.*

*But it didn't seem right. "Mama?" Anice asked.*

*She didn't reply.*

*"Mama, please rouse." Still she did not move.*

*"Mama," Anice pleaded. "You must rouse."*

*Marin put her arm around Anice's shoulder. "She's dead, my dear sister."*

She had died so quickly, so easily, without a word of protest.

That couldn't happen to James. She couldn't let him slip away so easily. He was too powerful for such a simple death; too patient, too wonderful. There hadn't been enough time for them yet.

He would never call her *mo leannan* again, or cradle her in those powerful arms, or see things in her that she never saw in herself. She was a better person with him. She could not lose him, not now, not ever.

Fear gripped Anice. He couldn't go to sleep. "James, open your eyes," Anice whispered. "Open them."

He did not. Isla gripped a dagger in her gnarled fist and split open his leine. The ruined linen drooped from his body, sodden.

But the powerful chest Anice knew every dip and curve of was now marked with wounds and blood.

"Open your eyes." Anice had not realized she'd said it aloud until Drake was at her side, offering her his arm.

"Let us leave him with the healer, my lady."

A knot burned in her throat. "My mother," Anice said. "When she had Leila. She lost too much blood; her body was too traumatized to live. She closed her eyes and…" Anice pressed her lips together, unable to speak. Instead, she went to James's side. She took his limp arm in her hand, his ring sparkled beside that of her mother's. "Wake, James. Wake. Please."

He did not respond. His arm in her grip was loose, offering no resistance to her subtle shake. A shadow loomed in front of her.

Isla's tawny eyes met hers, clear and bright beneath wrinkled lids. "He'll no' die on my watch, my lady." She gave Anice a pat on the head, the way she had so often done when Anice was a mere girl. "But ye may verra well kill him if ye keep shaking his arm like that. I canna keep my stitches straight."

Heat flared in Anice's cheeks and she immediately dropped her hold on him. A clatter of feet sounded outside, pulling her attention briefly from James. Panic raced through her anew. Had the new band of reivers broken through so quickly?

Grabbing a nearby sword, she raced with Drake to defend the great hall as best they could. For beyond the wounded and dying within the great hall were the deeper rooms of Werrick and the women and children hiding within them.

The footsteps did not come with the frantic thundering of marauders storming the castle. Figures filled the doorway, including her father's familiar frame. Anice stopped short.

At his side was Lord Bastionbury.

"The battle is over." Her father clapped the other earl on his back in the age-old show of camaraderie among men. "Bastionbury showed up at the perfect time to put an end to it all."

"You got James's message," Anice said.

Lord Bastionbury was a man only slightly older than her own father, with kind green eyes that crinkled in a smile at the mention of James. "Aye. I told him I will always be there should he need me. I was pleased to get his missive and came posthaste." He glanced about. "Where is he?"

*Injured. Perhaps dying. Maybe dead.* Anice's throat went thick. Rather than try to answer, she glanced back toward the great hall.

"He's been injured, my lord." Drake answered for her.

Anice heart squeezed as though in a vice. She had been the one to injure him. Suddenly, she regretted her decision to leave his side. He no longer needed her to protect him. There was no danger from an attack, only from slipping away as he slept. The same as her mother.

Anice dropped her sword and ran. Down the hall, through the doors of the great hall, and not stopping until she stood directly in front of Isla. The healer had a needle in hand, pulled taut while securing a stitch in James's torso.

Anice locked her gaze on James's face, yet unable to take in such a sight. "Is he still alive?"

Isla's hand swept down to James's body once more in Anice's peripheral. "Aye, my lady. I know yer Ma dinna wake up when she slept, but this is different, aye? His sleep keeps him from feeling my stitches. He's away from the pain. Let him be."

Away from pain, but also hopefully away from death. Anice wanted to hold his hand, to feel his embrace as it had always been, warm and strong and curled around hers like armor. She stared at his limp hand and stood helplessly at his side, for there was nothing to do now, but wait to see if he would live.

## CHAPTER 31

The sun shone on James's face, drawing him from the darkness with its brilliant heat.

"James," a soft feminine voice cried out.

One he knew better than any other.

*Anice.*

He turned his head toward the sound, the back of his skull grinding against something firm beneath him. Pain engulfed him all at once, burning, white-hot pain. His chest, his back, his side, every bit of him.

"James." Anice's voice again.

He groaned, a rasping snarl of a sound and blinked his eyes open. His gaze was waist-level. On his side. Confusion wracked through him. "What—"

"Nay, do not move." Anice's face appeared in front of him. Her eyes and nose were red, as though she'd been crying. She grasped his hand and lifted it to her mouth in a gentle kiss. Tears ran down her cheeks. "I thought…"

His fingers moved over the softness of her lovely skin, sweeping away the tear and savoring her.

Her eyes closed as more tears slipped silently from beneath

her lashes. "I feared I might never feel such a caress again," she whispered. "I'm so sorry, my love."

He shifted on the hard surface beneath him and pain screamed through him.

Anice leapt to her feet. "Don't move." She glanced about anxiously. "Isla, please come."

He frowned, not able to recall what happened to bring him to this hard table. A glance at his torso revealed two rows of neat stitches lining his stomach and side. "I was injured," he stated.

Anice pressed her lips together and lowered her head. "I stabbed you."

"Ye stabbed me?" he asked.

"And so did yer da," Isla replied as she approached. "Though it was yer da's blade which nearly did ye in."

It rushed back to him then, searing through the fog of confusion with startling clarity. His father had attacked Anice with the intent to kill. Except Laird Graham was now dead and James was laird.

"The reivers coming to attack." He wriggled on the table in an attempt to stand.

Isla gave a sharp hiss and put her hand to his arm to still him from moving.

"It was Lord Bastionbury." Anice smiled. "He came. Because of you. We are all alive because of you."

Not everyone. There were soldiers who lost their lives. Soldiers, and reivers too. But he did not state as much. "Together we have saved as many lives as was possible to save," he replied instead.

A man strode up behind Anice. Nay, not just any man. Lord Bastionbury. James tried to sit up.

Bastionbury shook his head. "Rest easy, lad."

"This is disconcertingly familiar," James grunted.

The earl smiled at that. "You've got a penchant for putting

yourself in front of others to save them." His head nodded with approval. "'Tis the mark of a good man."

The praise warmed through James and settled over his wounded soul, a balm for the hurt put there by his own father.

Bastionbury placed a solid hand on James's shoulder. "I'm proud of you."

The words glowed through James and filled a deep, wounded part of him that had always longed those words. Emotion caught at the back of his throat. So many years had gone by for James where he'd been told he wasn't good enough, strong enough, man enough.

*I'm proud of you.*

How many times had he craved these very words? And now he heard them, not only from his wife, but also from Lord Bastionbury, who had helped straighten James's life from a path of crooked morals.

James shifted his gaze away. "Thank ye."

"And I'm sorry for your loss." Lord Bastionbury spoke with a gentleness that conveyed his genuine sympathy. "It is always hard to lose a father, even when they are difficult to love."

Anice's hand tightened on James's, there at his side as he needed her most. This time, James could only nod, not trusting himself to speak.

"I must go see to my men." Lord Bastionbury removed his hand from James's shoulder. "We shall speak again when you are more recovered."

"Anice!" A feminine voice cried out.

Several girls edged around Lord Bastionbury as he made his departure. Three petite, chain-clad young women, two with blonde hair, one with dark hair. The daughters of Lord Werrick. Of course. James smiled in spite of himself.

They enveloped Anice in a hug so fierce, it pulled her hand from his. He let his arm fall and watched the reunion take place.

Though they had shared a month of happiness at Caldrick Castle, this was what Anice had been craving. This was what James had never truly known for himself: a family.

Anice's eyes were glossy with tears, her face bright with the brilliance of her smile. All three younger sisters chattered on with so much energy, it made James feel even more exhausted than he already was. All at once, they ceased their talking and came to him.

"Oh, James!" Ella put her fingers to her lips. "You nearly died protecting Anice. It was terribly romantic of you, but you could have been killed." She pulled something from a large pouch at her side, a bit of red fur, and plopped it beside his face.

A ratty looking beast stared at him with bright, black eyes, frozen with bewildered confusion at its new location.

"Don't put that there." Anice plucked the thing away from James, while Ella pulled it from her hand and back into her arms.

"This is Moppet," she said in a surly tone. "He was going to try to make him better."

"James." It was Catriona who spoke now, her face more solemn than he'd ever seen. "Your da. I'm so sorry, I—"

"He would have killed us all and taken Werrick." James shook his head. "The fault doesna lie with ye, lass."

Catriona nodded. "Then I'm sorry I did not act quickly enough to prevent you from being attacked. I..." Her face crumpled and she looked away in an obvious attempt to regain her composure. "I hesitated. I didn't want to kill him."

James drew from a dwindling well of energy and took her small hand. It was hot and damp against his fingers. "Ye did what ye had to, Cat, and ye saved the lot of us by doing it. Ye did well."

She nodded solemnly.

Leila took Cat's place and gazed down at him with a slight

furrow to her brow. "I'm sorry I couldn't tell you. How could one tell another their father was to die?"

"The failure of our union?" James prompted.

Leila nodded. "I could not see everything, but I knew. You are much stronger than I expected. I thought you'd side with your father." Leila held out a small bag toward him. "These are for you."

James peered inside and found several poultices and a few vials of cloudy liquid. Items that were not hurriedly made but had been prepared in advance. "Ye made these prior to the battle."

"Aye." She held his gaze. "Even though I thought you had betrayed us, you are still a part of our family." She brightened. "I'm pleased you did not, though."

He reached for the small bag. Anice rushed forward to take it as it began to slip from his weak grip. "You need rest." Concern showed in her eyes. "Go on, girls. Off with you. I'll be with you in a moment's time."

"The vial will help you sleep, while keeping the fever at bay." Leila turned away with Cat and Ella reluctantly following behind her. The creature Ella had rescued remained perched on her shoulder.

He wanted to ask what it was, to jest about it with Anice, to hold her hand and cradle her against him. But she was pulling the stopper from a small vial and assisting him in getting the bitter contents into his mouth and down his throat.

"Those girls love you." Anice put the empty vial into the bag, then leaned over him and pressed a kiss to his brow. "I love you." She kissed his lips, sweet and tender.

"I love ye, *mo leannan*." He tried to reach for her, but his arm wouldn't cooperate. The exhaustion and the injury had finally taken their toll.

"Say it again," she whispered and closed her eyes. "For I thought at one point to never hear it again."

"I love ye, *mo leannan*."

Anice pressed her lips together and opened her eyes. "Rest now, my love."

He let his eyes close, having no choice, but to do exactly as she bade.

James woke sometime later and discovered he had been tucked into a comfortable bed. Sleep tried to lure him back to its embrace, but laughter filtered into his room from somewhere below. Women's laughter. Most likely Anice and her sisters.

Warmth touched his heart at the thought of his wife. His bonny wife. Because after everything they'd been through, he now appreciated what it was to trust the woman he loved.

All the years of rage at Morna's betrayal eased away. After all, if he had not walked in on her, he might never have known of her infidelity. And he'd never have met Anice.

More laughter trickled in from the window, and James's lips lifted in a smile at the joyful sounds. They were a family like he had always wanted, one whose bonds went beyond blood. A family willing to accept despite wrongdoings, despite even being a Graham. He had lost a father, but he had gained a family.

"Ye dinna look like ye're resting." Drake peered in from the open doorway. He lifted a brow. "Does that mean ye're ready to spar?"

"Lucky for ye, I canna do it just yet," James countered. "Mayhap after I've moved around a bit, aye?"

Drake came into the room. Sunlight played over his face, highlighting the deep bruises and swelling of his skin. The lad didn't even seem to notice his own injuries.

"Thank ye." James nodded up at him. "For protecting Anice."

"I've got sisters." Drake lifted his shoulders in a helpless shrug. "Several. I've been protective of Lord Werrick's daughters since I met them."

A shriek sounded below followed by giggles.

"They're in the garden," Drake said. "Do you want to join them?"

James nodded. "More than anything else."

Drake came to his side and lowered his arm, putting it at the ready for James to use as a brace. "Come on, then. The sooner ye recover, the sooner I can get a new sparring partner."

∽

Anice kept an eye on the wild creature scurrying about Ella's feet. "What is it?"

Ella dropped a bit of food to her new pet and the animal fell on the treat. "Moppet is a squirrel."

Moppet did not resemble a squirrel. The beast was nearly too large to be one. It stood on its hind legs, fur mussed and standing every which way. It held the food in its one hand, while its shiny black eyes darted about. No doubt seeking out its next victim.

Piquette gave a low growl of warning when the squirrel set its gaze on him. Anice rubbed a loving hand over her dog's large head. Engelbart had personally brought Piquette to Anice as soon as he'd received notice it was safe to do so. Anice hadn't known the large dog could run with such haste, but he charged at her like a pup when he first saw her and nearly knocked her to the ground.

"Regardless, I'd prefer you not set Moppet near James while he rests." Anice glanced up at the castle to gaze at the window of their shared room. It had only been several days since his injury, but he had been resting a considerable amount. Thus far, the fever had not touched him, and she wanted it to stay that way.

Having a corpulent squirrel with a mischievous streak frolicking about on the sheets beside him would be a poor decision.

"He only wishes to help," Ella offered simply.

Moppet scurried up a tree, settled upon a low branch and flung a berry down at Cat. It bounced off her forehead. She started, then placed a hand over the point of impact and laughed good-naturedly. "He is such a feisty creature. I'm pleased he recovered so well."

Leila shifted slightly to put herself behind Cat, and out of Moppet's sight.

"Moppet," Ella chided. She lifted her hand up and the animal obediently scurried down from the tree and into her arms.

Piquette bristled but remained at Anice's side. In truth, he never left her anymore. He went about as though he were tethered to her hip, the sweet boy.

Anice laughed at the scene. While she hated her reason for returning to Werrick, it was so good to be home. Everyone was exactly the same as when she'd left. Her father still doted on his daughters and ruled the West March with fairness. Nan ran the kitchen seamlessly, grousing about the new butcher and his attempt to sweeten her disposition with an extra side of venison. William was still as uncompromisingly kind as he was knowledgeable about the castle and its land. Geordie was still madly in love with Cat, and Ella continued to follow the Master of the Horse with doe-eyed longing.

Anice's world had gone on in another direction, carving her own trail in life, while theirs had continued as it always had. Somehow seeing this, knowing that they would always be here, unchanged, gave her peace at going along her own path. In truth, she was beginning to miss Caldrick Castle. The land had just begun to show shoots to reward the Grahams for their hard work in their fields, and Ingrith had become the confidante

Anice had needed. Even the cook's brusque manner in the kitchen had started to soften toward Anice, and it made him all the more endearing.

A pang hit her heart. She was ready to go home. With her husband. Back to their shared life.

Piquette leapt to his feet with a whimper and dashed toward the castle. Startled, Anice jerked her attention up and found James coming toward them, supported by Drake at his side.

Geordie ran out from behind the two of them and waved with exuberance in Cat's direction.

"Piquette," Anice said in a gentle warning tone. It was caution enough for a dog as tender-hearted as Piquette. The great beast immediately slowed, his tail nervously wagging as he whimpered his frustration at not being able to leap upon James.

*James.* Anice's heart nearly sung at the appearance of her husband on the sunny, perfect day. She had to stay her own excitement, to keep from rushing toward him as Piquette had, and throwing her arms around his broad, powerful shoulders.

"I heard such bonny laughter from my room." James gave an apologetic smile. "I couldna stay in that bed any longer."

"I'm so glad you came." Anice went to James's free side. "Are you feeling well?" While she was overjoyed at seeing her husband, she could not stop her nervous glance at his tunic to ensure he had not begun to bleed through his bandages after the exertion of walking downstairs.

James put his arm around Anice's shoulders. He closed his eyes, turned his face to the sun and breathed in deeply. "I've no' ever been happier, *mo leannan.*" He opened his eyes and grinned down at her.

"I anticipate he'll be sparring with me soon." Drake led James to a bench in the garden and helped him sit. A nut flew down from the tree and bounced off the top of Drake's head. He ignored it, even as the younger girls shared a laugh.

Anice took the seat beside James and laid her head on his shoulder, mindful of his injuries. His wonderful, familiar smell surrounded her and brought with it the happy memories of their life together at Caldrick Castle.

"I'm looking forward to being home together once more." Anice entwined her fingers with his large ones.

"Home?" His voice was in her ear.

She lifted her head and regarded her handsome husband. "Our home. In Carlisle."

He smiled and lowered his head to kiss her. An acorn smacked into his temple. He lifted his brows without bothering to turn. "Moppet?"

Anice had told him enough stories of the little demon squirrel for him to know the beast simply by the action, which was funny enough for them all to laugh. Even Drake.

"Mayhap we'll be going home sooner than later." James winked at Anice as another nut flew down from the tree.

# EPILOGUE
## APRIL 1338, CALDRICK CASTLE, ENGLAND

The land had been good to them. In two years of crops, the rich soil of Carlisle had yielded enough to feed all its people and provide even more for sale.

It was not only the land that had been good to them. Life had been equally as good to them, perhaps more so.

Anice lifted her golden-haired babe from his cradle and curled him close in her arms. Sweet young Gavin gave a little coo of contentment and snuggled closer into her warmth on the cool spring morning. She sang softly as she swayed in that age-old way mothers do when holding their babes. Never had she imagined herself as a mother.

However, when Gavin was born, it was as though the final piece of happiness to Anice's life had been revealed. She gazed down at her son, staring at the perfect curve of his small nose, the brilliance of his blue eyes, the delicate curve of his lips, and her heart ached with indescribable love.

Piquette's tail thumped against Anice's thigh, impatient for a view of the small child. Anice gently lowered her son and let Piquette give him a nuzzling sniff.

Gavin opened his mouth in a wide yawn, revealing a small

tongue stained white with milk. Anice chuckled and drew him back against her. "You must be a tired boy."

"Was it from keeping us up last eve?" James asked from the doorway. He padded into the room and put an arm around her.

"'Tis exhausting preventing one's parents from sleeping." Anice slid James a playful smile.

Aye, she was tired, but she was happy.

She knew Ingrith would get up with Gavin, and she knew a wet nurse would allow her to sleep through the night. But Ingrith had her own son to wake up with in the morning, as well as a full day of work ahead of her. And after Anice had nursed Gavin herself, she would never hire a wet nurse. She loved those mornings rocking him, listening to the greedy gulps as her milk let down, and the drowsy warmth of her son as he grew full and tired once more.

"Ye're a good mother." James smoothed a loose hair behind Anice's ear. "I love seeing ye with our son."

"And you're a good father." She smiled up at her husband. "And a good laird as well."

It was true. He'd done everything he set out to do. Peace and prosperity had been restored to the land. His father's death had laid to rest the dreams of sacking Werrick Castle ever again. Or at least by the Grahams who remained in Carlisle. They were content to work the land with their families, to have a home and food and safety. The ones who did not wish to follow such a life had returned to the Debatable Lands.

Everything was going exactly right in their lives.

A knock sounded at the door. "My Lady, Mistress Davidson has just arrived."

James and Anice regarded each other curiously.

"Were ye expecting Marin?" James asked.

Anice shook her head. "Nay. Mayhap she's here to see Gavin, although it is rather early for a visit."

James held out his arms to hold Gavin, and Anice gave him their son. "Only until we see Marin, and then you know she'll want to hold him," she warned.

For as large as James was, he was the gentlest of men when it came to their son. Those powerful arms moved slow and tender as he cradled their small bairn against him and crooned soft endearments in Gaelic. Gavin stared up in adoring wonder at his father and reached a hand toward James's beard.

Gavin did that often, gripping the wiry hair of James's beard. But never once did James pull away or scold their son. He patiently held his head in place as Gavin's little hands tugged. Anice led them all from the room. "Give him a bit of time and he's going to hurt you."

"Ach," James said dismissively. "Unless he stabs me, I'll be fine." He winked at Anice and shifted Gavin in his arms as they went below stairs.

Her jaw dropped open in mock offense. "Mayhap I need to stab you again?"

He grinned. "Nay. Unless I deserve it."

"If you continue thus, you may well." She laughed in spite of herself and kissed James on the cheek.

They opened the door to the great hall to welcome Bran and Marin who were already sitting at a trestle with steaming mugs in front of them. Gavin gave a gurgling sound and Marin turned toward them. She got to her feet, strode several steps and went still.

Emotions played over her face, ones so raw Anice felt every one of them mirrored in her own soul. The surprise at the babe Marin already knew about, the immediate punch of hurt to her own empty womb, and then the joy for her sister. "Is this Gavin?" Marin asked in a whisper.

Anice's throat went tight thinking of her sister's inability to conceive. Of all the sisters, Marin was guaranteed to be the best mother after so many years of caring for everyone else. The one of them who wanted a child with every piece of herself, and yet Marin had been the one rendered barren. She had a happy life, but such a longing could not be easily quelled. Unable to find her voice, Anice simply nodded.

Marin held out her arms. "May I?"

Anice nodded again and James passed Gavin to Marin with gentle hands. Anice's elder sister took the baby in her arms and hugged him to her. The raw ache on her face, the hurt of not having a child of her own, nearly shattered Anice's heart.

Marin stroked a hand over Gavin's downy blond hair and pressed a kiss to his small forehead. Gavin looked up at her with his wide, curious blue eyes and poked his tongue from between his lips. Marin gave a sound somewhere between a laugh and a sob. Bran was at her side in a moment, hovering the way a concerned husband does.

Marin smiled up at him in a silent show that everything was all right. She met Anice's gaze with glossy eyes. "He's beautiful, Anice. Absolutely perfect."

"I pray God will give you one of your own soon," Anice said with heartfelt sincerity.

"We will take all the prayers we can," Marin said gratefully. "We have not lost hope."

After nearly five years without a child, most would have. But most were not Marin.

"Prayers, however, are not why we have come to you." Marin shifted Gavin in her arms, cradling him in the crook of her elbow. "Anice, the king is accusing Father of being a Scottish sympathizer."

Anice straightened at once. "How is that possible? He has been a loyal supporter, always serving the crown. We would not be safe in such dangerous lands were it not for his unwavering fealty."

Marin shifted her gaze back to the babe in her arms and smoothed a palm over his fuzzy head. Gavin had gone to sleep, his pale lashes resting against rosy cheeks. This was when Anice liked to kiss him best, when she could bestow a hundred kisses on his small face without him pulling back or opening his drooling smile.

"It's us," Marin said in a solemn tone. "We've both married Scotsmen."

"But—" Anice cut short her protest. They hadn't had a choice in the matter, neither she nor Marin. However, stating what they all knew would serve no good. "There must be some way to prove Father is loyal."

"There is, per the king's suggestion." Marin took a deep breath. "Ella will have to marry the Earl of Calville, by order of the king, to prove Father's loyalty."

Dread sucked at Anice. "Ella? Can it not be Cat?"

While Anice was loath to confine poor Cat to a forced marriage, Cat would go willingly to her fate. Ella, on the other hand...

Marin's chagrined expression echoed Anice's thoughts. "According to the king's missive, the union is to be held between Lord Calville and Lord Werrick's eldest unwed daughter. It is why I travel at such an hour, and why I have come to see you. We must go and convince her, for Father's sake."

Anice cast a glance at James.

"It's been far too long since we last visited," he offered. "Engelbart can see to things until we return." He was right, of course. Anice had ceased traveling to Werrick once she discovered she was with child and longed to visit with her sisters once more.

Anice nodded. "Aye, we'll go. And heaven help us convincing her. Ella has only ever planned to marry for love."

"Then let us hope it is fate which pushes her husband to her, and that she finds love," Marin stated. "As I have found with Bran."

"And as I have found with James." Anice shared a smile with her husband that warmed her to the soul. All her sisters deserved the life she had, and she hoped that no matter how it came, they would discover such happiness too.

<<<<>>>>

## ALSO BY MADELINE MARTIN

**Wedding a Wallflower**

The Earl's Hoyden

**The Borderland Ladies**

Ena's Surrender

Marin's Promise

Anice's Bargain

Ella's Desire

Catriona's Secret

Leila's Legacy

**The Borderland Rebels**

The Highlander's Lady Knight

Faye's Sacrifice

Kinsey's Defiance

Clara's Vow

Drake's Honor

**Highland Passions**

The Highlander's Challenge

A Ghostly Tale of Forbidden Love

The Madam's Highlander

Her Highland Destiny

The Highlander's Untamed Lady

**Matchmaker of Mayfair**

Discovering the Duke

Unmasking the Earl

Mesmerizing the Marquis

Earl of Benton

Earl of Oakhurst

Earl of Kendal

**Heart of the Highlands**

Deception of a Highlander

Possession of a Highlander

Enchantment of a Highlander

**Standalones**

Her Highland Beast

# ABOUT THE AUTHOR

Madeline Martin is a *New York Times, USA Today,* and International Bestselling author of historical fiction and historical romance with books that have been translated into over twenty different languages.

She lives in sunny Florida with her two daughters (known collectively as the minions), two incredibly spoiled cats and a man so wonderful he's been dubbed Mr. Awesome. She is a diehard history lover who will happily lose herself in research any day. When she's not writing, researching or 'moming', you can find her spending time with her family at Disney or sneaking a couple spoonfuls of Nutella while laughing over cat videos. She also loves research and travel, attributing her fascination with history to having spent most of her childhood as an Army brat in Germany.

Check out her website for book club visits, reader guides for her historical fiction, upcoming events, book news and more: https://madelinemartin.com